MATCHING MISS MOON

Hearts of Cornwall

K. LYN SMITH

ISBN: 978-1-7376579-5-8

"Have you seen any pleasant men?
Have you had any flirting?"

Lydia Bennet, from *Pride and Prejudice*

CHAPTER ONE

LATE SUMMER, 1819
NEWFORD, CORNWALL

*A*LMOST WAS A WORD WITH which Gryffyn Kimbrell was well acquainted.

From his pleasing manners (which were almost like his mother's) to his talent with a chisel (which was almost like his father's), he'd heard the comparative often enough. If he was familiar with the nuance of *almost* and its cousins *very nearly* and *not quite*, he'd convinced himself all was as it should be. He was not his father's son, after all, or his mother's.

Almost, but not quite.

Now he crossed his arms as Mayor Moon examined his new stone mantel. Newford's mayor had long been an admirer of the senior Kimbrell's

1

carving talent, but Gryffyn wasn't certain what he would think of the son's. He waited while the man ran an assessing palm along the intricately carved surface of creamy limestone, over delicate leaves and birds and a detailed rope banding that had taken Gryffyn days to complete.

Hodges and Payne, whom he'd engaged to assist with the heavy commission, stood in rough contrast to the drawing room's silken elegance. They twisted and tugged at their woolen caps as they waited to be released from the task of installing the mantel. A commotion sounded in the hall, and they shuffled to one side as the mayor's young son rushed in.

"Father, have you seen Keri?" Henry Moon asked, ignoring the room's other occupants.

"Henry," the mayor said with a hint of exasperation. "How many times have I told you not to interrupt when I have visitors? And why aren't you tending to your lessons with Miss Litton?"

The boy spotted the new mantel then and stepped closer, eyes large behind smudged round spectacles. "What's this?" He spied the bag of tools at Gryffyn's feet and asked, "Did you carve it?"

The mayor continued scowling at his son as Gryffyn replied simply, "I did."

"Henry," Moon said. "You will return to your lessons now."

The boy ignored his father's direction and traced

a stone vine with one short finger, exclaiming, "Why, there's a bird nestled in the vines, Father! Although," he added with a glance toward Gryffyn, "I think a dragon would have been quite stunning as well."

Gryffyn's brows lifted as he gave the boy a short nod of acknowledgment.

Henry spun back to the mantel and examined more of the carving. A satisfying expression of admiration lit his face. Admittedly, Henry Moon was naught but a lad of seven or eight, so perhaps his admiration was too easily won.

"Henry!" Moon said sharply, then, "Simons, return the boy to his governess."

"Come, Master Henry." The butler led the mayor's son away in a manner that appeared oft repeated. Henry's breathy declarations could still be heard in the hall as he continued to exclaim over the mantel. Moon released a heavy sigh then finally turned back to Gryffyn.

"You've carved a fine piece," he said, and Gryffyn's shoulders relaxed. "It's very nearly as good as the statue your father carved for my forecourt some years ago. I daresay you'll equal his skill in time, so long as you don't waste your talents on headstones and hedges."

Gryffyn's shoulders tensed again, but he replied, "Thank you, sir. It eases my mind to know you're pleased with the work."

"How does your father fare? I haven't seen him in some weeks or more."

"He's well, sir. His work keeps him occupied." With headstones and hedges.

Gryffyn's father had long since set his days of carving fine statues behind him. Before Gryffyn's time, his reputation had carried him to Truro and even as far as Plymouth and Bath, but now he opted instead for more sensible—and plentiful—commissions. Not a week went by when someone didn't need a headstone or a stone wall, and his father's refusal to accept more interesting work had become a source of quiet discord between father and son. Nothing to produce anything as serious as a raised voice, but Gryffyn couldn't deny the tension that bubbled and simmered between them. Why, even Gryffyn's undertaking of Moon's mantelpiece—which was hardly the ambitious carving of his father's youth—had turned his father's jaw to stone.

"I confess I was disappointed when Thomas declined to participate in the Truro exhibition," Moon said. "With his skill, I was certain we could have made a proper showing. It would have been a feather in our cap to have a Newford statue grace Truro's High Cross."

At Gryffyn's hesitation, Moon added, "Surely

your father has mentioned it?"

Gryffyn checked his frown. Of course, his father hadn't said anything of an exhibition in Truro. He cleared his throat and forced a smile. "As I said, he's been some busy these past weeks. I'm certain 'tis merely slipped his mind."

"Hmm," Moon said, then he brightened. "My entreaties fell on deaf ears, but to be sure, he'll listen to his son. You must persuade him to reconsider. We can't allow Falmouth to steal a march on us."

"I shall try," Gryffyn agreed, striving to sound more confident than he felt.

Moon shared what he knew of the upcoming exhibition and the requirements for the contestants. Then he cautioned, "Remind your father time is short. Enys—he's Truro's new mayor, you know— he's organized the judging for the end of the harvest festival. And you didn't hear it from me, but Falmouth has high expectations. Davies has carved an ambitious piece from Greek mythology. Or the Romans; I can't keep them rightly sorted."

Gryffyn's frown couldn't be helped at that statement. His displeasure wasn't because Davies meant to submit a piece from mythology; the gods were a common enough subject. His frown, rather, was for the carver himself.

He'd encountered George Davies a few months before when he'd gone with his cousin to Falmouth.

Davies' interest in Gryffyn's sketchbook had been flattering at first, then irritating as he'd frowned over a design Gryffyn had been perfecting for the lintels of Newford's new town hall. He'd turned the sketch first one way, then another before declaring it forgettable. "Attractive, to be sure," he'd said, "but mark me: in six months, no one will recall who the carver was."

Gryffyn disagreed, but that was only to be expected given the differences in their styles. Davies favored heavy, lurid subjects meant to shock and titillate—devils and demons and the like. Gryffyn supposed there was something to be said for a piece that aroused sentiment, but he preferred to arouse admiration rather than disgust.

Moon continued with a long stroke of his side whiskers. "Enys had it from Davies himself that his piece is one that won't soon be forgotten."

———

MISS KEREN MOON SET HER paintbrush back in the water and frowned at the poor creature gracing her paper. It was meant to be a fox, but he more closely resembled an overgrown terrier. She'd gotten the ears wrong again. And the body. Then she stilled, tilting her head, and listened.

There. The low sound of voices drifted up the

stairs. Not the murmuring tones of the servants but the low timbre of a masculine voice. One of her father's political acquaintances, perhaps, or the constable, returned with Henry again. Her frown deepened at the thought. Her father wouldn't look kindly on Henry's latest governess if she'd been lax in her duties.

Her brother needed something to capture his focus, to hold his interest for more than a few minutes at a stretch, but she couldn't imagine what that might be. She and Miss Litton had exhausted their creativity as it was.

She waited, breath held as she listened for the constable's voice. Although . . . the sound came from the drawing room, not her father's library.

The drawing room . . . Someone had come to call. That was a much more pleasant prospect as she'd grown bored with her own company some time ago. They rarely received social calls at Camborne—her father did much of his mayoral socializing at other people's homes, and while she had admirers, few took the time to call.

It was rather well known that while Mayor Moon's youngest daughter enjoyed the art of flirtation, she was not interested in marriage. It was also well known, owing to an unfortunate incident with one of her sister's suitors, that Mayor Moon was possessed of a strong arm and sure aim. As a consequence, many viewed a call at Camborne as an entertaining but potentially hazardous endeavor. A social caller was news indeed.

She hurriedly removed the smock covering her gown, groaning in frustration as the sleeves tangled on her arms. Then, fox forgotten, she smoothed her hair and raced toward the stairs. Her slippers skidded on the smooth marble as she descended to the ground floor. She paused at the table in the entry, frowning to see it empty of calling cards. Who had arrived?

The voices were indistinguishable as she approached the drawing room doors. Simons was nowhere to be seen, so she fixed a broad smile on her face, threw open the doors and entered. And stopped.

Why, it was only Gryffyn Kimbrell.

He glanced up at her arrival, brows lifting in mild surprise. Two workmen from Newford stood alongside him, caps in hand, as did her father. But no constable, thankfully. One of Mr. Kimbrell's hands rested atop an exquisite stone mantel. A mantel she was certain had not been there that morning.

Gryffyn Kimbrell turned to face her more fully, his lean form at odds with the shorter, rounder men beside him. Offering a polite nod, he said, "Good afternoon, Miss Moon."

She pressed her lips and returned his nod with a quick dip of her own. "Mr. Kimbrell."

It wasn't that she found Gryffyn Kimbrell disagreeable. Quite the contrary. The stone carver was the most agreeable of the Kimbrell cousins, but that was only because he was the quietest. It was hard to be disagreeable when one didn't speak. But agreeableness aside, his quiet, watchful manner had a way of suppressing any wit she may have claimed. No other gentleman of her acquaintance had such an effect on her manner, but like a fine champagne left to sit too long, her personality simply deflated in his presence.

Even now, he watched quietly, unsmiling, and waited for her to toss the first conversational ante. She gave a mental sigh, opened her mouth, and uttered something impossibly dull.

"Aye, Miss Moon," he agreed with a nod. "'Tis unseasonably cool for July."

The weather? It was ridiculous to feel irritation at his agreeableness, for what other response could he have for such an uninspired topic? He pressed his lips together as if he might be fighting a . . . smile? A smile, on Gryffyn Kimbrell? Although she supposed it could just as easily have been a yawn or a sneeze that he stifled.

Her father's greying brows were pitched over his nose in displeasure, no doubt at her hurried and undignified interruption. He was forever scolding her forwardness, and she was certain he would have something to say about it later. It was enough to make her wish the constable *had* returned with Henry in tow.

She searched her mind for something—anything—to convince the carver she wasn't a dim candle. Sadly, her mind remained empty, her bubbles fizzled.

Mr. Kimbrell straightened and said to her father, "I'll take my leave, Mr. Moon, if you've no other questions for me."

At her father's agreement, he collected his tools into a bag and left with the workmen, nodding agreeably as they passed. The front door clicked shut, and Keren's shoulders dropped. So much for visitors. She gave her father a brief nod and prepared to return to her poor fox, but she was not to escape his scolding, it would seem.

"Keren," he said, forestalling her exit. "I'll have a word, if you please."

"Yes, Father?"

He stroked his side whiskers as he studied her—never a good sign—then motioned for her to have a seat. Also, not a good sign. She sat and smoothed her skirts while he paced before her.

"You're two and twenty this year."

"Three and twenty," she corrected, to which he

scowled. Keren inhaled quietly and held the breath, waiting.

"I will grant that your age affords you some leniency in social behavior."

The lecture was not an unfamiliar one, and Keren resisted the urge to collapse against the velvet cushions. She supposed such an unladylike pose could not help her case.

"Your age does not, however, allow for the type of behavior of which I've recently been apprised."

Ah. This was not about her graceless entry this afternoon then. That had merely been one more straw on an already overburdened camel. Did he refer to her challenging the gentlemen at Mrs. Pentreath's picnic to a shooting competition? Or perhaps her flirtation last month—short-lived as it was—with a gentleman visiting from Bath? Mr. Wilkins, she thought his name had been? Wilson?

"The hurling," her father said, interrupting her thoughts. His face reddened as he continued, and he ceased his pacing. "I've been the recipient of more than one report that your behavior at the event was far from circumspect."

Ah. The parish's annual hurling was far more entertaining than any other event Newford would see throughout the year. The play was rough, and the gentlemen were quite stunningly, deliciously rumpled in the end. If Keren occasionally became caught up in the excitement, she was hardly the only young lady to do so. Granted, she may have pressed herself a little too closely to the winner, but it was practically tradition. Everyone *adored* a winner. Why, some of the townswomen even offered a kiss as a trophy. And she could, in good conscience, say she'd never gone so far as that.

The winner. Mr. Jory Tremayne was one of Gryffyn Kimbrell's many cousins. Had Mr. Kimbrell been the source of her father's latest report? A queasy warmth twisted her belly with equal parts irritation and embarrassment.

"It took months for the matrons of this town to forget your sister's havey-cavey marriage. My standing can't bear any additional scrutiny before the next election."

Keren refrained from suggesting that if he'd not taken a fist to Lizzie's then-suitor, the matter might have been viewed as somewhat less havey-cavey, but she didn't think he would appreciate the observation. She pressed her lips as he continued.

"You will conduct yourself with the propriety your station demands. I'll not have it said that my youngest daughter's bearing is not as it should be."

His youngest daughter. The label was telling. Not his artistic daughter or the musically inclined one. Not the beauty or the charitable one. She was his flirtatious daughter, but he could hardly refer to her as such, so she was known throughout Newford as simply the mayor's youngest girl.

She had no talent for art or the pianoforte, and her looks were rather ordinary. But flirting . . . the skill came to her quite naturally, so long as the gentleman wasn't Gryffyn Kimbrell, that was.

But she couldn't deny the truth of her father's words. She *had* played fast and loose with her reputation, and she wasn't so far gone she didn't realize the risks she took. Although she had no intention of marrying, neither did she wish to become a pariah.

"I will try to do better, Father," she promised.

"You *will* do better," he said, his voice as hard as the stone mantel behind him. He spread a hand over his forehead and pressed his temples. "One more infraction, Keren . . ."

She frowned, waiting, her pulse thumping heavily. Would he withhold her pin money? Refuse permission for her to attend the monthly assemblies?

"One more infraction, and I shall be forced to send you to Shropshire."

Keren stared at him. Surely, he didn't mean . . . ? "You don't mean to send me to Aunt Agnes?" she whispered.

Her father's hard stare was his only response.

Aunt Agnes, widowed at a young age, had never

remarried. She wore trousers, and her closest acquaintances were her deerhounds. To Keren's knowledge, there were no gentlemen of flirting age within fifty miles of her aunt. But Aunt Agnes's oddities were the least of her worries.

If he sent her away, she'd be separated from Henry. He'd have no one but their father, who didn't understand him, much less have patience for his eccentricities. Keren hadn't avoided marriage these past years to be sent away from Henry now, and over something so trifling as a hurling flirtation.

"But—but Henry," she said. "You can't wish me to be separated from him, or him from me." Her father's expression remained stony, so she added, "Who will coordinate his lessons with Miss Litton? Who will ensure he doesn't wander off to Weirmouth again and . . . ?" She stopped. No argument was strong enough to prevent her exile if her father was determined. He hadn't maintained his decades-long position as mayor without some measure of resolve.

"One more infraction, Keren," he repeated before striding from the room.

CHAPTER TWO

G RYFFYN LEFT HODGES AND PAYNE at the edge
of Newford. His cousin's inn, The Fin and
Feather, sat a few paces away where the
river joined the sea. Boats bobbed on the rippling
water as fishermen prepared to sail out for the
evening, and the warm scents of salt and fish hung
heavily in the air. It was midsummer and early still,
so candlelight had not yet begun to light the
windows along the high street.

He paused outside the Feather. Several of his
cousins sat at a table in the window as was their
custom when the weather and their work permitted.
Alfie leaned toward the window and waved
Gryffyn in, but as much as he would enjoy passing
a companionable evening over a whisky or two, he
was more interested in learning more about the
Truro exhibition. He shook his head at Alfie and

pointed his feet toward home instead.

He lived with his parents in a narrow but comfortable three-story home on a hill overlooking Newford and the sea beyond. It was the same home in which he'd been raised with four elder brothers, all of whom had married and set up their own households. His parents had insisted, and he had agreed, that the cost of setting up a bachelor's home far outweighed the benefits, and so he'd remained with them. And as time passed and his parents' steps grew slower, Gryffyn was pleased to help where he could and contribute toward their comfort.

He entered to the familiar smells of savory beef and pastry drifting up from the kitchen, and he inhaled. Mrs. Quick, who came several times a week to help his mother, could work wonders with a good joint of meat. Or a bad one, for that matter. She had a way with gravies and sauces, to be sure.

He found his mother sewing quietly in the front parlor, her chair angled toward the window's late afternoon light. He crept in quietly and leaned over to plant a kiss on her cheek. She let out a delightful gasp as she pressed one hand to her chest, her familiar rose scent fluttering the air.

"Gryffyn! You gave me such a start, love. Are you trying to put your poor mother in an early grave?"

He leaned down to retrieve the stocking she'd

dropped and returned it to her. He'd have felt repentant if not for the smile lurking at the corner of her lips.

"Never, Mother," he said. "And your heart would have to be a poor thing indeed to survive years of my brothers' antics only to fail at the slightest start from me."

She snorted and returned her attention to her mending. "You may not have been as devilish as your brothers, but you were not entirely blameless in their antics if I recall." She frowned as she tied off a stitch then said, "You've returned early. I thought you'd join your cousins at the Feather, to be sure. Or did Mrs. Quick's fine cooking lead your nose?"

He smiled. "No, although I won't turn down her beef pie. But I wished to speak with Father. Is he returned from extending Mr. Trammel's hedge?"

She nodded. "He's gone to dress for supper. You should as well if you wish any of Mrs. Quick's pie before your father eats the whole of it." She looked up from her sewing and something on his face arrested her thoughts. She set her scissors aside and turned to face him more fully. "Something troubles you, I can tell."

He couldn't abide the concern on her face, so he hurried to assure her. "No, 'tis only that I wished to speak with Father about an exhibition in Truro. There's a carving competition to be judged at the end of the harvest festival. Has he said anything of it?"

"Truro? No, I can't say he's mentioned it."

Was it his imagination, or was there a wariness in her gaze? She pulled a linen shirt from the basket at her feet and resumed her mending, the silver threads in her fair hair glinting in the afternoon light.

"Mrs. Quick has prepared her lemon cream for dessert," she continued. "I know 'tis always been your favorite." She smiled up at him, and he brushed his impression aside.

He left her to wash and dress for supper—something his mother had insisted on for as long as he could remember. She refused to share her table with boots and mud and carving dust. He feared to think what would become of him and his father were she not there to ensure the basic civilities were observed.

A breeze ruffled the lace curtain at his window, and he thought idly of Miss Moon's comments on the cool summer weather. As was typical of their interactions, his presence had done little to inspire her conversation.

He'd often witnessed her wielding her flirtatious manner against his acquaintances. His cousins, the squire's sons . . . Most recently, Gryffyn's cousin Jory had been the recipient of her interest at the annual hurling, although *Jory's* interest had been firmly fixed elsewhere.

But when forced to interact with Gryffyn, Miss Moon's words were uncharacteristically dull, without the liveliness she displayed for others. Not that he wished for her to flirt with him—he certainly didn't have the time or the desire to navigate such waters—but he was curious just the same. What was it that so turned her off him?

He toweled water from his head and dried his face and neck before pulling on a fresh shirt. He didn't think he was altogether unappealing, although he wasn't one to openly laugh and flirt like his cousin Alfie. Nor did he have the authoritative presence of his cousin Gavin. He supposed that came from Gavin's role as parish constable. And although Gryffyn was possessed of a mild temperament, he didn't have Jory's easy grin.

He didn't think any of these failings, in and of themselves, warranted Miss Moon's cool manner, but perhaps taken in total . . . Pushing aside thoughts of Miss Moon with a mental shrug, he donned a clean neckcloth then tugged on his coat before descending to the parlor.

His father watched the darkening sea from the window, hands clasped behind his back. Despite the comfort afforded by the Kimbrell name and fortune, Thomas Kimbrell was a man accustomed to work, and his hands bore the scars of his trade. Indeed, the backs of Gryffyn's own hands were acquiring a collection of fine scars as well, and callouses roughened his palms.

"Son," his father said, turning as Gryffyn approached.

"Good evening, Father."

"You delivered Moon's mantelpiece?"

"Aye, 'tis done." Gryffyn paused then added, "I believe he's satisfied with the work."

His father sucked his teeth then said, "O' course he is. You did a proper job of it." His father was not given to extravagance with his praise, but neither was he miserly. But his words were as puzzling as they were welcome, given his resistance to the more challenging carving work.

Gryffyn's mother joined them, and his father's staid expression relaxed into a fond smile. He lifted an arm, and she leaned her head into him as he escorted her from the parlor. Their posture was a familiar one, but the sight of the two of them—fair-haired and blue-eyed and so unlike Gryffyn's own dark looks—caused a slight pinching in his chest. His mother turned back at his hesitation and smiled, and he forced his feet to follow.

He'd never revealed to them what he knew—that he was not of their blood. It was a fact of his life he'd learned and accepted at a young age. He'd always wondered if they would broach the subject when he reached adulthood. They hadn't, and he wasn't sure it was a topic he wished to discuss either.

To be sure, no good could come of it.

———

MRS. QUICK BUSTLED ABOUT THE dining table, setting out platters of vegetables before placing her steaming beef pie at his father's elbow. She bobbed a quick curtsy before leaving and taking her bustling energy with her. The air in the room settled, and metal clinked faintly on porcelain as Gryffyn's father served beef pie onto their plates.

"I encountered Edith Pentreath outside the post office," his mother said as she accepted her plate. "It seems we're to have some new arrivals in Newford this winter."

"Oh? What have you learned?" his father asked. "Is there finally to be a new resident at Penhale?"

His father's questions were made out of politeness rather than any desire to learn the precise facts of these new arrivals. While there was usually a kernel of truth to Mrs. Pentreath's intelligence, the lady valued speed over accuracy, especially if it meant she could steal a march on Mrs. Clifton.

"It seems so," his mother replied. "Edith had it from Mr. Pentreath that the new owner is a gentleman from London. He'll send his man ahead to prepare for his arrival."

Gryffyn's father sopped his plate with a piece of bread and said, "My father will enjoy having a neighbor near to Oak Hill once more. What else does Mrs. Pentreath say about this London gentleman? Will he bring a family with him?"

"Edith is still ascertaining *that* detail, but I assume he must. What would a bachelor need with all that space?"

"'Twould be no different from Grandfather at Oak Hill," Gryffyn said. "He's but one man with more rooms than he's a need for."

"Well, yes, but Oak Hill is not so grand as Penhale. 'Tis more of a home than an estate, and where would the Kimbrells gather if not there?"

Gryffyn had to concede the point. His grandfather hosted frequent family gatherings on the lawns of Oak Hill when the weather was fine, or in the timbered, whitewashed hall of the rambling Tudor manor when rain threatened. While his uncles and many of his cousins enjoyed comfortable homes of their own, none were so large to accommodate fifty or more Kimbrells.

"If he *is* unwed, let's hope he's not too fine a gentleman," his mother continued with a crease between her brows. "The last thing Newford needs is another handsome bachelor." She looked at Gryffyn meaningfully.

He avoided her gaze and forked a buttered carrot. While his own brothers and many of his cousins had married, there were still quite a few as yet unwed, to their mothers' everlasting sorrow. Owing to the Kimbrell family's unfortunate tendency toward male babies—and lots of them—the sexes in the parish were distressingly disproportionate. One more unwed gentleman would certainly dampen maternal expectations.

"But if he should be a bachelor, that poor stroke of luck may be countered by yet another arrival," his mother said cryptically, leaning forward in her seat.

Gryffyn and his father lifted indulgent brows as they waited for her to continue. She allowed the silence to stretch a moment before adding, "Edith has also learned our vicar is to enjoy an extended visit from his niece. A pleasant and proper young lady by all accounts, and quite unmarried. A man could do worse, to be sure, than a vicar's niece."

Gryffyn chewed silently and pondered how a lady could be "quite unmarried." Such a statement of degree implied she could also be "somewhat" unattached or "slightly" unwed.

But as he had no great urge to marry, owing to the unanswered questions of his birth, he wasn't overly interested in the vicar's niece's unmarried state, "quite" or otherwise.

He and his father made polite sounds here and there as his mother continued speculating on the lady's many admirable qualities. Then, before his mother could suggest inviting the vicar and his incomparable niece to supper, Gryffyn cleared his throat and turned the subject to the one foremost in his mind.

"Father," he began. "When I delivered Moon's mantelpiece, he mentioned a carving exhibition in Truro. I think 'tis something we should consider."

His father chewed slowly, fork suspended over his beef pie. Even Gryffyn's mother grew quiet as she chased a pea about on her plate. Gryffyn drew a bolstering breath and continued despite the heaviness that had settled over the table.

"'Twould be a remarkable opportunity to carve something different. Moon says there's a purse of fifty pounds to be won, and the winning piece will have a place of honor in the High Cross outside St. Mary's. And as there's none can match your skill with a chisel, Father, I'm certain we could —"

"'Twould require more time than we can spare," his father said, lowering his head to resume eating.

"Aye, 'twould require time to be sure, but certainly a win would be good for the business. There's to be a council of judges to select the winner — a panel of gentlemen from throughout the county, headed by Truro's new mayor."

"We have all the custom we need without borrowing more from Truro."

Gryffyn inhaled slowly through his nose and held it. He wasn't an argumentative man, and neither was his father, but he couldn't let the subject lie. "Moon believes 'twould be a triumph for Newford to have our statue chosen."

"It sounds like nothing more than a puffed-up spectacle to curry favor for Truro's new mayor."

His father's expression was unyielding, and Gryffyn frowned. Then, decision made, he said simply, "I mean to submit a piece to the exhibition, Father. I would appreciate your guidance—your skill if you'd care to lend it—but with or without your assistance, I mean to send something to Truro."

"This conversation is upsetting your mother. You know she doesn't appreciate carving talk at the table."

Gryffyn's stomach dropped; he'd not meant to distress his mother, and he turned to her with an apology in his eyes.

She spoke up then, her voice soft in the silence. "You can't prevent him from entering this competition, Thomas. He's a man grown who knows his own mind."

A muscle flexed in his father's jaw before he said tightly, "Is there dessert?"

His mother jumped and excused herself to

collect Mrs. Quick's lemon cream.

A crease dented Gryffyn's brow as he waited for another argument. His mother had the right of it: at six and twenty, he didn't require his father's permission, but his heart would rest easier without the uncomfortable tension between them. He and his father worked together in their business, it was true, sharing in the workload as well as the profit. But that wasn't to say they couldn't take on their own projects, as Gryffyn had done with Moon's mantelpiece.

His father's blue eyes narrowed on Gryffyn's brown ones, but then his shoulders drooped a bit, and he leaned back in his chair. Rubbing his jaw, he exhaled and said, "You'll not let this impact your other work? We've the order for the town hall to consider."

Gryffyn tempered his surprise at the concession. "Of course," he said eagerly. At this late date, it would take long hours to carve a piece worthy of submission and still maintain his regular work, but he'd do what was necessary to see it done.

His father nodded shortly as his mother re-entered with bowls of creamy custard. Nothing more was said of the exhibition as bowls were passed, and Gryffyn hardly tasted Mrs. Quick's dessert as his mind was humming with ideas.

He excused himself early and retired to his room.

He had a lot of planning to do. Sketches to prepare. And he meant what he'd told his father. He'd not let the exhibition affect his work. There were lintels to be carved for the town hall, and a headstone awaited his chisel in the morning.

CHAPTER THREE

KEREN EXCUSED HENRY'S GOVERNESS FOR a well-deserved break and settled onto the floor of the nursery to hear the latest tale her brother had crafted.

His dark hair, which had a regrettable tendency to curl in the heat of summer, had sprouted unevenly from one side of his head, and she leaned over to smooth it down.

Henry, apparently, had been quite taken with Gryffyn Kimbrell's mantelpiece and was regaling her with a fantastical tale about a stone carver with magical abilities.

She'd never been able to make sense of her brother's odd starts, but she listened in amusement as his voice rose and fell with the excitement of his yarn. He'd always had a dramatic turn of mind, so Keren was not surprised when a copper dragon carved from the very cliffs above Copper Cove made an appearance.

"And the dragon breathed fire on the stone carver," Henry said with a flourish, "scorching his hair as the dragon's tail whipped at the man from behind. But the stone carver was armed and ready." Henry spun and wielded a small tool as a sword, and Keren's eyes narrowed.

"Henry," she said. "What is that?" She pointed toward the tool clasped in his small hand.

He straightened from his fighting stance and frowned at her.

"Why, 'tis a chisel," he said matter-of-factly. "Have you not been attending, Keri?"

"I can see that it's a chisel," she said with a wry twist to her lips. "But where did you find it?"

"In the drawing room. Beneath the couch."

"In the—did you not think it odd that there was a chisel in the drawing room beneath the couch?"

"Well, yes, but—oh. Do you think Mr. Kimbrell has left it behind?"

"I think it very likely, Henry. He's probably even this moment wondering what has become of his chisel."

"Botheration. We should return it to him, I suppose." Henry's disappointment at losing his new toy was poorly concealed.

"We should," she agreed with a sigh. "To be

sure, he'll be pleased to have it again. Collect your coat, Henry, then we'll collect Miss Litton."

———

GRYFFYN STARED AT THE TOOLS arrayed across his worktable, but his favorite chisel wasn't among them. He'd emptied his bag as well as the cabinets lining the walls of the workshop, but no chisel. He had others, to be sure, but none fit his hand as perfectly as the one he sought.

He settled his hands on his hips and considered the mess before him. His father would arrive soon, expecting to find their latest headstone ready to be delivered to the churchyard. He'd hoped to be finished by now so he could turn his thoughts back to his sketchbook. It lay open to his latest drawings for the Truro exhibition. He had a notion of what he wished to carve, but the lines, the energy of the piece, eluded him. It would take some time to capture his vision on the page before he could even begin to set his chisel to stone. He forcibly pulled his attention back to the pile of tools. He didn't have time to be woolgathering about Truro, much as he longed to.

He sighed and picked up his second-best chisel then turned toward a slab of Cornish limestone. It was depressingly tiny. The vicar had commissioned a simple headstone: name and dates only, as that was all the parents could afford. It shouldn't take him above a half hour to complete, and then he could return to his sketchbook.

He set his chisel at an angle and tapped the end with a mallet, and a satisfying sliver of limestone sheared away. He worked methodically to dress the stone, evening the edges until he was satisfied with the shape. Next, he reached for a smaller chisel to begin carving the dates. Year of birth: 1819. Year of death: 1819.

Such innocence surely deserved a more fitting period to the end of its sentence than a plain slab of stone. His throat thickened at the incomplete life that would soon be forgotten by all but two grieving parents. He eyed his sketchbook once more and released a slow exhale. Thirty minutes more wouldn't hurt. He brushed an arm over his eyes then bent to add an angel to the top of the stone.

His father would grumble about the extra time spent, but he wasn't a heartless man. Gryffyn had often caught him adding his own embellishments above and beyond what had been commissioned. He'd begun to put the final details on the angel's wings when he became aware of a shadow in the doorway. He brushed a calloused hand over the top of the stone, smoothing away a layer of dust, and looked up.

There, in the entry of his workshop, stood none other than Miss Moon. He couldn't prevent his eyebrows from lifting, and he set his tools aside as she entered with her brother and another young lady.

"Miss Moon," he said, "how can I assist you?" He was conscious of the dusty leather apron covering his shirt, his sleeves rolled high along his forearms and the dust covering his hands. He was in no condition to receive company. Then he reminded himself she'd come to his *workshop*, not his parlor, so this hardly amounted to a social call.

"I believe we may be of assistance to *you*, Mr. Kimbrell," she said, and his brows climbed higher. She nudged her brother forward. "Henry has something of yours, I believe. We've come, along with Miss Litton, to see it returned to you safely.

Gryffyn wiped his hands on a rag and approached the boy, curious. Henry pulled his arm from behind his back to present Gryffyn with his own chisel.

"You found it," Gryffyn said with relief.

"Yes," Henry said. "It was under the couch."

Of course. He'd left it at the Moon residence. He was normally more careful with his tools, but then he'd been distracted by Moon's conversation about the Truro exhibition. He rubbed a thumb along the edge, relieved to feel the familiar weight and smooth metal beneath his touch.

He looked up to see Henry had approached the headstone he'd been carving. The boy ran a small finger along the edge of the angel's wing and leaned over to peer at it more closely.

"How do you make it so lifelike?" he asked. "It's as if the angel will fly from the stone."

"And that is the secret," Gryffyn said. "To imagine whatever you're carving is a living thing trapped within. The skill of the stone carver is to release him from the stone. 'Tis a trick from the great sculptor, Michelangelo. You've studied him in your lessons?"

Henry nodded, and Gryffyn turned back to Miss Moon and Miss Litton. "Thank you for returning the chisel," he said. "I was some anxious over its loss."

Miss Moon looked about the workshop and the mess of tools he'd pulled from the drawers. "You've quite a number of other tools at hand, it would seem."

"Aye," he agreed, "but this was created specially to fit my hand. No other chisel will serve as well."

He rolled the steel chisel between his fingers and realized he was drumbling—boring her to tears, most likely, with talk of chisels and Michelangelo. Indeed, her expression remained carefully neutral without even the hint of a flirtatious grin. He suspected she'd dimple quite prettily were he anyone else.

Henry moved to the open window to study a collection of small carvings that rested on the stone sill. He picked up a tiny marble fox and turned it slowly in his hands. It was one of dozens of such figures Gryffyn had sculpted over the years.

"Henry," Miss Moon said gently, "you mustn't disturb Mr. Kimbrell's things without his permission."

Henry looked to Gryffyn. "May I hold the fox?"

"Aye," he replied, "but lift it to the light."

Henry's brows dipped for a moment before he understood. Then, lifting the fox to the window, he smiled to see the edges glow as light passed through the thinner parts of the stone.

"Marble has a translucent quality," Gryffyn explained. "'Tis why it's so well suited for carving people."

"Can you teach me to carve?" Henry asked as he set the fox back in the windowsill.

Gryffyn cleared his throat and forced the frown from his face. Given his regular work and now his Truro submission, he wouldn't have a single moment to provide carving instruction, no matter how flattering the pupil's interest.

Miss Moon must have been as surprised by the question as Gryffyn, as she stepped forward and placed a staying hand on Henry's shoulder.

"I'm certain Mr. Kimbrell doesn't have time for

carving lessons, Henry. Now we must hurry home so you and Miss Litton can resume your geography lessons."

Henry frowned much as Gryffyn would have done were he faced with such tedium, but he turned obediently toward his sister and governess.

Miss Moon, outlined by the sun much as Gryffyn's fox had been, nodded politely and prepared to take their leave. "Good day, Mr. Kimbrell."

It was then that Gryffyn's artist's eye took notice of her flowing lines. The soft lock of dark hair that escaped her bonnet to curl before one ear. The muslin skirts cascading over her trim form, folds draping softly in the morning light. A light breeze blew through the open window, and he could feel the movement of her hair and dress emerging beneath the chisel he still held. He frowned, eyes narrowed, and resisted the urge to lift the tress of hair at her cheek. Such an action, to be sure, would not be well received.

With effort, Gryffyn pulled his eyes back to hers. Recalling his manners, he said, "Thank you again for returning the chisel." He opened his mouth to say something more—he wasn't sure what, precisely—but she had already turned away.

—

So, THE EVER-AGREEABLE GRYFFYN KIMBRELL did have the power of speech after all. Keren pressed her lips against a smile as their party walked up the lane toward Camborne. Apparently, the topic of stone carving loosened his tongue much like brandy did for other gentlemen. Why, he must have uttered at least a dozen statements in the short time they'd been in his workshop.

The man's verbosity aside, she was pleased with the outing as her father could certainly find no fault in her behavior.

She'd very politely returned the man's chisel to him, in the unexceptionable company of her brother and his governess, for anyone watching from the windows along the high street. No one could take exception with Miss Litton, who was all that was proper, and Keren had maintained an even manner without any trace of forwardness. Admittedly, it hadn't been difficult, given her habitual lapse of personality in the man's presence. One might even say her behavior had been irreproachable.

Henry, on the other hand . . .

"Henry," she said gently, "you can't be so bold to ask Mr. Kimbrell for carving lessons."

He looked up with a frown angling his dark brows. "Why ever not?" he asked. "Did you *see* the angel he carved, Keri? I should like to carve something like that one day. Do you think I could?"

Faced with this barrage of questions, Keren selected the simplest for her response. "I did see the angel. To be sure, Mr. Kimbrell is very talented," she agreed, "but it isn't seemly to insist upon a man's time in such a manner."

"But I didn't insist. I asked, and very politely too," Henry said with a reasonableness beyond his years. "Was I not polite, Miss Litton?"

Miss Litton agreed with a silent apology in her eyes for Keren. Keren rubbed a finger against her temple and tried another tack. "Regardless," she said, "I don't believe Father would wish you to become a stone carver."

"Did he say that?" Henry asked.

"Not in so many words, but—"

"It's a respectable profession, is it not?"

"Well, it's not *un*respectable," she clarified. "But I'm certain Father must have loftier goals for you. Why, you could become mayor of Newford one day, or Truro." Even as she said the words, she doubted their father's expectations for his youngest son were so very high.

His first son, William, had died of an unexpected illness a decade before. When Henry came two years later, her grieving father had been quick to lay his empty hopes at baby Henry's cradle. But as Henry grew, so did his oddities, and their father's hopes had faded until they were hardly mentioned anymore. Now, any words the mayor had for his youngest son were spoken in frustration rather than pride.

"Politics is not for me," Henry said with bold self-assurance, blissfully unaware of their father's low expectations.

"Well, if not politics," Keren said, "perhaps the law. Or the church."

Henry frowned, as unimpressed with these options as he'd been with politics.

"You've plenty of time to decide," she said.

As her father's hopes had faded, Keren's had simply become more realistic. It was clear her young brother was different from other children. She'd heard the townspeople's whispers. At best, Henry was careless and imprudent. At worst, he suffered a "defect of attention" due to his "unstable nervous system." Her brother suffered neither defect nor instability to her way of thinking, but a staid life in the church or town hall would never suit his quixotic nature. But, she thought with a sigh, he probably didn't have the concentration required of a stone carver either.

CHAPTER FOUR

THANKS TO MISS MOON'S FLUTTERING hair and rippling muslin, Gryffyn's mind was loud with ideas for Truro. He set aside the small headstone and bent over his sketchbook, anxious to capture his thoughts on the page before they evaporated like Newford's morning fog.

While many sculptors began straightaway with the stone, he'd always taken the time to sketch first. He couldn't recall when he'd begun drawing, but the ritual of setting his vision to paper focused his energy. Without his sketches, what began as a fox might very well end as a dragon. With an angel's wings.

He thought if he'd ever been in love—which he hadn't—it might have felt something like the start of a new carving. The heart-thumping thrill of plotting and designing. The euphoria of discovery as his vision came alive, first on the page and then in the stone. Even the anxiety and sleepless nights . . . If love *was* anything like carving, he could understand why people made fools of themselves over it.

"'Tis complete?"

He started at his father's voice, surprised he'd not heard his approach. He looked aside at the headstone. "Nearly so," he said ruefully, setting his sketchbook aside.

His father brushed dust from the headstone's surface. He paused to frown at the additional embellishment then, lifting a chisel, he finished Gryffyn's angel with deft movements. Gryffyn placed the completed stone in a small cart to be carried to the churchyard. When he straightened, his father stood at his sketchbook. Gryffyn held his breath, waiting for him to speak.

"These are your drawings for Truro?" he finally asked.

"Aye. They're early still."

His father slowly turned the pages. "'Tis to be a figure from the Romans?"

Gryffyn nodded. "I'm thinking to carve Fortuna." He hesitated, uncertain how much his father was willing to discuss a project of which he'd so clearly disapproved. Taking a chance, he said, "I imagine her with flowing hair and skirts, but I can't capture the motion quite right. I'm not certain my ideas will translate well to the stone."

His father remained silent, a muscle tightening in his jaw as he turned the pages. His brows crouched over the bridge of his nose, and Gryffyn thought he might argue further against the Truro exhibition. Then his next words surprised him.

"'Twould seem there's some imbalance in the design as well." He pointed a blunt finger at the bottom of one sketch. "Her ankles may not be enough to support the weight of her."

"Aye," Gryffyn said slowly. "I see what you mean. Perhaps I can distribute the weight between her feet and skirts."

His father nodded, one hand stroking his chin. "It could work." Turning back to Gryffyn, he said softly, "They're fine drawings, son. I wish you luck."

"Good Fortuna?" Gryffyn said.

His father smiled, a rare curving of the lips that Gryffyn was pleased to see. "Aye."

His father may not have been in whole-hearted approval of the contest, but his words went a long way to easing some of the tension in Gryffyn's shoulders.

———

LATER THAT NIGHT, GRYFFYN'S CANDLE had burned to a flickering stub at the edge of his worktable, and he rubbed his eyes to clear his vision. A tap sounded at the door and he rose, relieved to set his charcoal aside. His cousin Jory greeted him, a paper wrapped package in one hand and his dog Trout grinning at his side.

"You were missed at the Feather, cousin."

Gryffyn pulled the door wider to admit the pair. Trout, a frequent visitor, immediately curled up in her favorite corner near the front window, her black fur blending with the shadows. She huffed a satisfied sigh as Gryffyn turned to his cousin.

"Is that what it appears to be?" he asked, motioning to Jory's wrapped parcel. His mouth watered at the thought of what he suspected lay inside.

"What does it appear to be?" Jory held the package out of Gryffyn's reach.

"'Tis shaped suspiciously like Wynne's raspberry tarts."

Jory frowned. "Aye," he said grudgingly. He handed the package to Gryffyn who eagerly unwrapped it, delighting in the sweet-tart scent of the flaky pastries. Their cousin's raspberry tarts were in nearly as much demand at the Feather as her ale and whisky.

As Gryffyn bit into one of the pastries, his cousin inspected the lintels he'd carved earlier in the day. Trout's eyes opened briefly as she tracked Jory's movements then drifted shut again. Gryffyn had intended to complete more of the town hall order than he had, but his thoughts had repeatedly been drawn back to his sketchbook.

"'Tis a popular design," Jory said, thumping the stone with a finger.

Gryffyn frowned as he licked raspberry preserves from his thumb. "What d'you mean?" he asked. The lintel's motif was a new one he'd not carved before.

"Aye. I saw it just a month agone when I delivered an order of bells to Falmouth. On the new assembly rooms, I believe."

Gryffyn straightened and pointed at the lintel with his half-eaten tart. "You saw *this* design?"

"Or something very similar. You've a better eye for these things. I don't think 'twas a lintel, though, but a plaque above the assembly room doors."

Gryffyn frowned. *Davies.* Davies, who'd dismissed his drawing as forgettable. He swallowed the rest of the tart, but it had lost its appeal.

"Are you going to eat the other one?" Jory asked, motioning to the remaining pastry.

When Gryffyn shook his head, his cousin didn't waste any time catching up the pastry. Trout's ears perked at the promise of a treat, and she wasn't disappointed when a small bit of crust "accidentally" fell from Jory's fingers.

"Is this what's kept you buried in your workshop all night?" his cousin asked around a raspberry mouthful.

Gryffyn shook his head. "There's to be an exhibition in Truro."

His cousin's brows lifted. "And you're carving a piece for it?" At Gryffyn's nod, he said, "Your father is a willing participant to this plan?"

"I didn't afford him much of a choice," Gryffyn said with a wince. "I told him I meant to carve a submission with or without his approval."

Jory swallowed the last of his pastry and leaned against the wall, arms crossed. "And did he give it?"

"I wouldn't say he's approved, precisely. But he's agreeable, so long as it doesn't affect our other commissions," Gryffyn said. "He's not in favor of the effort by any stretch, but 'tis no less than I expected."

Jory surveyed the dim workshop and Gryffyn's guttering candle. "'Twill be a challenge to manage both, to be sure, but you're a fine carver. You'll do a proper job of it."

As a bell tuner, Jory was well acquainted with the precision required for a man's chosen craft. One slip of the hand, one wrong stroke, could ruin a perfectly fine stone—or bell. Gryffyn appreciated his cousin's confidence, although he didn't share it.

"I'm not so certain," he said with a sigh. He

walked to a window at the back of the workshop and Jory followed. A slender moon lit the small stone yard where a large block of white marble awaited Gryffyn's chisel.

"I've a notion for what I wish to carve," he said, staring at the stone, "but I can't get the lines quite right." Then he described the trouble he was having capturing the movement of his figure's hair and skirts.

Jory rubbed his jaw, thinking. "Seems to me, you need a live model," he said.

"Aye, but I won't find one here. The ladies of Newford are the proper sort." Gryffyn realized how his words sounded and hastily added, "As they should be."

His cousin nodded his agreement. "I doubt you'll find one willing to risk her reputation, no matter how respectable the artist." They returned to the front of the workshop, and Jory's eyes brightened with inspiration as he said, "Perhaps you can convince Wynne to sit for you."

Gryffyn snorted at that. Although their cousin would be the first to argue she was neither a lady nor proper, she was the precise opposite of the gentle, flowing inspiration he needed. The soft drape of Miss Moon's skirts fluttered through his mind again, and it was a moment or two before he realized Jory had continued.

"—not certain what I was thinking. Wynne won't settle long enough for you to capture her lines."

Gryffyn nodded, frowning. "'Tis a carver's dilemma to be sure."

"I suppose this additional work means you'll miss tomorrow's assembly," Jory said.

Gryffyn winced. He'd forgotten about the upcoming assembly in the Feather's upper rooms.

Wynne had led a small rebellion the previous year when she'd wrested the town assemblies from the proprietor of The White Dove. Since then, many of their cousins had made a concerted effort to attend. If their participation wasn't entirely voluntary, owing to Wynne's frequent reminders and hints of bodily harm, it was appreciated. He frowned at the thought of more time lost, but perhaps an evening away from his workshop would help sort his mind.

"I'll be there," he assured his cousin.

———

KEREN'S SISTER CAST A CRITICAL eye on the vibrant spectrum of muslin and silk draped across the end of the bed. "These are lovely, Keri, but haven't you anything less . . ."

"Less cheerful? Less diverting?" Keren prompted.

"More demure, rather."

That her sister meant to truss her in debutante drab was a shame, given the vivid hues of plum, cerulean and emerald green to which she was accustomed. But the fact that, of all her sisters, Keren had requested Lizzie's chaperonage for the assembly spoke clearly of her desire to avoid Shropshire. Of the five Moon sisters, Lizzie had the greatest appreciation for proper decorum, which was to say the least tendency toward levity.

Keren waved an impatient hand at the wardrobe. "By all means," she said, "find something you deem more suitable."

Lizzie strode to the open cabinet, now nearly emptied of its contents, and inspected the dregs of Keren's wardrobe. She emerged moments later holding a short pile of pale muslin. "I think one of these shall do nicely," she said.

Keren inhaled and held the breath for a beat before releasing it on a sigh. "Look at me, Lizzie," she said. "I'm three and twenty, not a debutante fresh from the schoolroom."

"Three and twenty and *unwed*," her sister returned.

"Well, there's no need to put varnish on it," Keren grumbled. She was at ease with her choice not to marry, but sometimes the limitations of her unwedded state made her rather peevish.

"Sarcasm is unbecoming, Keri, and besides, you

don't wish to appear fast. If you're to avoid a future with Aunt Agnes, you'll not give Father any cause for complaint."

As Keren had requested her sister's counsel for the express purpose of avoiding Shropshire, she relented, albeit with little grace. "Very well, but I shall choose the ribbon."

Lizzie agreed and they set to work. Some moments later, Keren stood before the mirror and frowned at the bland confection Lizzie had selected. Botheration, but it was utterly forgettable.

She considered the unprecedented notion of forgoing the night's assembly. She'd never willingly given up a night of entertainment before, but then, it had been some time since she'd worn such a lifeless creation. There was a reason this particular gown had been in the back of her wardrobe. She did enjoy dancing, though, so she puffed her cheeks with a resigned sigh.

"Have you decided on a ribbon then?" Lizzie asked. "Perhaps something to match your eyes?"

Keren frowned at her sister. "My eyes are a very dull shade of brown, Lizzie." And she drew the line at wearing a brown ribbon. Then she saw the quirk of her sister's lips and realized she'd been having her on. Her own lips twitched, and she forced them to still.

"Perhaps I shall choose the indecent indigo," she

said with mocking determination. "Or maybe the scandalous saffron."

"Newford's matrons will be atwitter," Lizzie promised, then she added more earnestly, "You do look lovely, Keri."

Keren, however, didn't share her sister's confidence. The fabric had a lovely drape to it, but she struggled to find herself in the glass. White muslin simply didn't suit her. *Demure* didn't suit her. But if that's what it would take to remain in Newford, demure she would be.

———

GRYFFYN EXTINGUISHED THE WORKSHOP LANTERNS and made the short walk home to dress for the assembly. When he descended the stairs to take his leave of his parents, he couldn't miss the delighted look on his mother's face. Indeed, he felt certain the fishermen who'd sailed out for the evening couldn't miss it, so brightly did she beam.

"You're away to the assembly then, love?" she asked.

"Aye," he said, adjusting his sleeves. Then, to prevent her from becoming any more overdone, he added quickly, "But only for a short while."

Her face fell slightly before she smiled again. "Well, to be sure, you'll never meet a nice young lady if you don't venture beyond your workshop and the Feather's coffee room. Even for a short while." She reached up and adjusted the fold of his neckcloth as only a mother could do, then she patted his cheek.

"'Tis a proper shame the vicar's niece isn't yet arrived," his father said as he passed them.

Gryffyn resisted the urge to roll his eyes before stepping through the door. The night was mild for late summer, and a cool breeze rolled through the trees lining the lane. He reached the high street to find the top floor of the Feather aglow in soft candlelight. It spilled through the open windows as people approached the inn in pairs or groups.

One of the Feather's upper rooms had been set aside for cards and another for refreshments while the larger, central room was reserved for dancing. A small orchestra tuned their strings in one corner while a column of older gentlemen made their way to the card room. Wynne had arrived, of course, as it was but a short walk from the Feather's coffee room to the upstairs assembly rooms. She stood to one side with Miss Pepper, Jory's newly betrothed.

Gryffyn offered polite compliments to the ladies as several more of his relations joined them. When the master of ceremonies called the first set and Jory still hadn't arrived, he shared the set with Miss Pepper. He danced another with Wynne when she threatened to cut off his raspberry tarts if he didn't lead her out.

When he'd returned Wynne to her husband, he surveyed the crowd over his relations' heads and wondered if two sets amounted to a sufficient level of support for his cousin. Would his absence be remarked if he left? Then his eyes landed on Miss Moon.

She stood across the room in a demure white gown. He felt his brows hitch toward his hairline— the words *Miss Moon* and *demure* were not frequent companions, after all, but there it was. She held herself erect, her shining, dark hair arranged in a simple style that framed her face and accentuated the long column of her throat. A wall sconce lit her edges from behind, and he was struck by how much she resembled the creamy block of marble behind his workshop.

Smooth and translucent. Luminous.

He gave a mental shake of his head, certain no lady would appreciate being likened to stone, even marble. He knew he was considered odd by some, but that was a bit much, even for him.

Miss Moon looked up then and spied him watching her. Caught out, he tipped her a brief nod of acknowledgment before she pulled her gaze from his. He crossed his arms and watched the twirling dancers until his eyes slid back to Miss Moon. She walked with her sister, and as she moved, the white muslin of her gown rippled softly about her form. He patted his coat pocket, but he'd left his sketchbook back in his workshop. Frowning, he tried to commit the fluid motion of Miss Moon's gown to memory.

The strains of the waltz ended, and the master of ceremonies began placing couples for a quadrille. Before Gryffyn's intent was fully formed, his feet began moving. So focused was he on the folds and drape of Miss Moon's skirts that he didn't notice another man's approach until the squire's son joined her and offered a short bow.

Gryffyn stopped, and the crowd spilled around him. Miss Moon glanced up, eyes catching Gryffyn's once more before she placed a hand on Mr. Carew's sleeve. With a demure half-smile, she allowed him to lead her to their places on the floor.

———

KEREN SIGHED WITH RELIEF AS she stood across from Mr. Carew. She'd held herself in check all evening with nothing but demure glances and softly spoken words. Her teeth hurt with the effort, but Lizzie would be pleased. And if Lizzie was pleased, her father could have no complaint. She'd almost convinced herself she could manage the evening without incident, but then she'd seen Gryffyn Kimbrell approaching from across the room. He'd had a determined set to his face that had caught her up short.

She didn't think her confidence, which already suffered beneath her drab debutante garb, could withstand a dance with the silent carver. To be sure, they'd have nothing to say to one another unless she could prod him into speaking about his carving.

As she turned with the steps of the dance, her eyes found him again. With his height, he was hard to miss. She'd watched earlier as he stood up with his cousin and another young lady, his long form more graceful in executing the steps than she would have expected. Now he stood along the edge of the floor, arms crossed and brows lowered as his cousins laughed and chattered.

He watched the dancers roll about the room with an evaluative gaze, as if he were critiquing their steps. Then she realized he wasn't watching the dancers. He was watching *her*.

With each turn, she glanced over Mr. Carew's shoulder and found Mr. Kimbrell's dark eyes fixed on her . . . hem?

Her face, she would have expected, if he'd developed an interest in her. Her bodice, even, if he was that sort of unmannerly gentleman. But he continued to watch her *skirts*. She gave them an energetic swish with the next turn and his eyes narrowed. Her heart took up a pace she could only partially attribute to the waltz.

Mr. Carew executed a narrow. turn and she nearly missed a step. She drew a heavy breath and forced her eyes back to her partner before she caused them both to trip.

CHAPTER FIVE

KEREN HAD CHECKED ALL OF Henry's known hiding places—behind the sacks of flour in the larder, beneath her father's desk, behind trees and hedges in the gardens—but he wasn't to be found. It wasn't that her brother intended to hide himself, so much as he became easily distracted and often found himself in unexpected places. Last week, he'd dropped a marble in her father's library, and she'd found him beneath the desk, intently investigating a knot in the wood floor.

She emerged from the stables, and Miss Litton met her at the statue in Camborne's circular forecourt.

"He's not in the attic," the governess said. "I knew I shouldn't have allowed him a respite from his geography lesson."

Judging by Miss Litton's furrowed brow and twisting hands, Keren suspected she was regretting her decision to accept this post or worrying she'd be dismissed from it. Neither appealed to Keren as she didn't relish the thought of recruiting yet another governess. There had been quite a string of them, each handily dismissed as soon as her father learned of another of Henry's escapes.

But Miss Litton, despite her inability to keep track of her charge, at least had a firm grasp on geography. Henry's previous governess had insisted that Alexandria could not possibly be on the African continent with such a European name.

"Don't worry, Miss Litton," Keren said soothingly. "He can't have gone far so quickly. We'll find him, but I'd suggest we keep this to ourselves for now. There's no need to concern my father just yet."

Miss Litton's hands stilled. "Yes, of course, you're right. I'll check the icehouse."

"And I'll walk to the end of the lane to see if he's passed that way." Keren considered the heavy sky and wondered if she ought to collect her bonnet and half boots, but there was no telling how far Henry would stray in that time. Lifting her hem, she left the forecourt with quick steps.

The lane connecting Camborne with Newford's high street was well maintained, a consequence of her father's role as mayor. Thick shrubs bordered both sides and rustled with tiny, woodland footsteps. She called Henry's name as she walked, pausing every few steps to listen. Her voice disturbed a squirrel, who darted from the shrubbery, but there was no sign of Henry. Distant thunder rumbled, and she frowned to think of him caught outside when the rain came.

She soon reached the end of the lane and the high street. A cart laden with fishing nets trundled toward the harbor and further down, a carriage departed the Feather's stable yard.

She glanced along the shops bordering both sides of the cobbled street. The bakery lay to her left, but the windows were empty. She'd hoped Henry might have ventured there in search of one of Mr. Clifton's mince pies. The post office, the bank and Morwenna Williamson's dress shop were quiet; Newford's citizens had taken refuge ahead of the coming storm.

The Kimbrell workshop backed onto the river to her right, and a light shone from within. With a bit of effort, she pushed aside the memory of Gryffyn Kimbrell's disconcerting gaze from the night of the assembly, but then movement inside the workshop caught her eye. She recognized his tall stature alongside another, much shorter form.

Henry. Botheration. What did he find so fascinating about stone carving?

—

GRYFFYN SANDED THE TOP OF the headstone he'd just carved and blew dust from the surface. He'd been hurrying through the day's commissions, intent on returning to his sketchbook. But, judging by the volume and velocity of the questions being fired at his head, he'd not have a moment's peace to consider his Truro submission anytime soon.

"How did you manage the detail of the angel's hair? To be sure, it must require a fine touch. Do you have a special chisel for angel hair?" And before Gryffyn could formulate a proper response to that, "How do you know how long to sand the stone?"

Gryffyn watched Henry Moon from the side of his eye and wondered what had become of the lad's keeper. Shouldn't he be with his governess?

"Is the stone very heavy?" Henry asked. "How will you deliver it to the churchyard?"

"Master Henry," Gryffyn said before the boy could draw air for another volley. Henry looked up, eyes owlish behind rounded spectacles as Gryffyn continued. "I use a tooth chisel for the detail in the angel's hair. I sand the stone until it feels right."

Henry opened his mouth, and Gryffyn held up a hand to add, "And I'll secure the assistance of Mr. Payne and Mr. Hodges to transport the stone. Now, would you like to sand something?"

Henry's eyes widened before he gave a quick nod. "Oh, yes, that would be wonderful. Can I sand the headstone? Or perhaps you have something else in need of sanding. What about that urn over there?"

Gryffyn sighed and reached for a piece he'd carved that morning when he should have been working on his Truro submission. He'd been stumbling over his drawings, so he'd taken his chisel to a scrap of limestone instead.

"Why, it's a dragon!" Henry exclaimed, turning the small creature in his hands.

Despite Gryffyn's irritation, he couldn't help a low chuckle at the boy's delight. "Can you feel the roughness of the stone here and here?" he asked, and Henry nodded.

Gryffyn retrieved a piece of emery and demonstrated how to run it along the grain of the stone. "Be sure to use a light hand so you smooth the rough bits without rubbing out the detail, and pause after every second or third stroke to see how it comes along."

"Like this?" Henry rubbed the emery along the dragon's tail once, twice, then paused to blow dust from the stone. Brow wrinkled in concentration, he ran a short finger along the scales then glanced up at Gryffyn.

"Precisely," Gryffyn said. Henry ducked his head again, intent on his task, and Gryffyn thought perhaps he'd dammed the flow of questions for a time. He leaned down to examine the top of the headstone then took up his sanding block again.

"How long did it take to carve the dragon? May I carve one?" Henry asked, and Gryffyn sighed. It was several questions later before Gryffyn realized Henry neither required nor expected a response to all of his queries. He took up his chisel and refined the letters on the headstone to the soft buzzing of Henry's chatter.

Some moments later he looked up in surprise at the silence. Henry's head was bent toward the dragon, tongue poking from his lips as he concentrated on his task. His grip was tight about the dragon's neck as he sanded the poor thing to dust. Gryffyn settled a hand on the boy's shoulder and reached for the carving. Henry looked up and waited as Gryffyn examined the stone.

Gryffyn nodded once. "You did a proper job of it," he said. "Your hand was a bit heavy here—you can see the scale has lost some of its depth—but overall, 'tis a fitty bit of sanding."

Henry gave him a gap-toothed grin, then his attention was caught by something over Gryffyn's shoulder. "Keri!" he said. "I'm sanding. Come see what I've done."

Gryffyn turned to see Miss Moon framed in the doorway's dim light. She was bonnet-less, dark tendrils curling gently about her face. He nodded in greeting and not a little relief that Henry's keeper had arrived to carry him off. "Miss Moon."

"Mr. Kimbrell." She pressed her lips and watched him for a moment before turning to her brother. "Henry, Miss Litton and I have been searching everywhere for you."

"I'm sorry, Keri. I went to examine the bird nest outside the library, but I found a snail instead. He was a large one but slow, as you know snails tend to be. Miss Litton says that's because they have no legs. And then I saw Mr. Kimbrell carving. Well, sanding, rather." Miss Moon's expression didn't twitch even a little at this monologue, nor did she question how a snail outside the library had brought Henry to Gryffyn's workshop. Was she as barmy as her brother?

"Did you see the dragon I sanded?" Henry continued. He held the dragon up for her inspection, and Miss Moon advanced into the workshop with a tentative step. She glanced behind her as if concerned with the propriety of entering his workshop alone. But this was Miss Moon, who didn't concern herself overly with matters of propriety, so he could only assume she was reluctant to be seen entering *his* workshop.

Henry explained the process of sanding stone and the importance of a light hand, and his sister nodded at the appropriate places. When Henry moved to place his dragon among the windowsill's small carvings, Miss Moon looked at Gryffyn over the worktable.

"I apologize for Henry's imposition," she said. "Thank you for allowing him to visit."

"'Twas no imposition," he said politely, if a little untruthfully.

Miss Moon turned and studied her brother. She was silent while Henry lifted a tiny dolphin to the light, turning it first one way then the other as he examined the carved detail. Her eyes narrowed and, without taking them from her brother, she asked softly, "Have you ever considered taking on an apprentice, Mr. Kimbrell?"

"No." The word sprang quickly to his lips— perhaps a little too quickly for politeness. Miss Moon's own lips curved in a half-smile as she pulled her attention from Henry. "I know we've already importuned you once regarding lessons, but is carving instruction something you would consider?"

Gryffyn tempered his rejection and said simply, "I'm afraid I haven't the time, Miss Moon, to provide lessons."

"My father would compensate you, of course. And I'm certain it wouldn't require more than an hour of your time at any one go," she said, her look slightly pleading. "I don't think Henry's attentiveness could bear much more than that."

"I'm sorry, Miss Moon, but—"

"You see how the carvings have captured his interest. I'm certain my father would be willing to pay double whatever your time is worth."

Gryffyn felt his brows lift. "I don't need—"

The clouds beyond the window shifted then, and a damp breeze blew through the opening. Miss Moon turned toward Henry, and Gryffyn was struck again by the motion of her skirts and the movement of her uncovered hair as the breeze lifted a tendril at her neck. His brows drew down in thought as she turned back to him once more, and his cousin's words echoed: *You need a live model.*

"Triple?" she offered.

"I'll do it," he said, surprising himself as much as Miss Moon. He swallowed, uncertain how his next words would be received. "In exchange for your time."

She took a small step back, coming up against his worktable. "My—my time?"

"And permission to draw you."

———

KEREN STARED AT GRYFFYN KIMBRELL in confusion, one hand pressed against her pounding heart. He wished to *draw* her? He watched her through his lashes as he waited for her reply.

No one had ever made such an unusual request of her, not to mention inappropriate. Her father had commissioned an artist a few years before to paint her portrait, but what Mr. Kimbrell suggested was different. It was not a transaction sanctioned by her father, in his home, in his presence. To be sure, allowing Mr. Kimbrell to draw her for his own purposes was precisely the sort of forward activity her father did *not* wish her to undertake.

As it was, she'd been anxious since arriving at his workshop, worried one of the town gossips would report back to her father that she'd been seen entering the establishment alone, with no one present but an eight-year-old boy and Mr. Kimbrell himself. If she wasn't careful, she'd find herself on her way to Shropshire and Aunt Agnes before the week was out.

But then she'd been struck by how intently Henry regarded the man's little stone carvings. Her brother's attention had remained fixed for more than a fleeting minute on the curves and details of a small dolphin. She'd chastised him for appealing to Mr. Kimbrell for carving lessons, but perhaps Henry had the right of it; maybe stone carving was precisely the activity to capture his focus.

But then Mr. Kimbrell's proposal had confounded her. He waited, unsmiling.

"Why?" she asked simply. "Why do you wish to draw me?"

"I know it must seem a strange and bold request," he said, "but I aim to submit a sculpture to the exhibition in Truro. I need a model—"

"A model?" She lowered her voice, conscious of Henry behind her. "Mr. Kimbrell, I'm not the sort to permit a . . . an *artist* . . . to take my likeness." Heavens, had she truly allowed her reputation to falter so greatly? That thought—certainly not the forbidden nature of his request—set her heart to flapping against her ribcage.

"I assure you, Miss Moon, I mean no disrespect," he said somberly. "'Tis merely your hair and"—he waved a hand toward her sprigged muslin day dress—"your skirts I wish to draw, so I might capture the motion properly."

She stifled a surprised cough. *Merely* her hair and skirts? Somehow, that made the request all the stranger, and all the more inappropriate. She recalled his odd preoccupation with her hem at the assembly, and her cheeks heated at the thought of him studying her skirts while he sketched them. His eyes would be trained on her ankles, her legs . . . Lud, if her father found out, she'd never see Cornwall again.

"Will you do it, Keri?" Henry asked at her elbow. She'd been so caught up in Mr. Kimbrell's request she'd not heard her brother's approach. His eyes were wide and hopeful behind his lenses, and for a moment—only a fleeting beat—she nearly agreed to the carver's mad scheme. But she still had a shred of sense it seemed.

"No, Henry. I don't think it would be"—Sensible? Sane? Proper?—"appropriate," she finished.

Her brother's face fell, brows disappearing behind the metal rims of his spectacles, and she thought even Mr. Kimbrell's posture might have sagged a bit.

"But if Mr. Kimbrell changes his mind about receiving thrice the fee, he may find us at Camborne. Perhaps with such a generous payment, he could afford the services of an artist's model." Had that sharp, prudish tone come from her?

Mr. Kimbrell nodded but remained silent, although she supposed that was his normal state. The disappointment she'd detected in his stance was gone, and a polite expression settled on his face as he watched them take their leave.

Sketch her skirts, indeed.

CHAPTER SIX

GRYFFYN WATCHED MISS MOON AND Henry leave the workshop, the boy prattling to his sister about the clouds that were near to bursting above Newford. He closed his eyes on their departure and rubbed the back of his neck until he recalled the stone dust covering his hands.

The ladies of Newford are the proper sort, as they should be.

You'll not find one willing to risk her reputation.

Despite his exchange with Jory, he'd thought the mayor's flirtatious daughter might have been open to such an arrangement. Clearly, he'd been mistaken. Whether her reluctance was due to the improper nature of the request or simply a desire to avoid his company he couldn't say. He suspected it was the latter as much as the former.

He straightened and forced his jaw to relax then

crossed to his sketchbook. She may not have agreed to be his model, but that didn't mean the image of her skirts wasn't still fluttering through his mind. He picked up his charcoal and began to draw.

A sharp clap of thunder shook the rafters moments before a slashing rain pelted the slate roof. He closed the window and continued sketching, but then the thought of Miss Moon and Henry intruded on his concentration. Had they reached Camborne before the rain began?

He turned his attention back to the muslin flowing across the page before him, but the rest of the image eluded him. He squeezed his eyes shut, but it wouldn't be recaptured. Tossing the charcoal aside with a sigh, he stood and retrieved an umbrella.

Miss Moon and Henry were pure and soggy by the time he found them halfway up the lane to Cambourne. Henry seemed to be enjoying the experience as he skipped and splashed—quite deliberately, Gryffyn thought—through a deep puddle while his sister kept to the meager shelter of the trees lining the lane, hem trailing in the mud behind her.

"Miss Moon," he called as the rain pounded the leaves above them. She didn't stop. He raised his voice and called again, "Miss Moon!"

She stiffened for a moment then turned. Her

hair, which had curled so nicely in his workshop, hung limply about her ears, and her skirts were heavy and sodden. He'd heard of London ladies who dampened their skirts, and he couldn't help but notice how Miss Moon's drenched muslin outlined her form.

He quickly pulled his gaze back to her eyes as he contemplated how to capture such an adherent, liquid quality in his stone.

"Mr. Kimbrell," she said, lifting her voice to be heard above the rain. The soft fragrance of warm orange blossoms rose from her dripping hair, and her eyes were large beneath the thick fringe of her lashes.

"I've brought an umbrella," he said unnecessarily. He handed it to her, and she took it automatically as he tugged his arms from the sleeves of his coat.

"It's a kind gesture, to be sure, but I'm afraid the damage is done." She motioned to her hair with her free hand.

"Nevertheless," he said, "I can't allow you to continue without it. You and Henry will catch your deaths." Finally free of the garment, he stretched it toward her. "'Tis wet on the outside, but warm and dry on the inside."

She hesitated before allowing him to place the coat about her shoulders.

"Henry," he said above the rain. "Come walk with your sister."

Henry looked up from where he stood ankle deep in a puddle, surprise etching his features to see Gryffyn had joined them. He grinned and splashed to their side, spectacles fogged on his face.

"As a gentleman, you must avoid the puddles," Gryffyn said, "so your sister doesn't become any more dampened than she is. A gentleman must see to a lady's comfort above all things."

Henry's expression turned serious, and he nodded. Then he promptly stepped toward the center of the lane and the next puddle. Gryffyn rested a hand on his shoulder and steered him back under the umbrella with Miss Moon.

Gryffyn's hat kept the worst of the rain from his head and neck as he accompanied the pair to their home, but it did nothing to keep his gaze from straying to Miss Moon's sodden form. *That* required a strong will.

———

KEREN RELUCTANTLY CURLED INTO THE warmth of Mr. Kimbrell's coat as rain pelted his umbrella. She inhaled, her nose twitching slightly at the surprisingly soft, spicy scent of him that floated about her. She ought to be dismayed to be caught in such a condition, with her hair falling from its pins and rain dripping from the end of her nose. Indeed, were Mr. Kimbrell the object of one of her flirtations, she would have been mortified. But as she wouldn't be engaging in any flirtation for the foreseeable future, she allowed herself to relax.

He reached for Henry's shoulder and steered him back to the puddle-less parts of their narrow lane, and she breathed a soft sigh of relief. Her brother was a delight most of the time, but his energy knew no restraint, and she and Miss Litton were at a loss to know how to contain it. It was a relief to allow someone else the pleasure of guiding him, if only for a moment.

Mr. Kimbrell had surprised her with his sudden appearance, and she watched him from the side of her eye, curious about his intentions in following them. Did he think to change her mind about his proposal?

She thought again of Aunt Agnes and her deerhounds, and of Henry, who'd be left alone for all intents if she were sent to Shropshire. Her father was much too busy with his mayoral duties to pay him proper attention, and Miss Litton alone couldn't keep a rein on him any more than his previous three governesses. Keren's current, sodden condition stood as evidence to that fact.

No, she couldn't allow her father to send her

away, which meant she couldn't entertain Mr. Kimbrell's suggestion, no matter how intriguing she might find it.

———

LATER THAT AFTERNOON, KEREN—DRIED, newly curled and wearing a fresh gown—joined Henry and his governess in the nursery. A wrinkle of worry creased the space between Miss Litton's brows. She leaned toward Keren and asked on a low whisper, "You're certain your father is unaware that Henry was missing?"

Keren poured tea and passed a warm cup to the governess. "He wasn't *missing*, precisely," she said. "His whereabouts were simply unknown for a very short time." She wasn't certain her father's characterization of the day's events would align with her own, but that was a worry for another day.

Henry knelt on the floor before the fireplace, a painted army solider in one hand and a navy ship in the other as he enacted his own version of the Battle of Trafalgar. Neither he nor his army soldier were concerned that the event had been a naval engagement; Henry had never been one to sacrifice a good story for the sake of historical accuracy.

Miss Litton tapped her chin in contemplation.

"And Henry was attentive to Mr. Kimbrell's direction?"

Keren frowned but agreed with a short nod. "As much as you or I have ever seen him to be."

Miss Litton nibbled her thumbnail and nodded slowly. "It's a shame Mr. Kimbrell hasn't the time to provide lessons. Henry was quite intrigued with the man's carvings when we returned his chisel. He clearly has an interest there, and I think he could benefit from the instruction. Perhaps . . ."

Her voice trailed off, and Keren set her cup in the saucer. "Perhaps . . . ?"

Miss Litton sipped at her tea and watched Keren over the rim. "I was just wondering if Mr. Kimbrell might find he has the time for lessons if you offered recompense."

Keren shifted on her overstuffed chair and adjusted her skirts before admitting, "I did—offer to pay him, that is. But he's not a man motivated by money."

Miss Litton's brows lifted at that. "Well, certainly there must be something that could persuade him."

Keren rubbed at a loose thread with her thumb then blurted, "I believe there is." She cleared her throat and lowered her voice. "It seems Mr. Kimbrell would like to . . . sketch me. In exchange for instructing Henry, that is. Of course, I declined."

"Sketch you?" Miss Litton asked in a hushed whisper. "Never say he made such an improper suggestion!"

Keren, unaccountably, felt the need to defend Mr. Kimbrell. "His request was only on account of his work. He wishes to draw my skirts and . . . and my hair, so he can capture the motion in his stone carving." Even as she said the words, she cringed at how odd they sounded. At how odd they made Mr. Kimbrell appear.

Miss Litton leaned back against her chair and studied the low fire. "Your *skirts*?" she asked.

Keren nodded.

"And your *hair*?"

Keren nodded again.

"But not your face or anything of a more personal nature?"

Keren thought Mr. Kimbrell paying her skirts such marked attention was rather personal—far more than any harmless flirtation she'd ever engaged in—but she shook her head at Miss Litton's query.

"Perhaps it's not so improper then," the governess said hesitantly, and Keren's brows lifted.

Miss Litton set her tea on the low table before them and continued. "No one would need to know they're *your* skirts and *your* hair, after all . . ."

Her voice lifted with a question at the end of her

statement. It was clear Miss Litton wasn't wholly convinced of her own argument, but Keren straightened. Henry's governess was onto something. Even if Mr. Kimbrell's carved skirts and hair resembled her own, they were only skirts and hair. How would anyone ever know *Keren* had been his model?

Lizzie's face appeared in her mind's eye with a scowl for what she was considering. Keren pushed her sister aside none-too-gently and glanced toward Henry. Her brother had abandoned his naval battle and was attempting to walk on his hands across the nursery.

"If we're to do this," she murmured, "Mr. Kimbrell will have to prepare his drawings under the guise of providing Henry's lessons." She couldn't risk meeting with him separately, but no one would question their presence in his workshop while he instructed her brother.

Miss Litton nodded agreeably. "No one need ever know of the arrangement," she said.

Dimly, Keren thought she should be concerned with the ease with which Miss Litton had persuaded her of the scheme. Whether that was a reflection of her own deficits or Miss Litton's, she couldn't say, but she was going to do it.

She was going to allow Gryffyn Kimbrell to draw her hair and skirts.

The thought caused her cheeks to heat anew, and she pressed cool hands to soothe them. When had the mayor's flirtatious daughter developed such an irritating tendency to blush?

———

TWO DAYS LATER, GRYFFYN STOOD in the linney behind his workshop and eyed the charcoal outline he'd drawn on his marble. If he meant to have the piece finished in time, he'd need to begin roughing out the general shape of the thing. He could worry about the details later. He eyed the thin, dark lines with a critical eye then, taking up a linen rag, he rubbed them away to begin again.

Presently, he became aware of voices coming through the workshop's open back door. He set the rag aside and re-entered to see Henry Moon had arrived, along with his sister and the governess. Had Miss Moon come to quadruple her offer?

"Miss Moon," he said with a dip of his head. "Miss Litton. Master Henry. I'm pleased to see you've not suffered from your travels in the rain."

"Good afternoon, Mr. Kimbrell," Miss Moon said stiffly. Her gaze landed everywhere but on him, and Gryffyn knew a moment of regret for his impulsive suggestion from their last encounter. He'd not wished to cause her discomfort.

"Henry wished to examine the dolphin in your window again," she continued, "with your permission."

"O' course," he said with a nod toward Henry.

Miss Moon glanced once toward Miss Litton, who jumped to accompany Henry to the figures in the front window. Gryffyn watched curiously as Miss Moon stepped closer to him, hands twisting where she held them before her.

"Does your offer still stand?" she asked on a whisper.

He stilled. "Aye," he said hesitantly.

"I will allow you to sketch me in exchange for Henry's lessons, but I have some requirements."

Gryffyn's brows angled over his nose, and he forced his frown to relax. "Please continue," he said.

"You must do your sketching while Henry receives his lesson. I can't explain spending any more time here than is necessary for his instruction."

He considered her words then nodded. "Very well. D'you have other terms?"

"*No one* is to know about this, save you, me and Miss Litton. Even Henry—*especially* Henry—cannot know."

His frown returned. "To be sure, he'll see my sketches."

"But you're only sketching my hair and skirts, are you not? He needn't know they're *my* hair and skirts. You've heard how he goes on. He hasn't yet learned the art of discretion, and as I said, no one must know of our arrangement."

Gryffyn looked down at the charcoal staining his fingers before returning his gaze to her. "Miss Moon," he said, "I've no wish for you to do anything with which you're not comfortable."

She was silent for a beat before saying, "You still wish to sketch me, do you not?"

He hesitated then nodded once.

"And Henry will benefit from your lessons. All will be well, so long as you agree to my terms."

He watched her for a moment more before replying, "I agree."

She exhaled, her features relaxing, and asked, "When would you like to begin?"

"Now?"

"Now?" she squeaked.

"My submission is due in Truro in a matter of weeks. My time is short, Miss Moon."

CHAPTER SEVEN

THIS WAS SURELY A MISTAKE. If stupidity alone were sufficient grounds for exile, Keren thought perhaps she deserved to spend the rest of her days in Shropshire. She watched as Mr. Kimbrell stood over his worktable with Henry and explained how to "dress" a stone.

Henry's expression was rapt, his attention focused behind his spectacles, and she forced her misgivings aside. His attention was *focused*.

"Are we making a fox? Or a dolphin?" Henry asked.

"We're a fair distance from carving a fox," Mr. Kimbrell said. "Dressing a stone—'tis more the work of a mason than a carver, but 'twill help you master the use of the broad chisel."

"Where did you purchase your chisel? Did you craft it yourself? It seems sharp—how do you keep the steel so sharp?" Henry asked.

Keren and Miss Litton exchanged a worried smile at his endless questions. Keren thought Mr. Kimbrell would soon realize he'd gotten the poor end of this bargain, but he merely said, "All in good time, lad," before angling a flat chisel against a rough piece of stone.

He methodically tapped the end with a mallet, working his way around the stone, and Keren blinked when he lifted a perfectly smooth, "dressed" block from the rubble on his worktable. His hand was large with a wide palm and long fingers. Fine dark hairs disappeared beneath his sleeve, and Keren's breath caught at the male strength inherent in that single appendage. If she had any artistic talent—beyond terrier-like foxes, that was—she thought she might like to paint his hand.

She mentally shook herself; one modeling arrangement between them was quite enough.

He placed a smaller piece of stone on the table and handed the chisel to Henry, who struggled to wrap his smaller hand about the handle.

"Aye," Mr. Kimbrell said with a frown. "You'll need some proper tools of your own." He led a wide-eyed Henry toward a cabinet at the back of the shop where, after a moment's rummaging, he withdrew a small wooden crate. "These are the tools

I used when I learned to carve with my father," he said. "You may borrow them for your lessons."

He unrolled a leather cloth on the worktable then lined several of the smaller tools upon it. The handles were worn with faded blue paint, and Henry reached for a mallet.

As Mr. Kimbrell explained the proper way to hold the tool, Keren sighed and moved toward the open window. At this rate, Henry would require all of Mr. Kimbrell's time, and he'd have none to sketch.

A breeze carried the scents of Newford through the window. Salt and sea. Pies from Mr. Clifton's bakery. She lifted the fox Henry had studied on their first visit and held it to the light as Mr. Kimbrell had instructed. The little animal came alive in her hand as the sun lit the edges of the marble. The detail—from the hair about its ears to the bushy tail—was remarkable, and she knew a sudden curiosity to see what he would carve for Truro. If the tiny figurines in the window were any indication, it would be impressive indeed.

The steady thump of Henry's mallet continued behind her, and she turned to check his progress. And inhaled sharply to see Mr. Kimbrell seated on a stool across the room, studying her skirts, charcoal in hand as his fingers raced across his sketchbook. Her eyes flew to Henry, and she exhaled in relief to see his head was angled intently, and quite obliviously, toward his stone.

She approached Mr. Kimbrell. "Do—do you need me to sit somewhere?" she whispered. When her father's portraitist had painted her, she'd posed in a chair before the fireplace.

He looked up sharply, as if he'd been unaware of her approach despite the fact he'd been furiously sketching her skirts. "No," he said. "'Tis best to capture your natural movements."

"Very well," she said uncertainly, willing her heart to slow its rapid pace. "Shall I just return to the window then?"

"Aye, or you can move about the workshop if you prefer. There are more carvings toward the back." He waited for her to move, charcoal poised above the page as he watched her through impossibly thick lashes. His soft, spicy scent—familiar now after her walk in his coat—drifted up to tease her nose.

She lifted her skirts slightly with one hand and gave a little twitch of the muslin. "Do you need me to . . . I don't know . . . flutter my skirts?"

His lips, which she noticed were finely sculpted, tilted in an almost-smile as he continued to watch her. "Flutter your skirts? No, Miss Moon. I aim to capture the natural motion of the cloth as you move. No fluttering is required."

She felt her own lips twitch at his amusement. When he bent his head toward the page again, she leaned forward, curious, but she was unable to see what he'd sketched. She turned and walked as naturally as she could toward the back of his workshop, conscious of his eyes on her as she moved.

——

GRYFFYN WATCHED MISS MOON MOVE stiffly toward the back of his workshop. Sighing, he straightened and lowered his charcoal. He'd captured a few good strokes as she'd stood in the light of the front window, but now that she was aware of his regard, her movements had become wooden. Unnatural. He'd not achieve what he needed until she could become comfortable with him watching her.

And now he'd committed his time—hours he didn't have—to instructing Henry. He feared the arrangement he'd made with Miss Moon wouldn't be nearly as advantageous as he'd hoped. He set his sketchbook aside and joined Henry at the worktable.

"How did I do?" Henry asked as he lifted a partially squared block of stone with both hands. The stone was smaller, admittedly, but the edges were none too smooth. The boy's eyes were wide and earnest behind his spectacles as he awaited Gryffyn's assessment.

"'Tis nearly there," Gryffyn said. "You just need to smooth out the pointy bits." He bent down to show Henry how to do just that and belatedly realized he held his own chisel. The smaller tool he'd retrieved for Henry lay abandoned at the far edge of the table.

"Why are you not using the smaller chisel?" he asked.

Henry shrugged. "I forgot which one I was supposed to use."

"Oh, well aye. They look much the same, I suppose."

He looked to Miss Litton for help, but she merely shrugged, much as Henry had done. "Henry can be quite forgetful at times," she said. "We're forever leaving notes about Camborne to remind him to clean his teeth or complete his French lesson."

Gryffyn suspected many of the adults in Henry's life had simply come to accept his odd ways, adjusting their expectations to accommodate his eccentricities. But he recalled his own carving lessons from his father, which had been gentle but firm, and he knew such accommodations would not help Henry learn the trade properly.

"An accomplished carver always uses the best tool for the task," he told Henry gently, his father's words sounding odd in his own voice. "I think you'll find better success if you can remember to use the tools I've laid out for you."

Again, he wondered if he hadn't made a mistake in striking this bargain with Miss Moon. He looked up to find her studying his carvings at the far side of the room. Her skirts swayed softly as she leaned forward to examine his collection of stone frogs. She'd forgotten his observation of her.

He handed Henry the smaller chisel and hurriedly showed him again how to shear off the rough edges of the stone. Before he could return to his sketchbook, though, Miss Moon straightened and looked at him over her shoulder. She stiffened slightly when she saw he watched her.

Aye, to be sure, this had been a mistake.

———

KEREN DRESSED AND JOINED HER father in the drawing room as the day's light yielded to a pale moon. It had been some time since he'd been home long enough for them to enjoy supper together, but they were to dine before he left for business in Falmouth.

Miss Litton and Henry had arrived in the drawing room ahead of her, and she entered to hear her brother's rapid, breathless recitation of his carving lessons. She'd not told her father of

Henry's instruction yet, thinking his agreement would be easier to secure once the matter was a *fait accompli*.

She held her breath to see if Henry would say anything of Mr. Kimbrell's sketching, but he remained silent on that point. She felt certain if he'd noticed what the carver had been drawing, he wouldn't have hesitated to include *that* accounting in his monologue.

When Simons announced supper, Miss Litton led Henry back to the nursery to prepare for bed. Keren stood to move toward the dining room, but her father stopped her, greying brows dipped in a frown. "What are these lessons of Henry's?"

"Well . . . Henry has shown an interest in stone carving, as I'm sure you heard from his report, and Mr. Kimbrell has agreed to provide lessons." She spoke the words simply, as if the mayor's son receiving lessons from a stone carver was of little import.

Her father's frown intensified, and she hurried to add, "You should see Henry, Father. The attention he gives his carving lessons is quite remarkable. Certainly, more than Miss Litton and I have seen with any of his other subjects, and I believe the lessons will only reinforce his study of the classics. Mathematics, even." She crossed her fingers on that last bit, as she thought it might have been a stretch.

"Stone carving?" he said with a long stroke of his side whiskers.

Keren nodded, hands folded before her as she waited for him to follow along.

Finally, he said, "Well, if Kimbrell has time to provide instruction in the craft, I suppose there's no harm in it. Knowing Henry's tendencies, it's sure to be a short-lived pursuit anyway." Then, eyes narrowed, he said, "I assume Kimbrell's fee is fair?"

Keren hesitated for a beat before saying, "Yes, it's quite fair."

Her father nodded then said, "I'm afraid I won't be able to stay for dinner after all. I must leave directly for Falmouth."

"Oh. I see." Keren's smile fell, and she quickly lifted it again. "Would you like company for your drive? I can change and join you in a trice."

His gaze slid away before he replied, "No, that won't be necessary. It will be nothing but dreadfully dull talk of political matters, and I'm certain you'd not thank me for dragging you away from Henry." He tugged at the cuffs of his coat then adjusted his cravat.

She frowned at his odd behavior, at his over-explaining, then she noticed the coat he wore. It was his favorite one, a smart blue superfine he wore whenever he won an election. He kept his gaze from hers as he called for his hat and gloves, and she swallowed as the realization hit her. Her father was meeting a lady in Falmouth, and she was dining alone.

———

GRYFFYN CLEANED HIS TOOLS AND returned them to their places then began the short walk home. The day had been productive as far as routine commissions went. After Henry's lesson, he'd completed more of the lintels for the town hall and repaired several loose stones at Mr. Clifton's bakery before joining his father to work on a hedge near Weirmouth.

But as for his Truro project, he'd not made any progress. He couldn't even blame Miss Moon's stiff manner. His mind just wasn't forming the image he wished to carve. A rest from thoughts of stone carving was what he needed.

He joined his parents for supper, determined to set the Truro competition and Miss Moon from his mind. His mother began speaking while his father carved a joint of lamb.

"I encountered Edith Pentreath at Morwenna's," she said, referring to his cousin's dress shop. "She was admiring a lovely length of green ribbon Morwenna's just had from London, but I've never seen her wear anything besides blue or grey. I think she only means to get the better of Mary Clifton."

His father murmured agreeably as Gryffyn accepted a slice of lamb.

"She did mention," his mother continued, "that Miss Moon has been spending time at your workshop." The words were laid casually on the table alongside the peas with mint sauce, but his mother watched him carefully over the rim of her glass.

"Her brother"—Gryffyn cleared his throat and began again—"her brother wishes to have carving lessons. I've been instructing him."

"Aye?" his father said. "I hope Moon is paying handsomely for your time. The lad's a handful, by all accounts."

"The compensation is sufficient," Gryffyn said. His parents were silent as they chewed, and he felt their gazes as he speared a mushroom in a savory port sauce. "Mrs. Quick has outdone herself again," he said.

"You can do better than Miss Moon, son," his father said, and Gryffyn felt his brows climb. "The mayor's youngest daughter is quite the accomplished flirt, from what I've heard."

"Thomas, there's nothing wrong with a little flirtation," his mother said. "'Tis how I secured your affections, after all. Although I do wonder if constancy is in Miss Moon's nature."

"I've no interest in Miss Moon," Gryffyn said, "nor does she in me. Her brother's lessons are the only purpose to our meeting." He swallowed uncomfortably on the half-truth then added, "There's no flirting involved."

"Well, why not?" his mother asked, and he swallowed uncomfortably. "You're a fine and respectable gentleman. Kind and pleasing to look upon. She could do much worse, love."

"You're my mother," he said, although her defense warmed him. "By the very definition of the word, you're blind to my faults, and 'tis a requirement for you to say such things."

"On the contrary," she said with heat. "As your mother, I'm the most qualified to know your faults, although I will deny them to anyone who asks."

Gryffyn leaned back and set his fork down. His parents watched him with amusement in their eyes. "What are they then?" he asked. "These faults of mine? I don't deny they exist, but I'm curious to know if your list matches mine."

"Don't you worry if our lists match," his mother said. "Find a nice lady and match your list to *hers*. If she knows your faults and loves you anyway, that's the love of your heart."

He studied his plate for a beat. Should he tell them he had no plans to wed or let them work it out for themselves? It was true that men and women of questionable birth married all the time, and he wasn't so noble to let such circumstances alone prevent him from taking a wife. But he didn't even know his true name. How could he, in good conscience, offer the respected name of Kimbrell if it wasn't his to give?

And yet, he couldn't inquire about the matter without hurting his parents, and it wasn't as if there were a lady awaiting his suit anyway.

In the end, he simply nodded and returned his attention and his silence to the near-empty plate before him.

"Is there dessert?" his father asked.

CHAPTER EIGHT

GRYFFYN ASSISTED HIS MOTHER TO clear the supper things, then he took himself off to the Feather's coffee room. Many of his cousins would be at the inn, and he felt the need for their companionship, if not necessarily their conversation.

A mizzly rain had begun to fall, and he shook beads of moisture from his coat and hat as he stepped into the inn's flagged entry. Low laughter rolled from the coffee room, and he took himself in the direction of his cousins' table.

"Gryffyn," Wynne said as she passed him with a tray of empty glasses. "I thought you, at least, would have the sense to stay home in this weather. Not that I'm complaining, mind you. I welcome the custom, and Peggy and Anna will welcome the tips."

"'Twould seem my sense has fled along with that

of our cousins," he said.

Wynne rolled her eyes and left him to return her tray to the kitchens. The coffee room was empty save the table in the front window where his cousins sat. He took his seat in time to hear their impassioned debate on the merits of whisky versus ale, which was no debate at all to his way of thinking. He relaxed into his chair as Peggy, his cousin's barmaid, set a glass of amber whisky before him.

She winked and cast a friendly smile at him, as was her custom; Wynne's barmaid was not overly particular about where and with whom she shared her smiles. And that thought, of course, brought his mind around to Miss Moon. He wondered where she'd dined that evening—had she enjoyed supper with her father and Henry, or had she dined with friends? Perhaps she and her father had entertained some of his political acquaintances. Would she mention Henry's carving lessons?

"What d'you think, Gryff?" His cousins watched him expectantly as rain slid down the window glass, and he pulled his thoughts back to the coffee room.

"Sorry?"

Alfie smiled his broad grin. "Sometimes, cousin, I think you've as many rocks in your head as you have in your workshop. I'm thinking to purchase the old Penhollow farm. What d'you say to that?"

"The Penhollow farm? Whatever for?" To

Gryffyn's recollection, the property held little more than a ramshackle house, although its rolling orchards afforded pleasant views of Newford and the sea beyond. But Alfie shared a perfectly comfortable home with his father and seven younger brothers. Gryffyn couldn't imagine why he'd wish to acquire a new property, unless . . . "Are you courting a lady then?"

"Oh, aye," Alfie snorted. "Two or three, though never on the same day. I've learned my lesson there. But that's not what has me traipsing the mud at Penhollow. The farmland and orchards there are well suited for a brewery, and there's already a cider mill on the grounds. And a fair bit of work will turn the Penhollow cottage into a comfortable house."

Gryffyn sat back in surprise. "You're doing it then. You mean to start your brewery."

Alfie grinned. "Aye, although I'm thinking to begin with the cidery and expand from there."

"Congratulations, cousin," Gryffyn said with a nod and a whisky salute. Alfie had often spoken of creating his own establishment, but his words—while enthusiastic —had lacked the action to make such a declaration reality. Gryffyn considered his cousin more closely, surprised to see a determined set to Alfie's jaw.

"'Tis time," Alfie said. "I can't wait for Wynne to add a brewery to the Feather," he added a little more loudly than necessary.

Wynne passed their table with another roll of her eyes. "I can hear you, Alfie. There's no need to shout."

"What's finally persuaded you to do it?" Jory asked.

"You know how crowded my father's house has become now that my brothers are older. They take up an impressive amount of space, and they eat more than their share of Mrs. Beadle's cooking. 'Tis become a nightly battle to fill my plate."

Gryffyn and his cousins murmured their sympathy as all of them appreciated a full plate.

"And, to be honest, 'tis some difficult for a man to hear his own thoughts, much less think on his future amidst such mayhem. I thought a change of scene might be in order. The mere thought of it has set my mind to overflowing with ideas," Alfie finished, rubbing his hands together.

A change of scene . . . Gryffyn thought of Miss Moon and her unnatural stiffness as he'd sketched in his workshop. Surrounded by the tools of his trade, she'd been uncomfortably aware of their arrangement and of his regard. Perhaps different surroundings would set her at ease. He'd have to give the matter more thought if he hoped to see any success from their arrangement.

Wynne returned with a plate of her raspberry

tarts, and seven hands reached out before it landed on the table. Gryffyn took a large bite of one, enjoying the pastry's steaming sweetness.

"I hear Miss Moon has been spending time in your workshop," Wynne said, hands folded before her in a deceptive pose meant to disarm.

Gryffyn narrowed his eyes at her, certain she'd timed her words to catch him with his mouth full. He hurried to swallow, burning his tongue in the process. "Her brother," he clarified after a swallow of whisky. "I'm providing Henry Moon with carving lessons." How many times would he be required to explain their arrangement?

"Henry?" Gavin asked. "Moon has his hands full with that one. I found the boy hatless and halfway to Weirmouth last month. Claimed he'd been following a flock of birds." Gavin shook his head. "To be sure, 'taint the sort of task I imagined when I took on the role of parish constable."

"You're keeping company with Miss Moon?" Alfie asked.

"I'm not *keeping company* with anyone."

"Aye, well, you'd do well to keep yourself clear of Miss Moon," James said. "She's quite the flirt."

"I've heard Miss Moon doesn't intend to marry," Merryn said.

"Which should give you pause, Gryff. The lady is disingenuous at best, as every lady intends to marry," James stated, crossing his arms.

"Regardless of the lady's intentions," Cadan added, "her father won't hesitate to force the issue if it comes to it. You recall what happened with the other daughter."

"Aye, the beauty," Alfie said and everyone nodded. Although it had been some years, they all recalled the incident in question when the mayor had leveled Miss Elizabeth Moon's suitor with a well-aimed punch. The vicar had promptly called the banns the following Sunday.

"Miss Moon doesn't flirt," Gryffyn said.

"Doesn't flirt?" Wynne said, her voice rising as she fisted her hands on her hips. "Where were you during the hurling?" Jory quirked a brow of apologetic confirmation in Gryffyn's direction as Wynne continued. "If Miss Moon doesn't flirt, then Alfie Kimbrell doesn't drink all my ale and whisky." Alfie frowned at that but held his tongue.

"What I meant is that she doesn't flirt with *me*," Gryffyn amended with a frown.

Merryn eyed him with a mouthful of raspberry tart. He swallowed then said, "To be sure, Miss Moon flirts with everyone. Perhaps you just don't recognize flirting when you see it."

"I'm certain I can recognize flirting," Gryffyn said, turning his glass between his hands.

"All right," Alfie said, leaning back with a broad

grin. "Name three ways a lady may flirt to gain a gentleman's notice."

"To what end?" Gryffyn asked. He reached for the last tart, but Gavin beat him to it.

"To demonstrate your knowledge of the art. Enlighten us."

Gryffyn inhaled heavily through his nose. His cousins would be insufferable until he played along. And to think he'd actually sought their companionship this evening. They watched him, waiting, familiar grins on their faces, and he sighed. As irritating as they could be, he'd take their good-natured teasing as an indication of their affection, feeble as it was.

"Only three?" he said, leaning back and crossing his arms. "Well, there's flirtatious conversation. And o' course, a lady may flirt with her eyes. And how a lady holds herself in the presence of a gentleman can be flirtatious. I suppose it would depend upon the lady."

His cousins murmured their agreement, save Wynne.

"So, 'twould look something like this?" she asked, twining a curl about her finger. She pursed her lips in a pout and glanced at him through her lashes. Then, fluttering a hand above his arm, she settled it with a gentle squeeze.

Gryffyn frowned in exasperation as his cousins

erupted into laughter. "No, Wynne," he said. "Truly, how did you secure Roddie's affections? Flirtation must arise naturally, without artifice. Otherwise, 'tis naught more than trifling."

Wynne straightened and smiled approvingly, and he shifted under her gaze.

"So, lads, 'twould seem he does know flirting, after all," Merryn said.

"O' course I know flirting. I'm not daft."

"We wondered, cousin."

"And you are equally certain Miss Moon hasn't displayed any of these flirting behaviors?"

"Not with me."

"Perhaps she falls more in the triflers' camp."

And on that note, Gryffyn put an end to the discussion. "To be sure, 'taint proper to discuss the lady in such terms." Despite what he'd told his cousins, he wasn't always clear on the signals that ladies sent out. But whether Miss Moon was a flirter or a trifler, she'd been pleasant and polite to him, and he was certain she didn't deserve to be discussed so openly.

"Our cousin is right," James said with a frown, and they grudgingly returned the conversation to Alfie's pending purchase of the Penhollow property.

Gryffyn relaxed his arms again, but he couldn't deny the twinge of disappointment in his chest.

Although he certainly didn't have the time for it, he thought he might have enjoyed the experience of flirting with Miss Moon. So long as she was more accomplished at the craft than Wynne.

———

KEREN, MISS LITTON AND HENRY arrived at Mr. Kimbrell's workshop promptly at nine on Monday morning, the time they'd arranged for Henry's next lesson. On entering, though, they found the space empty. Miss Litton looked at Keren with a question as Henry skipped toward the worktable.

"He's left a note, Keri." He lifted a folded sheet of paper. "And it's addressed to me," he added in surprise.

Had Mr. Kimbrell changed his mind then about Henry's lessons? "Well, what does it say?" Keren prompted.

Henry unfolded the paper and traced one finger beneath the words as he read.

"'Please come to the cove for today's lesson. There are plenty of stones to carve there.' He's signed it with a 'G' and look! He's added a little sketch of a dragon at the bottom." Henry held the page up to Keren's face for her inspection. "Hurry," he urged.

The cove, which could only refer to Copper

Cove, wasn't far from where they stood, and the weather promised a fine day for a walk. "Very well," Keren said. "Let's go find your carving tutor."

They left Mr. Kimbrell's workshop and traveled to the end of Newford's high street. The harbor lay to their right, luggers and cutters bobbing on the sparkling folds of the sea. A path to their left broke off to edge the cliffs above the sea, and they followed it for a pleasant mile to Copper Cove.

The small cove, Porthkober in the old Cornish, lay tucked in a sheltered portion of the cliffs. Although thin copper deposits lined its rugged face, the cove had been named for the heavy bracken that would light the cliffs with copper fire in autumn.

They reached a set of stone steps carved into the cliffside. From their vantage point, Keren saw Mr. Kimbrell seated on a flat rock below, shadowed by the towering cliffs. He was hatless, dark hair curling about his collar as he bent over his sketchbook. He sat with his back to them, and she was struck by the width of his shoulders. Had they always been so broad?

Henry skipped down the narrow stone steps, and Miss Litton lifted a hand in caution. "Have a care, Henry!"

He ignored her warning and hurried to the sand below. Miss Litton's shout caught Mr. Kimbrell's attention, and he rose to greet them. As they reached the final, steep step, he extended a hand to assist them down. Despite the strength Keren had witnessed as he'd carved with Henry, his grip was gentle, his fingers warm through the lace of her glove.

Once she was safely on the sand, she pulled her hand from his, the delicate lace catching slightly on the callouses of his palms. Her hand tingled where he'd held her, and she flexed her fingers to clear the sensation. Heavens, her hand had been held many times before, by men much more dashing than Gryffyn Kimbrell. She adjusted her short spencer and collected herself before looking up to face him.

"I thought we should have our carving lesson out of doors since the day is so fine," he said. "I've brought your tools, Master Henry, and there are plenty of stones to select for your practice." Indeed, the beach was strewn with boulders awaiting Henry's eager chisel.

"And there are some fine, flat rocks as well, if you ladies would like to sit while Henry carves. Although"—he cast a frown at Keren—"I should have thought to bring a blanket for your comfort. My apologies."

"No apology is necessary," Keren assured him. "We often come to the cove to search for shells. Miss Litton and I shall entertain ourselves while you provide Henry's instruction." She began tugging the gloves from her fingers in anticipation of shell-hunting.

Mr. Kimbrell led them to where he'd laid out a selection of carving tools on a strip of leather, and Keren's lips quirked to see he'd considered his tools' comfort, if not that of the ladies. It was safe to say Mr. Kimbrell was unlike anyone she'd ever met.

A breeze fluttered her ribbons and the hem of her gown then, and heat rose in her cheeks to think of him sketching her skirts again, but it was the bargain she'd made. She glanced toward Henry, who stood wide-eyed as he received his instruction, and she knew she'd made the correct choice. And Mr. Kimbrell was right—it *was* a fine day—so she resolved to enjoy the cooling breeze and the soft sounds of the sea and forget the uncomfortable thumping of her heart.

Mr. Kimbrell turned to Henry and asked, "D'you remember which mallet we should use for letter carving?"

Henry studied the tools for a moment then reached for a mallet with a rounded head.

"That's the correct style," Mr. Kimbrell said, and Henry beamed. "However, you'll want to use this smaller one here."

Henry, with his usual absent-mindedness, had picked up Mr. Kimbrell's much larger mallet instead of the one provided for his own use. He nodded and swapped his mallet for the smaller one, and together they went searching for the perfect carving stone.

Keren watched them pensively, Mr. Kimbrell's lean form towering alongside her brother's slight, much shorter one. It was unfortunate that her father's duties—not to mention his lack of patience with Henry—prevented him from spending more time with his son.

She wrinkled her nose against the uncomfortable sting of tears and joined Miss Litton to explore the cove's offering. Waves rolled in to lap gently at the shore's edge, and a tiny crab scuttled beneath a piece of driftwood as they walked. The charred remains of last week's bonfire were a dark, acrid scar upon the pale sand. Together she and Miss Litton combed the shoreline as the sun climbed, scooping their finds into their hands until they couldn't hold any more. She should have thought to bring her reticule.

"You may use these if you like," Mr. Kimbrell said from behind them. "For your shells." Keren turned to see he held three handkerchiefs, and she gratefully deposited her shells into one of the linen squares.

"Thank you," she said, looking up into his eyes. They were a rich, delicious shade of brown, with amber glints that sparked in the sun. Her cheeks warmed as she realized she was staring, but how had she never noticed the color of his eyes before? Then her lips quirked in amusement, for what sort of gentleman carried *three* handkerchiefs?

"I prefer to be prepared," he said, reading her thoughts.

"For what?" she asked with a slow grin, eyeing him through her lashes. "An excess of damsels in need?" The flirtation—meager as it was—slipped out easily, despite her attempts to maintain a more dignified manner. Lizzie would have simply thanked him for his courtesy. She pressed her lips together lest she do something truly disastrous, like set her lashes to fluttering.

He frowned. "For an excess of dirt. And shells, I suppose," he added with a wave toward her collection.

She relaxed with a smile. Gryffyn Kimbrell was as oblivious to the art of flirting as one of his stone carvings.

"Keri," Henry said as he ran up to her side. "Come see what I've carved." He reached for her hand and tugged, pulling her along behind him as Mr. Kimbrell tied the corners of his handkerchief over her shells.

They reached a large, flat boulder and Henry pointed proudly at the lettering carved on the face of it. "HM," he said, "for Henry Moon." The letters were smooth and even, to her surprised delight. "You did a fine job of it, Henry," she said, and Miss Litton murmured her agreement.

Henry explained in exacting detail how he'd carved each stroke, and Keren listened attentively, thrilled beyond measure to hear him craft such a cohesive account. There were no distracted side comments about the bird that flew overheard or the color of the damp sand. Miss Litton's brows lifted as she smiled at Keren above Henry's head, and even Mr. Kimbrell's expression bore the unfamiliar traces of a smile.

"You're fortunate in your monogram, Henry," he said. "'Tis naught but straight lines."

Keren looked to where Mr. Kimbrell had carved his own letters opposite Henry's, a simple but perfectly curved G alongside a straight-lined K.

"I think your parents did you an ill turn, Mr. Kimbrell," she said with a smile. "What must they have been thinking to burden you with such a complicated given name? At least they were more considerate in your surname."

Mr. Kimbrell's expression froze for a moment, and Keren took a small step back at the change in his demeanor. Yes, any measure of flirting was definitely lost on Gryffyn Kimbrell. But rather than confound her, the thought set her at ease. She could be herself, at least out of earshot of others, without worrying that her actions would be construed as overly forward.

Henry bent his head to resume his carving. "Shall I carve your monogram, Keri?" he asked, and Keren agreed. When her brother's attention was firmly fixed on his task once again, she turned back to Mr. Kimbrell.

"Do you wish to sketch?" she whispered with a wave toward her skirts and a silent curse for the blush that heated her neck.

"'Tis done," he said, nodding to where his sketchbook lay on the sand beyond their carving rock.

What? He'd already sketched her? She thought of the hour or more she'd passed collecting shells with Miss Litton, unguarded moments when he must have been drawing her, and her color rose higher. She should have felt relief, but her stomach was heavy with . . . disappointment.

She frowned, because on the heels of her disappointment came an uncomfortable realization. No matter that he remained unaffected by her, *she'd* been anticipating the tingling warmth she'd felt beneath his intent regard.

CHAPTER NINE

THE PAST MORNINGS HAD BEEN more successful than Gryffyn had anticipated. The notion of drawing Miss Moon in a more relaxed environment had been an inspired one. Today was their third such outing to the cove, and her movements had been fluid and natural as she and Miss Litton walked along the edge of the foaming sea to collect their shells.

And Henry . . . Gryffyn had become somewhat accustomed to the boy's flowing chatter, which slowed to a heavy trickle whenever he directed his attention to the stone before him. He had a natural talent, to be sure, even for a lad of his tender years. Today, Gryffyn had graduated him from carving straight edges to curves. He'd been surprised at Henry's quick grasp of the technique and motion required for his lessons and satisfied to see the level of concentration he applied to the tasks put before him.

Miss Moon seemed pleased with Henry's progress as well. She approached them and watched her brother for a long moment before shading her eyes to study the cliffs behind them. Her profile had the now-familiar effect of causing his heart to thump painfully in his chest, and he averted his gaze so his pulse might calm.

"The cove is much different in the light of day," she said. "More peaceful than it is on bonfire nights."

"Aye," he agreed. With its curving cliffs, the cove was a sheltering haven.

"As a girl, I often came here to think. To ponder ponderous thoughts, I suppose."

"And what sorts of 'ponderous thoughts' did you have?" he asked.

"The usual, I suppose. The meaning of life. Why bad things happen to good people. Why the sky is blue. I used to study the cliffs for hours. I thought that protrusion there"—she pointed toward a small, low outcropping—"looked like the bow of a ship emerging from the side of the cliff. It's silly, I know," she said. "As I look on it now, it doesn't appear to be anything more than what it is. A lump of stone poking out from the cliff."

He cocked his head to the side and studied the

place she indicated. He could see a ship if he squinted, but only just. It was like the vague shapes one could spy in woolly summer clouds if one stared hard enough.

Her gaze was hidden by the brim of her bonnet, and he wondered what she must think of him. Of his less-than-witty conversation and his odd fascination with rocks. He tried to think of a way to prolong the conversation, and, if he were honest, encourage her to flirt with him just a bit. But nothing came to mind, and he said only, "A ship. Aye, I can see it."

She turned from him to survey Henry's progress again. He sighed and returned his attention to the cliff face where her ship lay anchored, trapped in the stone, and it struck him then.

The perfect rendering of Fortuna.

The image came alive in his mind, and he knew what he needed to carve for Truro. He straightened quickly, drawing Miss Moon's attention.

"You're brilliant, Miss Moon," he said, reaching for her. She started at his abrupt actions, her head jerking slightly as she watched him. He dropped his arms before he could do anything untoward, like grip her ungloved hands in his own. Instead, he spun in the sand and strode toward the stone steps. And stopped.

Tools. He needed his tools. Then he realized he

couldn't leave Henry and the ladies behind either. It would be ungentlemanly, and his mother would box his ears if she ever learned of his poor manners. No, he couldn't leave them, but the image in his mind was tap, tap, tapping to get out, and his impatience grew.

He rushed back to them and said, "Hurry along, Henry. We must go."

Henry's head remained fixed on his task, tongue darting between his lips as he concentrated on carving a precise Q. Gryffyn hastily collected his tools, and Miss Moon was finally moved to action.

"Henry," she said. "We must go. Mr. Kimbrell has a pressing engagement, it would seem."

She sounded a bit snappish, and while he didn't fault her for it, he couldn't be concerned with polite niceties. Henry blew dust from the final stroke of his letter and looked up, beaming and oblivious of Gryffyn's urgency.

"'Tis well done, Henry, but we must go now," he said as he held an arm for Miss Moon. She took it hesitantly, and he guided them toward the steps. Before they could begin the climb, though, he recalled her shells. Dropping her arm, he jogged back to the fallen log where Miss Moon had left her small pile.

"Your shells," he said as he handed the bundle to her. She watched him with a tiny line creasing the space between her brows, and he was certain he must appear a perfect timdoodle to her observation.

"My Truro submission," he explained. "I've the perfect notion of how to proceed, thanks to your ship's bow." He nodded in the direction of the stone protrusion and her frown eased.

"I—I see," she said, although he wasn't certain she grasped the import of the situation.

"I have to return to my workshop," he said, mentally reviewing the commissions that awaited his return. Once he'd finished them, perhaps he could devote the rest of the day to his neglected block of marble. His heart raced at the notion, and he became aware of Miss Moon watching him closely. He colored under her regard and guided her and Miss Litton up the steps.

Henry's chattering questions returned in full force on the walk back to Newford, but Gryffyn was only mildly aware of his answers. When they reached the high street in front of his workshop, he paused, aware that his manners had gone wanting.

"Thank you for your escort," Miss Moon said, "but we shall continue to Mr. Clifton's bakery from here." She spoke the words with a small smile, and he breathed a relieved sigh.

"And thank you, Miss Moon, for your inspiration," he said earnestly. He lifted her hand, unable to stop himself, and squeezed her fingers.

She'd re-donned her gloves, but even so, he imagined the softness of her hand beneath the lace. He was surprised by how much he wished to retain his hold of her despite Fortuna's urging, but he supposed any artist would feel the same toward his muse.

She pulled her hand from his, mouth open in a small O of surprise. He nodded at Miss Litton and Henry then hurried into his workshop, where he tossed his hat on a nearby stool and ran restless fingers through his hair. With any luck, he had a long afternoon of carving ahead of him.

———

KEREN FORCED HER MOUTH TO close and watched Mr. Kimbrell disappear behind the door of his workshop.

"He's an odd man," Miss Litton whispered, and Keren couldn't say she disagreed. But the light—the passion—in his eyes as he'd spoken of his Truro submission had lit an answering spark in her own chest.

And *she'd* inspired him? Or rather, her silly comment about a ship anchored in the cliffs. But if he found inspiration in the notion, she wouldn't gainsay him.

"Yes," she said to Miss Litton. "He is a trifle odd.

But a little . . . intriguing, don't you think?"

Miss Litton's brows lifted before she said skeptically, "I suppose so."

"Why did Mr. Kimbrell have to hurry back to his workshop?" Henry asked. "Do you think he had too much sun? Do you remember the time I had too much sun and was too ill to eat my supper?"

Keren smiled at her brother. "I think Mr. Kimbrell was struck with an idea for his project. We shall have to wait to see how it develops." And she knew a sudden urgency to do just that. Then she realized that, in their haste, they'd not set a time for Henry's next lesson.

CHAPTER TEN

THE NEXT MORNING, KEREN DEBATED sending a note round to Mr. Kimbrell to inquire about Henry's lesson. There was no point venturing down the lane only to find he had no time for them today. But she was curious about his cliffs-inspired project, and she hoped to sneak a glimpse of his carving, so she collected Henry and Miss Litton, and they made their way to Newford.

She paused outside Mr. Kimbrell's workshop and peered through the window, but she couldn't see anything. Had he gone ahead to the cove, then? Did he expect them to join him there?

"Do you think he's waiting for us at the cove?" Miss Litton asked, echoing Keren's thoughts.

"I'm not certain," Keren said, then she tried the door. The knob turned easily in her hand. "Let's see first if he's within."

His workshop was cool and still in the shadows, and weak sunlight filtered in to light the figurines in the window. Keren called out to him, but there was no answer.

Then she heard it. Tapping beyond the back door. After a small hesitation, she led Henry and Miss Litton past the worktable, past shelves of tools and small carvings.

The back door was ajar. She pulled it wider to find an open stone yard in a linney of sorts. A roof protected it from the sun, but the sides were open, and the river flowed lazily just beyond the far edge. And in the center, Mr. Kimbrell crouched next to a large block of white marble. It rested on a low wheeled dais, and the sizable pile of rubble at his feet suggested he'd been there for quite some time. He was down to his shirt sleeves, the linen rolled to his elbows to expose fine, dark hairs and corded muscles. A pair of braces defined the firm line of his shoulders, and dun-colored trousers outlined strong legs as he bent lower.

He lifted a large mallet in one hand, and with one quick tap another piece of stone dropped to the ground. The muscles in his forearms bunched with powerful efficiency, and Keren's breath caught at the sight.

She lifted a hand to her throat and said, "Mr. Kimbrell," as he raised his arm once more.

He lowered the mallet then turned and gazed up at them through a shock of dark hair that had fallen across his forehead. When had Gryffyn Kimbrell become so . . . arresting? she wondered as her heart skipped in her chest.

Then she peered more closely at his eyes, which were reddened. "Have you—have you slept?" she asked.

He set the mallet to the side and stood. "Miss Moon. 'Tis time for another lesson?" he asked.

Henry craned his neck to see the block of stone behind Mr. Kimbrell.

"Mr. Kimbrell," Keren said again. "Have you been here all night?"

He speared a hand through his hair, dislodging a shower of stone dust and causing his hair to spike on one side. "Aye, the better part of it." he said with a sheepish twist of his lips. "Fortuna—she awaits no man."

"May we see?" she asked.

He hesitated, and she thought he'd deny her request, but then he stepped back. "Aye, although 'taint much to see as yet. I've merely been roughing her out." At their confused looks, he added, "Removing the excess stone to create the general shape of her."

Henry stepped up to the carving, running small fingers over the smooth facets where Mr. Kimbrell's chisel had sheared away large slabs of rock. Keren studied the piece, frowning, but she couldn't see Mr. Kimbrell's vision. Indeed, she couldn't make out much of a figure at all, general or otherwise. Certainly, it didn't bear any resemblance to the goddess of fortune, and she wondered if perhaps Mr. Kimbrell wasn't a bit touched in the head.

Henry, however, had no such concern. "'Tis marvelous," he said with reverence. "This will be her arm here?" At Mr. Kimbrell's nod, Henry said, "You can almost feel her warmth."

"Henry," Mr. Kimbrell said, smiling beneath the dust covering his face. "You've the spirit of a true stone carver."

Henry beamed, and Keren's stomach dipped just a little toward her toes.

—

GRYFFYN REACHED A HAND TO the back of his neck, frowning to feel bits of stone and a layer of dust there. What must Miss Moon think?

He looked up, surprised to see a fixed expression on her face as she watched him. Not an expression of distaste so much as . . . interest? He wasn't sure what to make of it, but he didn't have time to reflect further as a voice called out from inside the workshop. His mother.

He lifted a rag and wiped his hands then motioned to the Moon contingent to precede him through the door.

"There you are," his mother said with a smile of greeting. Her face didn't show any surprise to find him entertaining visitors. "When you didn't come home last night, I told your father you must have remained at the workshop. Hello, Miss Moon."

Miss Moon gave his mother a pretty greeting before introducing Henry and Miss Litton.

"Mr. Kimbrell is carving a magnificent piece, Mrs. Kimbrell," Henry said. "Although, as he's your son, you probably already knew that. Has he always been a skilled carver?"

His mother chuckled at Henry's energy. "I've no doubt that my Gryffyn is carving something truly wondrous," she said. "And that's not just the mother in me saying that. He's a remarkable carver, much like his father. But sometimes even remarkable carvers forget to eat, so I've brought something to break his fast."

Gryffyn noticed then the basket she'd placed on his worktable. He moved toward it and lifted the cloth, delighted to see some of Mrs. Quick's sausages and kidney pie. Several Bath buns and a stoppered jug of ale. His stomach made its emptiness known with a low rumble, and the back of his neck heated at the sound. He turned from the basket to find Miss Moon watching him and his mother watching Miss Moon.

"Gryffyn was much like Henry as a child," she said, and Gryffyn nearly choked to hear himself described so. He saw little resemblance between his pensive self and the lad who was now rifling the contents of his tool bag.

Miss Moon's brow lifted in mirrored surprise. "Was he indeed?"

"Oh, don't mistake me. Gryffyn was a quiet child—he's never been one for talking—but he was easily distracted. Of all my boys, his head was in the clouds more than any of them."

Gryffyn fumbled for a new topic of conversation—anything to put an end to his mother's disclosures—but his words remained stubbornly out of reach.

Miss Moon merely smiled and said, "Henry's head is so often in the clouds that I wonder it doesn't part from his body. But it's a comfort to know he may come out all right in the end."

She angled an amused glance toward Gryffyn, and his brows dipped. She thought he'd come out "all right?"

His mother chuckled. "Aye, I've raised five boys. Every child is unique, of course, but I imagine Henry benefits greatly from your guiding hand and perhaps a little extra creativity to keep him focused on the task at hand. Now, I've packed plenty of food," she said. "Would you like to share some kidney pie?"

"Oh, no," Miss Moon said. "We thank you, Mrs. Kimbrell, but we must return to Camborne."

"What about my lesson?" Henry asked. He turned from the tool bag, eyes large behind his spectacles. Clearly, he'd been more attentive to the conversation than they'd credited.

Miss Moon placed a hand on his shoulder. "I'm certain Mr. Kimbrell would like to enjoy his breakfast and then find his bed. We'll return another time for your lesson."

Gryffyn's brows dipped in disappointment—and not a little surprise at that unexpected sentiment, for he'd rather continue carving Fortuna. But then the hours of carving caught up to him and pressed on his shoulders until they sagged. He *was* tired, and thoughts of breakfast followed by a bath and an hour or two in his bed sounded heavenly.

"Of course," his mother said to Miss Moon. "But perhaps you'd all like to join us next week for a picnic on the grounds of Oak Hill? There will be a lot of children Henry's age, and of course, your father is welcome as well."

Gryffyn studied his mother, wondering at her scheme in inviting Miss Moon to his grandfather's picnic. Miss Moon must have been equally surprised, but she hid it well. After a brief hesitation, she nodded and said, "It sounds delightful, Mrs. Kimbrell, thank you for the invitation. I shall be sure to extend it to my father."

Gryffyn escorted them to the door then turned back to find his mother watching him. "Miss Moon is very attentive of young Henry," she said.

"Aye."

"I confess, she's not the flighty bit she's been painted."

Gryffyn frowned. "I wouldn't call her flighty, precisely, no," he said, unwilling to agree to anything more than that. He recognized the animated light in his mother's eyes; he'd seen it most recently when she'd speculated on the vicar's niece.

And he could count, too: there were more tin plates in his mother's basket than a man alone required. He must remember not to underestimate the Newford ladies, for how else would she have known to bring extra plates?

He crossed his arms and leaned against the worktable, waiting for her next bowl across the pitch. She didn't disappoint as she smiled broadly and said, "Twill be a pleasure to become better acquainted with her at Oak Hill."

He chuckled. "Your technique requires some refinement. 'Tis far too obvious to be called subtle."

"Aye, well, you can't blame a poor mother for wishing for her children's happiness. And I recognize a budding flirtation when I see one. A gentleman may be blind to a lady's interest, but another lady will certainly see it."

He coughed in surprise. Surely his mother was seeing only what she wished to find. He said gently, "Miss Moon has no interest in me beyond her brother's lessons. Don't mistake her pleasant manner for anything more than that."

"Miss Moon is agreeable, to be sure, but 'twasn't her pleasant manner I was referring to, love. I suppose you shall have to come to see it for yourself."

He had no response to that, so he sought another topic and asked, "Was I truly a distracted child?"

"Oh my, yes." She smiled in remembrance. "Your father has always had the patience of a saint, but I'll admit you tested it often as your attention was hard to gain, much like Henry's."

He frowned to hear her description of his younger self, then he had a sudden, fleeting memory. The smell of paper and charcoal and stone dust. The scent of his father's cologne as he sketched something for Gryffyn's amusement—a bird or a fox, he couldn't recall.

As a carver, he'd said, *you must learn to focus your thoughts and plan ahead. Draw before you carve. 'Twill settle your mind.*

"You were always a quiet child," his mother continued, "as I said to Miss Moon. But there came a point when you would become so lost in your own head, we feared you'd not come back. You weren't much older than Henry, I would guess, but sometimes I still see that lost look in your eyes." She watched him speculatively for a moment then touched a palm to his whisker-roughened cheek, despite his dust. "Your father and I love the man you've become, but I often wonder if something caused such a change, or 'twas merely the mind of a brilliant carver in the making."

Her blue eyes studied his, bright and clear and so different from his own dark brown ones. His jaw worked as he considered his reply. He could guess at what might have caused his thoughts to turn inward.

Should he tell her about the afternoon he'd played sardines with his brothers? He'd tucked his eight-year-old self into a cupboard and was later surprised to overhear his parents—who never argued—arguing. Should he tell her he knew they'd returned from an extended stay in Bath eight years before, with a babe that wasn't theirs? A child they'd argued about returning.

When his brothers finally found him long after the game had ended, he'd been shaking so hard it had taken two of them to unpack him from the cupboard.

Her smile slipped as she awaited his reply, the fine lines at the corners of her lips becoming more pronounced.

In the end, he gave her a slow grin and said only, "I suppose it must have been as you said. 'Twas naught but brilliance in the making."

Her face relaxed, and he knew he'd given the right answer.

CHAPTER ELEVEN

SOME DAYS LATER, GRYFFYN CROSSED the high street with thoughts of Fortuna's waving hair on his mind. He'd made some progress roughing out her form and would soon begin the arduous but satisfying detail work.

Mrs. Clifton, the baker's wife, moved to the opposite side of the street with quick steps, and he realized he was frowning to himself. He forced his face to relax and nodded politely, tipping his hat in the matron's direction.

As he neared his workshop, the door opened and an animated Henry came through, followed by Gryffyn's cousin, Gavin. Gryffyn frowned in confusion and lengthened his stride.

"—and the angel's wings fairly fly from the stone. Have you ever seen anything like it?" Henry spied Gryffyn then, and his face lit. "Mr. Kimbrell," he said. "I was telling the constable about your carving."

"Gavin?"

His cousin tossed him a wry smile as he kept a firm hand on Henry's shoulder. "I found this one lurking about inside. I'll return him to Camborne. I imagine his sister must be some worried for him."

Henry's eyes were as round as his spectacles as he watched the two of them.

"I can see Master Henry home," Gryffyn said. Gavin's brows arched, but when he saw Gryffyn was in earnest, he quickly lifted his hand from Henry's shoulder.

"I won't argue with you, cousin," Gavin said. "Mrs. Pentreath has registered another complaint about Mr. Morgan's cow. I anticipate 'twill take some time to sort." His expression was pained as he left them.

"Henry," Gryffyn began. "Why have you come alone? Your sister and Miss Litton must be concerned over your absence."

"Do you think I've caused them to worry?"

"Aye. To be sure, 'tis a man's right to enjoy his solitude, but you mustn't leave your home without telling someone."

"All right." Henry frowned, eyes narrowing, but any concern for the trouble he'd caused his sister and governess was soon forgotten. "Can I remain with you since I'm here now? You said you would teach me how to carve angel wings at my next lesson," Henry reminded him.

Gryffyn sighed and thought again of Fortuna's hair, but it had been a few days since Henry's last instruction at the cove. "Aye, I'll show you—quickly, now—how to carve angel wings, but then I must return you to your sister. 'Taint gentlemanly, giving her cause to worry."

Henry nodded, and Gryffyn led them inside to the worktable. They set out their tools, and when Henry began to reach for the largest chisel, Gryffyn steered him toward the smaller tools.

"See the paint on the ends here?" he asked, pointing out the newly painted handles.

Henry nodded, a crease pleating his brow.

"You told me your favorite color is red—"

"And sometimes yellow," Henry said. "Or green, although—"

"Aye, well, when you're carving, your favorite color is red. You can see I've added a dab of red paint to the handles so you can easily choose the proper tool."

Henry's eyes widened as he gazed at the row of red-handled tools, and he smiled. "That's quite clever, Mr. Kimbrell."

"Aye, well, 'twas my father who did the same for me years agone, only with blue. Now, about those wings . . ."

Much later than Gryffyn would have liked, after numerous fits and starts and conversational diversions, he was finally able to maneuver Henry into his father's cart, and they set off for the Moon residence.

As Gryffyn drove along the high street, Henry twisted from side to side and maintained a steady commentary on the shops and individuals they passed. At one point, he leaned precariously over the cart's edge to watch a kitten chase a mouse behind the blacksmith's shop. Gryffyn grasped the back of his coat with one hand and gently steered him back onto the seat with a sigh.

To be sure, Fortuna's hair would have to wait.

———

KEREN STUDIED HER LATEST FOX with a critical eye then examined the thick pile of her previous paintings. She'd still not been able to get the poor thing's ears right. As she set her paintbrush aside, she wondered about Mr. Kimbrell's carving project and hoped he was having more artistic success.

She'd not seen his progress since the day they'd found him behind his workshop, eagerly chipping away at an indistinct block of marble. As each of Henry's carving lessons came to a close, she'd hoped to have another peek, but he'd always taken his leave of them outside his workshop. There'd been no plausible excuse to follow him inside, much less to the linney in back.

She'd sent a prettily worded note the previous day to inquire about Henry's next lesson, and Mr. Kimbrell had returned her query with an exceedingly efficient message of his own. *Wednesday, if that is agreeable.* Nothing more, nothing less.

Henry had been counting the hours since they'd received his reply, and Keren found herself oddly eager for the clock to advance as well. Not so much for Henry's lesson, as Wednesday was still some days away, but for the Kimbrell picnic tomorrow. The thought of encountering Gryffyn Kimbrell away from his workshop and Henry's lessons both intrigued and terrified her. Would they find anything to speak of?

She reached for her paintbrush once more and dipped it in her cup. As she rolled the excess water from it, Simons stepped into the room with a modest throat clearing.

"Miss Moon, Mr. Gryffyn Kimbrell has arrived—"

Her heart tripped in her chest. He was here? She looked down in dismay at the apron covering her dress.

"—with Master Henry," Simons finished.

"With Henry?" Keren stood, sending water to splash over the side of her cup. Mr. Kimbrell entered behind a beaming Henry as she sopped up the mess with a cloth.

"Keri," Henry said, advancing into the room. "Did you know Mr. Kimbrell can drive with one hand? I should like to learn to drive. Do you think he could give me lessons?"

"Henry," she said sternly. "Where have you been? You should be with Miss Litton."

Henry shrugged and Mr. Kimbrell took up the explanation. "My cousin came across him in my workshop, eager for his lesson on angel wings," he said with a wry twist of his lips.

Henry lifted a scrap of limestone for her inspection, and Keren could see feather-patterned scratches where he'd been practicing his angel wings.

Miss Litton entered then on a cloud of frantic energy. She visibly deflated on seeing Henry. "Oh, thank the heavens," she said on a low whisper. "Henry, you gave me such a fright."

"Did you see my angel wings?" he asked, turning toward the governess. His questions faded in the hall as Miss Litton led him back to the nursery.

Keren turned back to Mr. Kimbrell. "Thank you for seeing him returned safely."

"O' course." He hesitated then asked, "Does he often go astray?"

"Too often for my peace of mind. And that of Miss Litton. She worries my father will turn her out without a reference if he finds out, and she's not wrong. That's why Henry's previous governesses left."

"Your father doesn't know he escapes Miss Litton as well?"

She shook her head. "So far, we've been able to retrieve him before too much time has passed." At Mr. Kimbrell's silence, she puffed her cheeks and added, "I know we must seem mad, but Henry's curiosity is limitless, and sometimes he simply can't control the impulse to follow his questions. Miss Litton may have trouble keeping up with him, but she's had far more success than his previous governesses, and we'll be hard pressed to find another if she leaves."

Dark brows dipped over Mr. Kimbrell's eyes as he regarded her. "You seem more a mother to Henry than a sister."

"I'm all he's known, although . . ." She swallowed and looked away before continuing. "I believe my father may be courting someone. It's possible Henry will have a new mother before the year is done." She forced a smile to her face as she looked up to find his regard hadn't wavered.

"'Twould be a difficult change to weather, I imagine. For both of you."

She opened her mouth on a denial then swallowed it. "Yes."

His attention shifted then to her easel and paints. "D'you enjoy painting?"

She snorted softly, relieved at the change in topic. "I do, but the true question—the one you should be asking—is whether I have any talent for it."

"All right," he said with a small, rare smile. He stepped closer and asked, "D'you have any talent for it?"

"No," she said flatly. "I've been painting the same poor fox for weeks, but I can't get him quite right."

He studied her for a moment more then turned to her pile of discarded paintings. "May I?"

She nodded her agreement then winced as he lifted the top one. The proportions were dreadfully off, and she couldn't imagine what Mr. Kimbrell, with his artist's eye, must think. He cocked his head to one side as he scrutinized her work. His spicy scent teased her nose and she inhaled slowly. She avoided closing her eyes as she breathed him in, but only just.

She fixed her gaze instead on the fine shape of his hand as he lifted a long finger to the fox's ear. He angled it to cover a small sliver of her painting. Intrigued, she leaned closer and watched as he did the same to the tail. She pulled back with a gasp on seeing the image revealed by his actions.

"Why, the proportions are perfect!" she exclaimed. "Do that again, please."

He obliged her, and she marveled at how easily he'd uncovered the problem with her fox.

"In my experience," he said, "'tis more about removing the bits that don't belong to uncover what lies beneath."

His voice was low and rich, and she felt it in the soles of her feet. She looked up to see him watching her, dark brown eyes steady on hers. She was mesmerized by the flecks of gold and amber in the irises, and she realized how closely they stood. All of him—his scent, his voice, his long fingers and fathomless eyes—all of him combined to addle her wits and she couldn't think of a thing to say.

"Wednesday?" he said, and she frowned.

"Wednesday?"

"Henry's next lesson," he clarified.

"Oh!" She took a small step back, breaking the hold he had on her. "Yes, of course. Wednesday."

———

GRYFFYN'S HEART DIDN'T RESUME ITS normal pace until he reached the high street. Miss Moon had imposed her quickening effect upon the poor organ once more, and he feared he was well on his way to a full-on infatuation.

If he were pressed to mark the start of it, he supposed it must have begun with their walk in the rain. Despite the impending weather, she'd come to retrieve her brother, without regard for the state of her hair or her slippers. He'd glimpsed the lady within and had been intrigued, as his image of her didn't fit with the one all of Newford shared. She was much like one of his carvings in that way, a delicate creature waiting to be released from the stone. Their regular encounters for Henry's lessons had only worsened his condition until now, whenever he was in her company, he was hard pressed to recall his own name, much less think on whatever task he was about. And that, with not a bit of flirtation between them.

This preoccupation with a lady was an utterly novel experience, and not one he was sure he welcomed. At best, it set his heart to racing and his stomach to twisting, which couldn't be good. At worst, it threatened his concentration. With the short time remaining before the Truro exhibition, he couldn't afford any delays or mistakes.

They'd not set a duration for their arrangement. He could manage with the sketches he had; how much longer would she expect him to provide lessons for Henry? His grandfather's picnic was tomorrow. Perhaps there would be an opportunity to speak with her about setting an end to Henry's lessons. And *that* thought set his heart to thumping once more. There was no pleasing the thing.

He returned to the workshop to find his mother waiting inside. "Mother? Is anything amiss?"

"No," she hastened to assure him. "All is well, but you've taken so little time to eat, and I merely wished to know if you'd like me to send Mrs. Quick round with luncheon."

"'Tis thoughtful," he said, "but unnecessary."

She idly lifted one of the figurines in the window and turned it in her hands. "I thought you'd be here when I arrived and was surprised to find you'd gone out."

"Aye, I've just returned Henry Moon to his sister. 'Twould seem the lad has a penchant for escaping his governess."

His mother chuckled. "I imagine his father must remain very busy with his mayoral duties. 'Tis unfortunate Henry hasn't a mother to see to his care."

"He has his sister," Gryffyn said. Then, at his mother's raised brows, he added, "Although, to be sure, no love can compare to that of a mother's."

Her brows relaxed and she smiled sadly. "And poor Miss Moon, without a mother as well. To be sure, 'tis difficult for any child to lose a parent, but her heart must have still been aching over the loss of her brother . . . My own heart nearly broke for her, alone in her grief when young William died."

Gryffyn recalled the summer well. He'd just turned sixteen, and the last of his own brothers had married and set up house in the hills above Newford. Gryffyn had always been comfortable in his own company, but the silence of his parents' house, with just the three of them to fill the space, had been loud. More and more, he'd sought his cousins' company just to escape it.

They'd often encountered William Moon and his sister Keren pitching stones into the river or cajoling treats from Mr. Clifton's bakery. The siblings had been inseparable, until the day they weren't. Gryffyn had helped his father carve the headstone.

"Miss Moon must have had the comfort of her parents and sisters when her brother died," he said.

"Aye," his mother replied with a sigh. "But her sisters had families of their own by then, and her parents' grief was keen. I suspect Miss Moon's loss was often overlooked."

Gryffyn's chest tightened at his mother's words. In the moment before the Moons' butler had announced him, he'd spied Miss Moon beyond the paneled doors. His carver's mind had immediately begun to separate her form into its component lines and curves, from the long elegance of her neck as she bent over her painting, to the smooth sleekness of her dark russet hair swept and twisted behind her. There'd been something about her figure that had defied his sorting, but now he knew what it was. Loneliness.

—

"YOU'RE CERTAIN TOMORROW IS SUNDAY?" Henry asked as Keren tucked the counterpane about him. Miss Litton had already retired, and the nursery was still and dark in the long shadows of Henry's bedside candle.

"Yes," she assured him. "Tomorrow is Sunday."

"And we're to picnic with Mr. Kimbrell?"

"We're to picnic with Mr. Kimbrell's *family*," she replied. There was a distinction, and she wanted to be sure Henry—and she—recalled it. She was resolved to keep her wits about her going forward—she would not be distracted by Mr. Kimbrell's eyes or his firm jaw or any other portion of him.

Henry smiled. She smoothed his hair then lifted the spectacles from his face and set them on the table beside the candle. He blinked up at her, and she swallowed. If she was correct and her father was courting someone in Falmouth, Henry might have a new mother soon. Someone else to smooth his hair and settle him into his bed. Her eyes burned and she blinked to clear the moisture there before he could see. Leaning over, she kissed his forehead then pulled back as something poked her rib. Lifting the counterpane, she found a steel chisel in the folds of the linen.

"Henry," she said, lifting the tool. "Did you take one of Mr. Kimbrell's tools?"

"He said I could bring it home to practice."

She exhaled in relief. Henry's odd ways were enough to manage without adding thievery into the mix. Then she narrowed her eyes on the end of the handle. "Did you—did you *paint* his chisel?"

"No, Keri," he insisted. "Mr. Kimbrell did that. He painted all of my tools red so I can remember which ones I'm to use. He's quite clever, don't you think?" He grinned, a gap in his smile where his front tooth had been, and Keren's heart twisted for Mr. Kimbrell's unexpected thoughtfulness.

She set the chisel on the bedside table and took up the candle. "Yes, I think Mr. Kimbrell must be very clever indeed."

CHAPTER TWELVE

GATHERINGS AT OAK HILL WERE always festive occasions, and Sunday's picnic was no exception. The vicar had that morning read the second banns for Jory and his Miss Pepper, and they'd marry soon. Gryffyn watched as the couple arrived on the terrace to warm greetings from his relations. Jory's broad grin was visible even across his grandfather's expansive lawns.

"Jory's some pleased with how things have come about then," Gryffyn's father said as he lifted a cup of cider.

"Aye," Gryffyn agreed. "After five years, 'tis fitting he's finally found joy with Miss Pepper." Joy was a bit of an understatement; Jory had become absolutely barmy with love for Miss Pepper. Gryffyn was pleased for his cousin. No one deserved happiness more than Jory, but a tiny, shameful bit of him was envious. Like Gryffyn's brothers, Jory would soon begin his own family. His cousin had found a soul to match his own. A place where he *belonged* and—Gryffyn ended the thought before it could become maudlin and pitiable.

"I see Miss Moon has arrived," his father said with a nod toward the terrace.

Miss Moon had indeed arrived, along with Henry and their father. She wore a demure gown of pale muslin, her eyes shaded by a simple straw bonnet trimmed in blue. It had been less than a day since he'd seen her at Camborne, but the sight of her caused Gryffyn's heart to race anew in uncomfortable anticipation. Today, he reminded himself, he'd find a way to put an end to their arrangement. His thoughts and his heart would be his own again soon.

He watched as the mayor greeted his grandfather and several of his cousins. The man's smile was jovial, as befitted a politician, Gryffyn supposed. Moon motioned to his daughter, and she offered his grandfather a pretty curtsy, her motions fluid and elegant, before turning her attention to those gathered on the lawn.

Her eye stopped when she spied Gryffyn, and his breath caught in his chest. His feet urged him to go and greet her, but then Alfie approached her side. Even from a distance Gryffyn could feel the warmth of her smile as she flirted with his cousin, and he frowned.

His mother joined her then with a greeting of her own and introduced Henry to several of the younger Kimbrells. With a nod of assent from Miss Moon, Henry left to join their game of tag.

Truly, he should do the polite thing and greet her, but what could he have to say that would be of interest? Entertaining a lady on his grandfather's lawn was not the same as sketching her at the cove. Her eye caught his again before she returned her attention to his mother.

"To be sure, she's the most beautiful sight these eyes have ever beheld," his father said, and Gryffyn coughed in surprise.

"Father?" He turned to see a warm smile on his father's face and realized the words were for his mother, not Miss Moon.

"Nearly forty years I've loved her." His father's smile straightened, and he turned back to Gryffyn. "If you're ever presented with such a gift, son, don't let it go."

His father left him with those words and moved off to speak with some of Gryffyn's uncles. Gryffyn turned to the food tables in a bid to distract himself from Miss Moon's, well, *distracting* presence. The lady, though, would not prove so cooperative.

"Good afternoon, Mr. Kimbrell." She spoke from

Gryffyn's side as he collected a plate of cold chicken and sliced fruit, and he turned to face her.

"Miss Moon, welcome to Oak Hill." She eyed the plate in his hand, so he added, "May I help you fill a plate?"

She agreed and fell in step with him as they navigated the tables set out on a corner of the lawn. He motioned to a bowl of strawberries, and she nodded her assent.

"I've been watching you watching me," she said, eyeing him from the shadow of her bonnet.

The plate bobbed in his hand and he righted it. She continued before he could respond.

"Are you studying me for one of your drawings?" she asked in a low voice. "You're only supposed to be drawing me during Henry's lessons, you know."

She smiled then, a teasing light flashing from her eyes, and his own lips twitched as he considered his reply.

He was surprised to realize that, despite all the minutes he'd spent observing her across the lawn, drawing her had never entered his mind. His interest had merely been captured by *her*, not by her lines and form or the drape of her dress. He could deny her assumption, but that would force him to explain why he'd been caught watching her. And that . . . that was an explanation as unclear as it was uncomfortable. He opted to let her assumption stand.

"My apologies, Miss Moon. I shall endeavor not to study you further, at least for the duration of my grandfather's picnic." He cleared his throat. "Are you enjoying yourself? 'Twould seem your father's found an attentive audience."

They both turned to see her father laughing with several of Gryffyn's uncles. Miss Moon's smile slipped, and the humor dimmed in her eyes.

"Is anything amiss?" he asked.

She looked at him through her lashes as she took the plate from him. "My father believes my behavior has been too forward of late," she said. "It's not that he's wrong, but I think the world must be a very unfair place, indeed. He's free to laugh and go on precisely as he wishes, while I must wear insipid gowns and carry myself as a lady with no spirit or thought of my own."

He frowned, unsure which of her assertions to address. "I wouldn't call your gown insipid," he began hesitantly.

"It's *white*," she said, holding her skirts with her free hand. "How would you describe white, if not boring and insipid?"

He recalled his impression of her the night of the assembly, with the candlelight limning her white-clad form. "'Tis light," he said simply. "Like the finest marble, 'tis pure and absolute, unmarked by the other colors."

She stared at him, frowning, and his neck heated beneath her regard. The urge to look away was strong, but he forced himself to hold his gaze steady. Finally, she relaxed her frown, and her expression turned thoughtful.

"You make white sound sublime, like something all the other hues should aim to achieve."

"A futile effort, to be sure," he said. "Such an unattainable goal will only leave the other colors feeling poorly about themselves."

She snorted a soft laugh. "Against all reason, you have very nearly convinced me of white's noble qualities," she said. Then, with another glance at him through the fringe of her lashes, she asked, "Do *you* find my behavior too forward, Mr. Kimbrell? Imprudent, perhaps?"

Gryffyn's brows lifted, and he drew a large breath before responding. "I'm not your father nor your husband, Miss Moon. 'Tis not for me to judge."

"But if you *were* my father or . . . or my husband, would you find my manner forward?" she asked.

She plucked a ripe strawberry from her plate and bit into it, smiling at him around the fruit. Warmth rushed from his belly to his fingertips. What was her question? Ah, yes. "Generally speaking, Miss Moon, I've found no fault with your behavior. But at this moment," he said, "with these questions . . . yes, I would say your manner is a bit forthy."

Her eyes sparkled as her coral lips curved in a gentle half-smile, and his breath caught. Her manner, though forward, was light and teasing, her enjoyment genuine.

Miss Moon was *flirting* with him.

———

KEREN PULLED HER EYES FROM Mr. Kimbrell and the firm hold his gaze had on her. Heavens, if she wasn't careful, her father would be sure to find fault in her behavior. And what was she thinking anyway, to flirt with Gryffyn Kimbrell? It was one thing to tease him at the cove, away from prying eyes. But here, where anyone could comment on her behavior . . .

She should walk away and find a nice group of ladies to speak with. She should, but she didn't wish to. And besides, if a man was oblivious to a lady's flirting, it didn't truly count as flirting, did it? And never was a man more oblivious than this one. Or was he?

Even as his eyes flashed at her now, she couldn't tell if her arrows had reached their mark. Gryffyn Kimbrell was inscrutable and quite unlike any other gentleman of her acquaintance. If she'd aimed her flirtation at someone else—someone like Alfie Kimbrell, for example—he'd have returned her fire in equal, indisputable measure. She'd not be left wondering.

But she found to her surprise that the notion of flirting with Alfie Kimbrell—or with anyone for that matter—didn't cause the same excitement to rise in her chest as it once had. Certainly, there was no fluttering in her belly that her meager flirtation with Gryffyn Kimbrell had wrought.

Interesting.

"You're studying me again," she said, delighted when his cheeks reddened and he looked away. She tapped a finger on her chin and added, "But if we're being honest—and truly, there's no reason not to be—I've been studying you as well."

His eyes cut to hers. "D'you wish to draw me then?" he asked. "Perhaps for one of your paintings? I hope you manage my proportions better than you did your fox's."

A laugh erupted from her, and she quickly muffled the sound with her hand. Then she considered his words. Considered drawing him. From his tall form and finely chiseled lips to his broad shoulders and calloused hands ... An annoying blush stole along her neck, and she welcomed the slight breeze that lifted the ribbon of her bonnet and cooled her skin. His brown eyes watched her, and any response she might have made withered on her tongue.

Botheration.

She turned her attention to the sweeping lawns, as much to still her heart's hurried pace as to allow her breathing to catch up. And that's when she spied Henry.

He'd lost interest in the children's game. Or to put it more accurately, he'd found another interest with which to occupy himself. He sat beneath the spreading leaves of an ancient oak and studied something on the ground. An insect or a blade of grass, perhaps. The other children continued their game around him, racing to and fro as they strove to catch one another. As she watched, one young boy nearly tripped over her brother as he fled his pursuers, and Henry was oblivious to it all. She sighed.

Mr. Kimbrell followed the direction of her gaze. "Henry has a rare talent for finding joy in the smallest things," he said.

"That's putting it kindly," she replied.

"'Tis a gift that will serve him well, I think, to be at ease in his own company."

She thought for a moment and wondered if he spoke from experience. "You seem to be of a similar temperament—a man at ease in his own company. Have you always been so?"

He nodded in reply to her question then, in a rare elaboration, he said, "The ability to find my own amusement has served me well. I have four elder brothers, but they're closer in age to one another than to me. They were often going off on larks, and my mother was forever reminding them to take me along." He stopped, brows dipping before he added, "I see the pitying look on your face, but 'tis unnecessary. I'm fortunate to have the love of my family."

"It wasn't pity you saw on my face, Mr. Kimbrell, but empathy. I see myself in the child you described." She stopped, surprised at her own words, at the easy comparison between herself and Mr. Kimbrell. She hesitated then continued. "My older sisters were much like your brothers. I think that must be why my brother Will and I were so close. We had one another to stand with against the world. At least for a time. But Henry . . . Henry has no one."

"You're wrong, Miss Moon. Henry has you, and I—I think he's better for it."

Her brows lifted at his statement. He could have complimented her eyes or her bonnet or her dress— she still couldn't call it anything but insipid, despite his impassioned defense of white. But none of those tributes would have caused the warmth that spread through her limbs at his simple statement. *Henry has you, and he's better for it.*

She smiled before ducking her head and allowing her bonnet to shield her face. "I should go see to him."

"D'you think he'd enjoy visiting Oak Hill's ruins?" Mr. Kimbrell asked. The words were said in a rush, as if he'd no more wish to end their time together than she did.

She turned back to face him. "I've heard about the ruins, but I've never seen them for myself. Are they far?"

"They're just beyond the stables. 'Tis naught but a short walk to where the cliffs overlook the sea."

She looked about them. Her father was still occupied with several of the Kimbrell clan, and others milled about with plates of food. There was no harm in walking with Mr. Kimbrell to view the ruins, was there?

At her hesitation, he said, "My cousin Wynne is just over there. I'm certain she would enjoy walking with us as well."

Keren glanced to where his cousin stood and thought Mr. Kimbrell might have overstated the matter. Keren and Wynne generally maintained a wide berth.

It may have had something to do with the fact that as girls, Keren had flirted shamelessly with Wynne's husband. Although, in her defense, Roddie

Teague had not been the lady's husband at the time.

Mr. Kimbrell awaited her answer. "That would be lovely," she agreed with a slow nod. Then, more firmly, she said, "Let's collect your cousin and Henry and go see these ruins."

CHAPTER THIRTEEN

WYNNE FROWNED WHEN GRYFFYN INVITED her to walk with them, and he recalled her disapproval of Miss Moon. But he kept his gaze steady on his cousin, willing her to agree with a minimum of fuss. Eventually, her frown eased and she relented.

He held an arm for Miss Moon and offered the other for Wynne, which she ignored. Together they followed Henry down the path that edged the cliffs beyond Oak Hill.

The ruins were naught but the crumbling remains of an old huer's hut. In its day, the hut had served as a smuggler's lookout as well as a station for the huer to watch the sea. On spotting shoals of fish, the huer alerted the fishermen so they could ready their nets. A newer structure further up the coast had long since replaced the hut, and the ruins had been a point of interest for visitors to Oak Hill ever since.

Henry ran and skipped along the sandy path, pausing every few steps to comment on the wild thrift and heather that grew in waving abundance and the vast expanse of sea that rolled below them like fine French silk.

They weren't the first to arrive at the ruins. As they neared the top of the path, a flash of blue disappeared behind the whitewashed hut. The low murmur of voices floated on the air, followed by a light giggle, and Gryffyn slowed his steps. If he wasn't mistaken, they'd nearly come upon a trysting couple. His cheeks warmed and he glanced sideways at Miss Moon, whose own lips were twisted in wry amusement. The heat on his neck only intensified.

"Henry," she called, but her brother continued his skipping dash toward the hut.

"Henry," Gryffyn said, adding his voice. To his surprise, the lad stopped and spun toward them.

Their voices had been enough to flush the couple from behind the hut, and Gryffyn was not overly surprised to see Jory emerge with a grin, his betrothed's hand tucked in his. Miss Pepper's head was angled down, but Gryffyn couldn't miss the smile that lit her face, or the blush that stained her cheeks.

"I was just giving Anna a tour of the ruins," Jory

said, rubbing the back of his neck with one hand.

"She's already seen the ruins," Wynne said unhelpfully.

"Aye, well, she wished to see them again," Jory insisted. Wynne smirked as Anna plucked at her skirts.

"The view is quite lovely from here," Miss Moon said, neatly turning everyone's attention to the sea stretching before them. Gryffyn thought she must have a bit of her father's political polish. "You can almost imagine a smuggler's cutter sailing onto the beach below to empty their cargo," she continued.

"Smugglers?" Henry asked, twisting about to look up at his sister, eyes owlish behind his lenses.

"Aye," Gryffyn said as he led Henry toward the hut. "They used to stand here to alert the ships below with their lanterns. To let them know when it was safe to land their cargo. There are caves all along this stretch of the cliffs, where they used to hide their barrels and tubs. When the way was clear, they'd carry them overland, although the paths are long since eroded or overgrown."

Henry stepped precariously close to the edge of the cliff and Gryffyn reached out a hand to draw him back.

"Were you a smuggler?" Henry asked and Gryffyn started. "I? No. I haven't the temperament, or the desire, to always be looking over my shoulder for the revenue men. I'm afraid I'm not that dauntless."

Henry's face fell at his admission, and Gryffyn looked to the side to gauge Miss Moon's reaction. She must find him dull indeed. But the smile on her face indicated otherwise, and he felt an answering tug on his own lips.

"You're not that foolish, d'you mean?" Wynne said. She spoke from experience; her husband Roddie had enjoyed the smuggler's lot for years before finally settling down to the placid life of an innkeeper. It was a change that well suited him— and Wynne—Gryffyn thought.

"I think I should like to be a smuggler," Henry announced.

"Why on earth would you wish to do that," Miss Moon asked, "when you've such a talent for stone carving? It takes a much more clever man to create something beautiful from a lump of rock than to sneak about in the night."

Henry, eyes wide, nodded slowly at this logic, and Gryffyn's heart twisted a little in his chest.

———

AFTER VIEWING THE RUINS, MR. Kimbrell led them back to the Oak Hill lawns, where Keren passed a pleasant time with some of the female Kimbrells.

Accustomed as she was to the disapproving gazes of Newford's high street matrons, she'd been hesitant at first, but their laughter and friendly manners gradually eased her reticence.

Indeed, the afternoon had been idyllic, with enjoyable conversation, plenty of sunshine to warm the sea breezes and plenty of food to fill the numerous bellies. Keren thought Mr. Alan Kimbrell, the Kimbrell patriarch, must be very flush indeed to host such a gathering so often, given the number of hearty men in his family with equally hearty appetites. Many of the women, she'd noticed, had brought fare from their own kitchens, with the result being an incongruous but delightful assortment of dishes. It was a very familiar and convivial gathering that caused just a pinch of wistfulness in Keren's chest.

Over the course of the afternoon, she'd witnessed Gryffyn Kimbrell eat what must have amounted to an entire chicken. *Not* that her attention had been fixed solely on him, as the Kimbrell lot was both numerous and welcoming, but she couldn't deny her gaze had strayed to him more often than she might have intended.

Gryffyn. In a crowd of Mr. Kimbrells, she'd begun referring to him by his given name, at least in her thoughts. Gryffyn. She silently tested the name on her tongue. It suited him. Solid and strong.

Hushed and slightly mysterious.

She glanced across the lawn to see him enjoying the company of his cousin Jory and Jory's betrothed. A tiny bit of envy wriggled its way beneath her skin. An irritating little itch that she wished to rub away. Envy of Jory and Miss Pepper, because anyone could see their love for one another was the rare sort, the kind few were fortunate to find. And, if she were honest, envy of Gryffyn, who had the pleasure of such a large and loving family. Why, they'd even folded her father into their midst. As mayor, his favor was often courted, but Keren suspected the friendship offered today was of a more genuine sort.

And Henry . . . despite his oddities, her brother had been accepted simply, with no questions or measuring glances.

Henry . . . Where *was* Henry? She scanned the lawn in search of his dark hair and spectacles. The children had long since abandoned their game of tag for a more organized cricket match. The pop of a willow bat sounded from the far side of the lawn, but she didn't see Henry anywhere. She craned her neck, glancing from group to group, seeking his short frame.

"Is all well, Miss Moon?" Gryffyn asked from her side.

She glanced at him quickly then resumed her search. "I don't see Henry anywhere," she said, trying to keep the note of panic from her voice.

"Perhaps he's joined the other children on the pitch?" he asked. She turned to him, brows dipped over her nose in a truly-you-can't-be-serious expression. "No, o' course, you're right," he said quickly. "Why don't you search this side of the lawn, and I'll check the other."

She nodded, and he paused to add, "To be sure, he's found something to capture his interest. We'll find he's discovered a new species of insect, Miss Moon."

Some moments later, with still no sign of Henry, Keren turned to see Gryffyn speaking with one of his uncles. He nodded at something the man said then turned and strode in the direction of the stables. Keren lifted her skirts with one hand and hurried after him. His long stride swiftly increased the distance between them.

He reached the stables and continued through the thick hedge that bordered the cliffside path. She stepped through the shrubbery and called after him. "Mr. Kimbrell!"

He stopped and waited while she hurried to reach him. "My uncle thought he saw Henry walking toward the stables," he said, "but I suspect he may have returned to the ruins."

The ruins, above the smuggler's cove that had so fascinated her brother. Of course. She lifted her skirts higher and hurried her steps. Gryffyn fell into step alongside her, but she sensed he restrained his steps to accommodate her shorter stride. "Go," she urged.

He nodded and raced ahead.

"Henry!" she called, but there was no answer. Gryffyn's voice echoed her call yards ahead.

She crested the path to see Gryffyn had reached the whitewashed huer's hut. There was no one else about, and her stomach sank. Then she watched as Gryffyn leaned over the side of the cliff, hands on his knees as he gazed at something down below, and her knees threatened to buckle. Ice crusted her veins for half a heartbeat before her legs began pumping. She sped toward the cliff's edge, and a wail she didn't recognize burst from her chest. "Henry!"

CHAPTER FOURTEEN

ROCKS JUMPED AND SKITTERED OVER the edge of the cliff as Gryffyn stopped her with firm hands on her arms. "Henry's fine," he said, and she stared at him mutely, uncomprehending. "He's on a ledge."

Her head turned back and forth, from the cliff's edge to Gryffyn's face and back again. "What?"

"Keri!" Henry's thin voice called from a distance, and she pulled from Gryffyn's grasp to lean over the edge. And there was Henry, gap-toothed and bespectacled, grinning at her from a narrow ledge thirty feet below.

The cliffs fell away from him in a steep drop, and Keren's heart spun in her chest.

"Henry," she ordered. "Don't move." He frowned and she begged again around the lump in her throat. "Please, Henry. Don't move."

"I wanted to see the smuggler's caves," he said.

"How did you get down there?" she asked. He pointed to the side of the cliff, but she couldn't see anything resembling a path to where Henry now stood. There were dips and crannies along the vertical face of the cliff, but none so large for a boy to stand.

She turned to Gryffyn. He'd removed his coat and vest and stood before her in his shirt sleeves.

"What can we do?" she pleaded. Her breath came in short gasps, and she thought she might suffocate.

He gripped her arms again, his hands warm through the muslin of her dress, his voice a low whisper as he assured her, "'Tis not so far down. I'll fetch him up."

She stared as he knelt in the grass and studied the stone face below. When he swung his legs over the edge, she dropped to his side. "Wait," she said. "Let me find help. Ropes or something."

"Aye," he said. "Ropes would be helpful."

His shoulders dropped below the edge and then his head. Eyes wide, she leaned over to see him hugging the side of the cliff. His hands gripped small handholds in the stone, and his feet had found unlikely purchase in a couple of awkwardly placed crannies.

Keren's breath sat heavy in her chest as she

watched his progress. Like a crab, he moved across the face of the cliff, angling himself to where Henry perched on his ledge. Pebbles skipped to the beach far below with each movement. His foot slipped once, dislodging a larger stone to bounce down the face of the cliff, and she stifled a cry with her fist. Her heart stopped as she waited for him to regain his footing, then it thumped heavily while he continued his crawl across the cliff face.

If Henry came out of this, she was putting him on a lead. She'd tether him to her, so she'd never need worry over his whereabouts again. And if Henry didn't come out of this . . . she refused to contemplate the possibility.

She forced a calming breath into her lungs. Gryffyn had reached a point about five feet from Henry's ledge. Even from her vantage high above, she could see that sweat beaded his brow and pressed the white linen of his shirt to his skin. His shoulders flexed beneath his braces, hard muscles rolling and shifting, tempered by hours spent wielding a mallet and chisel.

He reached Henry's ledge, and her breath stuttered in her throat as he maneuvered himself to a sitting position next to her brother. He glanced up, feet dangling over the boulder strewn beach forty feet below and nodded at her.

She pushed herself up from the cliff's edge and

raced toward the stables. Rope. She needed to find rope.

—

GRYFFYN INCHED ALONG THE NARROW stone ledge and flexed his hands to ease the cramping there. His heart raced in his chest, a heavy, steady thumping that only increased when he glanced up to see Miss Moon watching them from above. She scrambled back from the edge, and he turned to Henry.

"Henry," he said on a heavy exhale. "How did you get down here?"

Henry shrugged. "I wanted to see the caves," he repeated. "But when I got to this ledge, I couldn't find a way to go any further. Do you see how far down it is? Do you think I've caused Keri to worry?"

Gryffyn puffed an amused snort. "Aye. I believe you've caused your sister some worry. What"—he drew in another heavy lungful of air and wondered if his heart would ever be the same—"what was your plan for returning once you found the caves? When the tide comes, the caves will fill with water."

Henry's eyes widened and he shrugged again, and Gryffyn's admiration for Miss Moon—who suffered Henry's oddities with limitless patience and affection—expanded.

"Henry," he said, leaning his head back and wincing when a sharp stone poked his neck. "You must learn to focus your thoughts and plan ahead. 'Tis a lesson any good stone carver must master. Otherwise, you'll have naught but a pile of dust where you meant to carve a masterpiece."

Henry considered his words with a furrow pleating his brows, eyes magnified behind his spectacles and dirt mingling with the freckles across his nose. "How do you do it?" he asked.

Gryffyn sighed. "I was a preoccupied lad much like you, or so my mother tells me. But drawing helps me rein in my thoughts so they're not so scattered about."

"I like to draw," Henry said. "Although I'm not nearly so good at it as you are. Your sketches of Keri are quite magnificent."

Gryffyn stilled, watching Henry from the corner of his eye. "You've seen my sketchbook?"

Henry nodded. "I shouldn't tell my father, though, if I were you. He tends to go into fits about that sort of thing." Henry hesitated then asked, "Do you think drawing could help me?"

"I don't know," Gryffyn said honestly. He wasn't sure that anything could have prevented *this* particular scenario. "But I suppose it's worth a try," he finished.

Sounds from above caught their attention then,

and Gryffyn leaned out from the ledge to peer up. Faces began to appear at the top of the cliff—his cousins Gavin and Merryn as well as Miss Moon, followed by a bevy of his other relations.

"We've brought rope," Merryn called down. "We'll have you both fetched up in no time."

"Aye," Gryffyn said. "Toss the end down and I'll loop it about Master Henry."

Miss Moon twisted her hands and asked, "Is Henry all right?"

"Aye, he's well."

"Don't worry, Keri," Henry said, leaning out from his position against the stone wall. "Mr. Kimbrell is here, and he thinks drawing will help me focus."

Miss Moon nodded in confused acceptance of Henry's *non sequitur* then returned her gaze to Gryffyn. Her eyes were intent on his and he nodded, willing her to see more confidence than he was feeling. Her face relaxed, and she stepped aside as Merryn lowered a length of rope over the cliff's edge.

"Are you ready to return topside, Master Henry?" Gryffyn asked.

Henry nodded, and his blind trust caused the backs of Gryffyn's eyes to burn. He hoped he didn't let the lad—or Miss Moon—down. He brushed aside such ineffective thoughts and knotted the end of the rope to form a harness of sorts.

"Aye, then. We'll loop the rope beneath your arms then I'll guide you up. I shall be beside you the entire time, and if you should slip, my cousins will catch you with the rope. You won't fall, but 'tis important not to look down."

And with such an end to his pretty speech, of course Henry looked over the side of their ledge to the boulders below.

"Henry," Gryffyn said firmly. Once he had the boy's attention again, he said, "I need your vow that you won't look down. Can you give it?"

"Yes," Henry said. "I won't look down."

"Excellent. Now, let's return to your sister." Henry held his arms up and Gryffyn slid the rope harness over him, tightening the knot behind Henry's shoulders. When he was confident it was secure, he said, "Now, take hold of that bit of rock there. That's it. And place your right foot in the cranny here. You're doing a proper job of it, Henry."

In this manner, they slowly navigated the face of the cliff, Henry reaching and stepping where Gryffyn indicated and—thankfully—not looking down. Gryffyn marveled again at how the boy had found himself in such a position, but he pushed the thought aside. There was no sense worrying over questions without answers.

At one point, Gryffyn indicated a narrow

foothold some distance above Henry's position.

"I can't reach it," Henry said. "I'm too short."

"Oh, aye," Gryffyn said. "I can see that." He looked about for another foothold for Henry to take, but there were none. He surveyed his own position, which was precarious but not as unbalanced as he'd been a few steps back. Satisfied there was no other option, he crooked his right leg next to Henry and said, "Use my knee. Place your foot here and you should be able to pull yourself up."

Henry's eyes widened. "Won't you fall?"

"No," Gryffyn said with a silent prayer. He brushed sweat from his left eye with his arm and turned back to Henry. "'Tis the only way."

Henry nodded then lifted his foot and placed it gingerly on Gryffyn's braced knee. Gryffyn grunted slightly as Henry pushed off, but he maintained his position and sighed in relief to see Henry reach the higher foothold. Only another ten feet to go.

When Henry's head finally neared the edge of the cliff top, strong hands reached down to haul him the rest of the way over amid shouts of relief.

"Henry!" Miss Moon's shaky voice was followed by Henry's muffled reply, and Gryffyn pictured him folded in his sister's arms. He rested his forehead against the stone in front of him and puffed his cheeks on an exhale before reaching for the next handhold.

As he neared the top, Henry's grinning, bespectacled face appeared above the edge. Then the boy scooted aside as Merryn and Gavin took his place. They assisted Gryffyn as, with one final effort, he pulled himself over the edge of the cliff.

Once he was on firm ground, he flopped onto his back. The sky was brilliant overhead—surely it had never been such a vibrant shade of blue before—and he closed his eyes against the light. His arms and legs throbbed as his heart struggled to resume its normal pace. A shadow passed behind his eyelids, and he opened them to see Miss Moon bending over him, moisture dampening her cheeks.

"Thank you," she whispered, and his heart resumed its dangling-from-the-edge-of-a-cliff pace.

———

KEREN BRUSHED AT HER CHEEKS as she gazed down at Gryffyn lying on the grass. She was at turns hot and cold, nauseous and euphoric, smiling and teary-eyed. But above all, she was exhausted. The energy that had propelled her when she'd raced for help had burned off, and now she wished nothing more than to crawl into her bed and sleep for days. A week, perhaps.

Henry stood with their father, who was thanking the Kimbrell cousins who'd assisted in his son's rescue. Her brother seemed no worse for his ordeal, oblivious as only Henry could be. Gryffyn blinked up at her, and a grin lit his face—the first true smile she'd ever seen on him. It threw tiny creases to the corners of his eyes and nearly brought her racing heart to a fatal standstill. She offered her own shaky smile in return. Then she spied the blood staining one of his palms, and she gasped.

"You're injured."

He stared at her mutely for a moment before he followed her gaze. Turning his palm from side to side, he examined it before letting it drop. "'Tis naught but a scratch," he said.

"'Naught but a scratch'," she mimicked, kneeling in the grass beside him. "Never say you're one of those men who scoffs at pain even as his life's blood stains the ground."

He pushed himself to a sitting position then brushed pebbles from his hand with a wince. "I doubt I'm in such dire straits. As I said, 'tis naught but—"

"I know," she interrupted. "Naught but a scratch. Here, let me see." She lifted his hand and after some minor resistance, he allowed her to pull it toward her. She removed a handkerchief from the sleeve of her dress and gently blotted his palm where blood beaded along a thin gash.

"You're fortunate it's not worse," she said, "as

I've only the one handkerchief. I'm dreadfully unprepared, it would seem."

"Woefully so," he agreed, and she bit her lip against a smile.

He watched her as she worked, and she marveled again at the size of his hand, so much rougher and larger than her own. Strong and capable, as evidenced by his deed today. The fine hairs on the back tickled her fingers where she held him before disappearing beneath the edge of his sleeve. Heavens, one would think she'd reached the ripe age of three and twenty without ever seeing a man's bare hand.

Then, to her utter mortification, tears pooled in her eyes and her own hand began to shake. She blinked and willed it to settle, but the shaking only intensified. He folded his fingers about the handkerchief, capturing her hand in his and holding it steady. The warmth of his fingers soothed the chill in hers. She pulled her eyes up to see his dark gaze steady on her, his lips curved in a gentle smile.

"To be sure, 'tis been a trying day," he said. "'Tis all right to feel it in your bones."

She inhaled a stuttering breath, unsure how to respond but grateful for his compassion.

"Keren," her father said from behind her.

She jerked her hand from Gryffyn's, and they both hurried to stand.

"The hour grows late," her father continued. "We should return Camborne."

"Yes, of course," she said.

Her father turned to Gryffyn. "I'm indebted to you, Mr. Kimbrell. It's very possible you saved my son's life today."

Keren hid a smile as Gryffyn colored at her father's words. "I assure you, sir," he said, "'twas no more than any of us would have done."

"Nevertheless, you were the one Fortune placed at my son's side today, and I thank you for your efforts." He flashed one of his mayoral smiles, then he spied Keren's handkerchief in Gryffyn's hand. He sucked his teeth for a moment before turning back to her. "Shall we?"

CHAPTER FIFTEEN

T HE MORNING AFTER THE EVENTFUL picnic at Oak Hill, Gryffyn woke to find golden sunlight piercing the lace curtains his mother had hung some years agone. He rubbed his eyes and—sunlight! It was late—long past the time when he and his father normally began their day.

He threw off the quilted counterpane, groaning as his muscles protested the motion, then quickly washed and cleaned his teeth.

He felt the effects of the day before keenly. His arms and legs ached from the strain of scaling the cliffs, and his neck was stiff—probably from all the tension that had gripped his body as he'd guided young Henry. Despite his assurances to Miss Moon, there had been moments when he'd doubted his ability to return her brother safely to her. He turned his head from side to side in an effort to loosen the stiffness before shoving stockinged feet into his worn boots.

His mother's soft voice and that of Mrs. Quick rose from the kitchen as he descended the stairs. They looked up at his arrival and his mother smiled.

"Good morning, Mrs. Quick," he said. "Mother." He leaned down to kiss her cheek. "Why didn't you wake me?" he asked.

"Your father thought we should allow you to sleep," she replied, "and I agreed. 'Taint every day you save the life of the mayor's son. We were certain you'd be feeling the effects of your heroics this morning. How are you, love?"

He winced at her characterization of the events but allowed her statement to go unchallenged. "Right enough," he said, rubbing the back of his neck.

"Your father went to tend to Dr. Rowe's hedge — the one that runs between his north field and Mrs. Treleven's farm. He said 'tis naught but a minor repair, and you can use the day to catch up on your carving."

Gryffyn eased his sore muscles into a chair as Mrs. Quick poured a cup of hot coffee. She slid it across the kitchen's oak table, and he accepted it with gratitude.

"You keep yer thanks to yerself," she said pertly. "Yer mother told us how you rescued that dear boy.

A warm cup of coffee and a late mornin' be the least you're due."

He ducked his head and sipped the dark brew carefully as the ladies bustled about. His mother was preparing herbs for drying while Mrs. Quick, he noted with interest, added sausages to a pan of eggs. Soon, the tantalizing odor caused his mouth to water, and his stomach rumbled as she emptied her pan onto a plate and set it before him.

It had been some days since he'd enjoyed Mrs. Quick's hearty morning fare, as he'd been rising well before the sun to accommodate not only the workshop's regular commissions and Fortuna's demands but Henry's lessons as well. He tucked into the eggs with relish, barely catching an audible moan before it could escape.

Presently, Mrs. Quick left them to tend the wash, and his mother pulled a chair across from him. She sat with a smile and sipped her own coffee.

"How does your Truro piece fare?" she asked.

He didn't wish to tempt fate—or Fortune, as it were—with boastful thoughts, so he said only, "'Tis coming along well enough, although 'twill be a challenge to finish in time."

His mother stretched a hand across the table and squeezed his. "You'll manage it, and very well I should think. You've nearly your father's skill with the stone, after all."

He hesitated, studying his plate before returning his gaze to her. "Why d'you suppose Father was so set against it? By everyone's account, he was an accomplished sculptor in his younger days. Does he not long to do more than . . . repair hedges?"

Her hand stilled on his and her gaze sharpened. "Your father's hedges are straight and strong, Gryffyn. The finest in the duchy," she said, and guilt poured through him.

"O' course they are," he said quickly. "No one would think of engaging anyone but him for their hedge work. But does he not miss the carving? The excitement of watching a thing of his own creation emerge beneath his chisel?"

She squeezed his hand once more before releasing him. "Your father's a talented carver, to be sure," she said. "But he's much more than that. He's also a husband and a father, and he's always placed his family above all else. He's always *chosen* his family above all else. You will feel the same one day when you have a wife and child to protect."

He frowned. His mother's words didn't make sense. Despite the prosperity behind the Kimbrell name, many of his relations had made their own way, and his father was no exception. Thomas Kimbrell was a proud man, and Gryffyn could understand his desire to provide for his family by virtue of his own livelihood. He could even understand—to a point—his preference for the steadier commissions over the more irregular but fancier work. But his mother's choice of words—*a wife and child to protect*—struck him as odd. Protect from what?

"Mother," he said. "His children are grown. We are all of us well prepared to make our own way in the world. What can he have to fear?"

After a short pause, she replied. "A father will always fear for his children, love. You must accept that he's living the life he's chosen for himself. 'Tis an abundant and honorable life that's served us well."

Gryffyn swallowed. His mother was right. Just because his father's path wasn't one he wished for himself didn't diminish his father's choices. But he couldn't help wishing his father were more accepting of his own desires.

"Now," she said, neatly turning the subject. "I had a thoroughly enjoyable conversation with Miss Moon when she and her family arrived at Oak Hill yesterday. And judging by Miss Moon's *pleasant manner* toward you, 'twould seem she enjoyed the day's conversation as well."

His ears heated at her not-so-subtle reminder of their previous discussion about Miss Moon's interest in him.

"I do hope Henry has recovered from his ordeal,"

she continued. "Will you call at Camborne?"

"I hadn't thought to, no," he said, forking a piece of sausage. He avoided her gaze; she'd always been able to tell when one of her sons was stretching the truth.

His earlier resolve to set an end to their arrangement had crumbled like pebbles falling from Henry's ledge, and he had, in fact, just been wondering if he ought to call on them. The lad had seemed blissfully unaffected by the entire cliffside incident, but what of Miss Moon? He couldn't forget the trembling of her cool fingers as he'd held them in his own.

Then he thought of her teasing conversation prior to Henry's disappearance. Even as a smile tempted his lips, he wondered if her flirting had been an aberration. An effect of the agreeable weather and convivial atmosphere. If he called at Camborne, would Miss Moon flirt with him again? Did he wish her to?

While he couldn't deny his pride appreciated the possibility, a more sensible part of him rejected the notion. He had no intentions to marry, and, as his cousins had pointed out, the lady herself had no desire to wed. No, 'twould be better not to call—for both his pride and his sense.

His mother took another sip of coffee then continued. "'Tis no matter," she said. "You'll have an opportunity to inquire after Henry tonight, as the mayor has invited us to dine. I'll be sure your best coat is pressed."

—

"I'VE INVITED THE KIMBRELLS TO join us for supper," Keren's father said from behind his newspaper.

The Kimbrells? Keren pleated the edge of the tablecloth as her heart gave a heavy thump. But since "the Kimbrells" could number two or two hundred, she asked, "Which Kimbrells, Father?"

"Mr. Thomas Kimbrell and his wife and son. I thought we should show our appreciation for Gryffyn Kimbrell's efforts on Henry's behalf."

Keren had thought to call at the Kimbrell home with a basket later that day — perhaps a collection of jams and jellies from Camborne's larder — to express their appreciation for Henry's rescue. Paltry though the notion was, such an act would have been unexceptional. Respectable, even. But supper was a much more fitting expression of their gratitude. And it meant Gryffyn Kimbrell would return to Camborne.

"I'll inform Cook," she said with a short nod.

"Your sister and Langford will be joining us, and I've invited some acquaintances from Falmouth as well to round out our party. A Mr. Davies and his widowed sister, Mrs. Richardson. They'll be staying a few nights."

Keren's brows climbed. This was the first he'd mentioned any overnight guests, but Camborne was well-managed and would accommodate the visitors easily. Her father's attention remained fixed behind the wall of his newspaper, so she couldn't read his gaze. His visits to Falmouth had increased over the past month, and she wondered if the widowed Mrs. Richardson hadn't been the object of his travels.

"How are you acquainted with Mr. Davies and his sister?" she asked.

Her father's reply was brief and uninformative. "I was acquainted with the lady's husband before he passed last year." He lifted the pages of his paper higher then, a sign the conversation was concluded.

She frowned and sipped her tea before saying, "I'll be sure the guest chambers are prepared."

Later that afternoon, Keren was tidying her brushes and paints when her sister breezed into the morning room.

"Lizzie," Keren greeted, drying her brush on a linen cloth. "Did Langford accompany you?"

"Yes, he's with Father in his study, and you know one can't pry the two of them apart once they get to discussing the elections." Lizzie removed her gloves and stepped around Keren's easel to inspect her painting. "You've finally mastered your fox's proportions," she said with unflattering surprise.

Keren gave her sister a wry smile. "I believe I have. The secret, you see, is to remove the bits that don't belong to uncover what lies beneath."

Lizzie's delicate brows dipped. "If you say so."

Keren waved the topic away before placing her paints back in their box. "So, sister. Have you come to dress me like a Christmas goose, or to ensure I don't embarrass Father before his friends tonight?" At her sister's silence, Keren pressed her lips together. "A little of both then."

"Keri—"

"Very well," Keren said with a sigh. "Why don't we find something suitable for trussing my wings?" She rose and led the way from the morning room.

"I'm sure Father only wishes to see you happily settled," Lizzie said as they ascended the stairs.

"What nonsense," Keren said. "You and I both know the source of his concern is his political standing." Her sister had no reply to that, so Keren turned the subject. "A Mr. Davies and his sister, Mrs. Richardson, are to join our party for supper. Are you acquainted with them?"

A crease formed between Lizzie's brows. "Father mentioned some additional guests, but I don't believe I've had the pleasure of their acquaintance. Are they from Newford?"

Keren's tension eased to know she wasn't the last

to hear *everything.* "No, I believe they hail from Falmouth. Father has been traveling there more frequently of late." At her sister's silence, Keren prodded, "Do you think he intends to marry again?"

"Father? I imagine he must one day. Henry needs a mother, after all, and Father needs a hostess for his political dinners. He can't rely upon you to perform that duty forever."

"But he must see that I'm better suited to care for Henry than any stepmother."

"Well, yes, but you'll leave Camborne one day."

Keren avoided a reply and removed a bit of lint from her sleeve. They entered her bedchamber, and she led her sister to the wide oak armoire. Her maid, Molly, waited patiently as Keren set aside gown after gown until she'd narrowed her choices to two: a soft, pale blue with a lace overskirt—which Lizzie approved as suitable for entertaining in their own home—and a simple white silk.

Molly hesitated when Keren finally indicated her choice then took the white silk to see that it was properly pressed and aired.

"It's a good choice," Lizzie said with an approving nod. "Father can have no complaint."

While Keren was still not enamored of white on principle, she couldn't deny the quickening of her pulse as she imagined greeting their guests in the gown. Or rather, one guest in particular. What would Gryffyn think? Would he see light in her? Would he liken the gown—would he liken *her*—to the finest marble, pure and absolute? And was she truly wishing for a man to compare her to a . . . a *rock*? There was no question that her association with the carver was the strangest flirtation she'd ever engaged in, but she couldn't help the feminine thrill that chased her spine when she thought of his warm brown eyes on her.

"Keri? You appear flushed. Are you feeling quite the thing?" Lizzie asked with concern.

Keren puffed a cooling breath toward the curls at her temple. "I'm well. It's merely the warmth of the day." As she spoke, a cool breeze wafted through the open window, belying her words.

Lizzie eyed her suspiciously before taking a seat on the chaise longue. "Father said some of the Kimbrells will also join us this evening. Thomas Kimbrell, I believe, and his wife and son."

Keren nodded and fussed with some ribbons at her vanity. "Yes. Gryff"—she cleared her throat—"Gryffyn Kimbrell."

Lizzie tipped her head to one side. "Gryffyn Kimbrell . . . Isn't he the quiet cousin? The one who always seems a bit aloof?"

Keren thought of the hours spent in his company at Copper Cove, of his measured observations and, more recently, his teasing flirtation at Oak Hill. *Aloof* was not the word she would have applied to him. "He's the more reserved of the cousins, yes, but I think perhaps he's just . . . thoughtful."

Lizzie stared at her for a beat more before her lips eased into a smile. "And why, precisely, has Father invited the Kimbrells to dine with us?"

"Why, Gryffyn Kimbrell saved Henry's life. Did Father not tell you?"

Lizzie shook her head, so Keren related the tale of how he had rescued Henry from a certain and horrific death at the base of the cliffs. When she finished, her sister fanned herself with one hand, despite the breeze cooling the room.

"My, that's quite a feat of strength and courage, to scale the cliffs in such a manner. And in his shirt sleeves?"

Keren nodded and moved to stand closer to the open window.

"You could do worse, Keri," Lizzie said.

"What do you mean?"

"Gryffyn Kimbrell. His family is respected and well situated thanks to his grandfather's holdings. And he's fine to look at as well. You could do worse." At Keren's frown, Lizzie's eyes widened. "You *do* intend to remain unwed then. I've heard it whispered about, but I didn't believe it. It's unnatural, Keri."

"You know I can't leave Henry. He's the reason I

allow you to dress me in *this*." She waved a hand at the pile of pale muslin decorating her counterpane. A tiny voice reminded her she'd chosen the white silk for reasons not entirely related to Henry, and she ignored it.

Her sister watched her silently for a moment then said, "You can't sacrifice your own happiness, Keri."

"Henry needs me. Father doesn't understand his eccentricities, and I can't leave him alone at Camborne."

"He's hardly alone. He has Father and a governess and servants to see to his every need. Are you certain it's not *you* that needs *Henry*?"

Keren shifted uncomfortably before the window until Lizzie relented with a small shrug.

"My apologies," she murmured. "I only said what I did about Gryffyn Kimbrell because you have the *look*." Keren turned back to her with a confused frown and Lizzie continued. "The look I despaired of ever seeing on you—the look of a lady well on her way to falling in love."

"Love?" Keren asked, her voice rising.

For a lady who'd spent the past years intent on flirtation—and only flirtation—she could think of nothing more disastrous than *love*. Flirtation was light and amusing and harmless. Easy to begin and easier yet to end. Love was something else entirely.

She lowered her voice and asked, "Why do you say that?"

"I can see it in your eyes, Keri. You're uncertain about your Mr. Kimbrell, and that's a sure sign. Tell me: Do you think of him often, even when you're shopping for ribbons or, I don't know, reviewing the menu with Cook?"

Keren shook her head slowly, resisting her sister's words. Although . . . she'd taken twice the normal time to tally the household accounts last week, as her mind had insisted on returning to their last meeting with Gryffyn. Or speculating on the one to come.

"Do you wish to speak of him, to share details about his manner or his conversation or the precise shade of his blue eyes, perhaps?"

Keren frowned. It was all she could do most days not to bore Miss Litton by speaking her incessant thoughts of Gryffyn aloud. And his eyes were a lovely shade of brown, at turns rich and dark like fresh-poured coffee or amber-flecked like whisky. They were most definitely not blue. She stopped herself from correcting her sister, but only just.

"I can see from your expression that one has hit the mark. What do you think of his attentions toward other ladies?"

That one was easily managed. "Gryffyn—Mr.

Kimbrell—doesn't pay any particular attention to anyone." He'd danced a couple of sets at the last assembly, but his manner, while polite, had been perfunctory. He'd not shown a preference toward any particular lady, but the thought of him doing precisely that put her stomach in an odd twist.

"And if he's written you a letter, I'm certain you've read it a hundred times."

"A letter! That would hardly be appropriate," Keren protested. Despite her father's despairing of her, she did have some sense.

Lizzie waved aside her concerns in an odd reversal of their roles. "To be sure, it wouldn't be the proper course, Keri, but I know the way of these things. How do you think Langford and I came to discover our feelings for one another?"

"A letter? *That's* why Father took a fist to Langford?"

Lizzie nodded, a smile tipping the corner of her lips.

Keren had been twelve at the time, but she recalled the incident well. The debacle of the mayor engaging in fisticuffs with his daughter's suitor had generated talk from the butcher's to the baker's and the surrounding parish beyond. And that was on account of a *letter*. Keren could well imagine her father's reaction if he ever learned his youngest daughter had *posed* for a man, no matter how innocent their bargain. Although, in truth, she'd done less posing than she'd anticipated and more shell collecting.

"So, your Mr. Kimbrell hasn't written any letters, I take it."

"No." Keren smiled her relief. This, at least, was not a portent of looming disaster. Gryffyn Kimbrell was a man of few words, not one to expound on his feelings—whatever their nature—in a letter.

She thought of his terse note, hastily scrawled in reply to her query some days past: *Wednesday, if that is agreeable.* Words, she realized with a start, she'd rubbed her finger across at least a hundred times.

Botheration.

CHAPTER SIXTEEN

GRYFFYN'S MOTHER HAD BEEN TRUE to her word: his best coat was pressed and waiting for him when he returned home later that afternoon. Nerves set his stomach to twist and turn as he dressed for the evening.

His mother, for her part, was delighted with the prospect of their outing. She flapped and fluttered about him like a mother wren when he descended the stairs. Reaching up to adjust his cravat, she smoothed a hand along the front of his coat with a satisfied smile. At six and twenty, he'd long since outgrown such fussing, but he suspected she'd still be fixing him when he was forty to her seventy.

"You grow more handsome every day," she said.

"Even though I don't match you and Father in looks?" he asked. "Or my brothers?" The words escaped before he could stop them, and she cocked her head to one side. A heavy moment of silence hung between them before she spoke.

"Even though," she whispered, and unexpected relief washed through him. Whether for her assurance or her avoidance of his question beneath the question, he couldn't say.

"You're my mother," he reminded her. "There must be a handbook that instructs you to say such things."

"There is no handbook for mothers, I assure you," she said as she patted his arm.

His father joined them then, dressed in his own best coat, and together they walked to the carriage. It was an old equipage, a relic from days long past when his parents had used to travel to Truro and Plymouth and Bath for his father's commissions. Their old cart horses shuffled in their traces, the weight of the carriage unfamiliar at their backs.

His father handed his mother in then settled next to her. The carriage dipped and rocked slightly as Gryffyn entered and took the rear facing seat. While their family may not have had a frequent need for the carriage, his father believed in keeping his things in top condition, and the old velvet cushions were clean.

Mrs. Quick's husband, who'd once driven for Squire Carew, had been happy to earn some extra coin for the evening. He climbed on the box, and they reached Camborne in minutes. Indeed, they could have walked there in less time than it took to ready the horses, but his mother had insisted that arriving on foot to a fine supper with the mayor would not have been the thing.

Lamps lit the exterior of the mayor's residence, and candles shone from within. The carriage was opened, and they were shown into the drawing room—the same room where Gryffyn's mantelpiece had been installed some weeks before.

Despite the presence of several others in the room, his eyes immediately found Miss Moon. She sat near the pianoforte, back straight, gloved hands folded one atop the other, and she . . . glowed. There was no other word for it. Her face was serene as she watched his arrival. As she watched *their* arrival, for surely her gaze was not for him alone. Nerves fluttered again in his stomach, and he pulled his eyes from Miss Moon as the mayor stood to greet them.

"Mr. Kimbrell," Moon said to his father. "I'm delighted your family could join us." The mayor bowed over his mother's hand and greeted Gryffyn before indicating the others in the room.

Gryffyn was surprised to see George Davies, the sculptor from Falmouth, alongside a delicate, fair-haired woman he estimated to be on the near side of forty. Another couple were seated across from Miss

Moon, and he recognized another of the mayor's daughters.

"My daughter and her husband, Mr. and Mrs. Langford," Moon said, making the introductions. "And I believe you're acquainted with Mr. Davies. He and his sister, Mrs. Richardson, have traveled from Falmouth to join us."

Polite greetings were exchanged, and Gryffyn couldn't help the feeling that he was being measured by Miss Moon's sister. Her gaze was intent as she watched him from her position next to her husband, and he wondered if his cravat had gone askew since his mother's fussing. He shook off his discomfort and crossed to the pianoforte.

"Miss Moon." He greeted her with a dip of his head.

"Mr. Kimbrell." Although she wasn't precisely frowning, neither was she smiling. Her eyes, which lately had sparkled at him with humor, were dim, and his brows dipped in confusion. Gone was the warm, vibrant grin he'd come to expect and, in its place, cool composure.

"I hope the evening's weather made for a pleasant journey," she said.

He checked his surprise. They were back to the weather, were they? Where was the teasing lady from his grandfather's picnic? It would seem her flirtation *had* been an aberration then. An unexpected weight settled in his chest at the thought, but perhaps it was for the better.

"Aye, Miss Moon," he said shortly. "The weather was fine indeed, and we passed a pure and pleasant three minutes in our carriage."

Her serene expression remained in place for a beat then her lips twitched as she fought a smile. Finally, she succumbed. Her eyes brightened as her lips curved, and the weight lifted from his chest. How was it possible for another person to have such authority over his body's highs and lows? Whatever the reason for her initial coolness toward him, he was glad for its thawing.

"I'm relieved to hear it, Mr. Kimbrell. I would not have wished you discomfort for such a long journey."

Their conversation was nothing of significance. Certainly, anyone overhearing their remarks would think them dull indeed, but his heart, it would seem, was easily moved. It expanded with each word from her lips.

"How d'you fare?" he asked softly. "Are you and Henry recovered from yesterday's events?"

"We are quite recovered, thank you for asking. Although, I'm not certain Henry ever truly grasped the gravity of the situation."

"'Tis for the better," he said. "Gravity would not have served him well on the cliffs."

"Mr. Kimbrell," she said, her finely carved brows lifting in surprise. "Have you made a jest?"

"A poor one, yes. I can see I've surprised you."

"I confess," she said, "nothing you say or do is as I expect."

He wasn't certain if that was to his favor or not. "My manner may not be as open as some or as easy as others, but I assure you, Miss Moon, I do have a sense of humor."

"So you do," she said softly. "And I think your manner is as it should be. If it were any different . . ." She paused.

"Aye?" he asked, curious.

"Well, if it were any different, you wouldn't be . . . you. And that would be a shame."

Gryffyn's breath caught at her simple words, and he stared at her. She didn't measure him against his father or his mother or his legions of brothers and cousins. Absent were the qualifiers *almost* and *nearly*. She couldn't know it, but her words had the effect of a chisel to his heart, shearing off layers of stone to reveal what lay beneath. And what lay beneath was raw and elemental as it thumped frantically, trying to escape the confines of his chest.

"And now," she said, "I can see from the frown on your face that *I've* surprised *you*." She returned his words neatly to him, and he forced his frown to relax. Her eyes dropped to his hand and softened. "And how do you fare, Mr. Kimbrell?"

How did he fare? He couldn't rightly say. His thoughts were a drumbling mess and—

"How is your hand?"

His hand? He blinked then followed her gaze, his fogged brain finally sorting her words. He flexed his fingers. "Aye, 'tis well, Miss Moon, despite your poor planning. What manner of lady carries naught but a single handkerchief to a picnic?"

She laughed then covered the sound with her gloved fingers.

"You ought not hide your laughter," Gryffyn said. "'Tis a lovely sound."

"Kimbrell." The greeting behind him prevented any reply she might have made, and Gryffyn turned to find Mr. Davies. The sculptor eyed them curiously before saying, "'Tis an unexpected surprise to find you at Camborne."

Gryffyn resisted the urge to point out that surprises, by their nature, were unexpected. He replied instead, "Mr. Davies. 'Tis been some months since last we met."

"Moon tells me you're preparing a piece for the Truro exhibition," Davies said. "My sister and I will remain in Newford for a few days, and I'd love to see how your work progresses." He leaned too closely toward Miss Moon and added, "I'm certain it must be impressive, eh, Miss Moon?"

"I'm certain it must be," she agreed.

"You've not seen it then?"

"I understand artists can be very secretive." Miss Moon's words were for Davies, but the teasing glint in her eye was directed at Gryffyn. "Being an artist yourself, Mr. Davies, perhaps you've a similar temperament."

Davies merely nodded and Gryffyn added, "I'm afraid 'taint much to see as yet."

"But the date is fast approaching. Surely you must have made *some* progress by now?"

Miss Moon cast a look of expectation toward Gryffyn, then her smile slipped a tiny bit at his hesitation. As much as he longed to reassure her that he would, indeed, have a piece worthy of submission, he said only, "I understand you also mean to submit to Truro, Mr. Davies. I don't think 'twould be fitting to share our work before the exhibition."

"Ah, but the distinction is that my piece is *finis* and has been done for some time now," Davies said. "Surely, there can be no harm in sharing at this late date, and perhaps I can advise you on yours."

His words were unexceptionable, but Gryffyn recalled Jory's report of the assembly room carvings in Falmouth. He certainly didn't need the man learning anything of his own plans, no matter how much Miss Moon's brows knitted in disappointment.

———

SIMONS ANNOUNCED SUPPER AND KEREN marshaled the guests to the dining room. The ladies were seated near her father at the bottom of the table, the gentlemen near Keren at the top. They were a motley assortment.

Mrs. Richardson was a fragile, if fading, flower with white-gold hair and a slim nose that twitched when she spoke. She put Keren in mind of an overly clever rabbit, plotting to steal the cabbages. The lady cast frequent and obvious glances at Keren's father, settling the question of his recent trips to Falmouth and causing Keren's stomach to knot.

Lizzie watched them with unmistakable interest while her husband enjoyed his meal with unmistakable ignorance. How Langford could fail to notice Mrs. Richardson's interest in their father was beyond Keren, but when it came to romance, she suspected Langford's only awareness was for her sister.

Gryffyn's father was a polite man with few words but sharp eyes that she suspected missed very little. Although he and his son looked nothing alike, his quiet manner reminded her of Gryffyn. And Mrs. Kimbrell . . . The more Keren was in the lady's company, the more she found to like. Gryffyn's mother was kind and warm with a ready smile. Precisely the sort a lady might wish for her own mother, were there choices to be made in such things.

Mr. Davies wore his classically handsome looks with ease and a good bit of cologne. With a straight nose much like his sister's and flaxen hair that lay perfectly across a smooth forehead, he resembled a languishing poet more than a sculptor. As she eyed the narrow cut of his coat, she couldn't imagine the man wielding a mallet to any great effect, for all that he boasted of his completed carving. He certainly didn't have Gryffyn's quiet strength or enigmatic dark looks.

And yet another mark against the man: his overblown attempts to flirt with Keren were, in a word, uninspiring. She feared Gryffyn's understated teasing had broken something in her; more than once she'd barely stopped her eyes from rolling at some ridiculous thing or other that Mr. Davies said. All her prior flirtations came back to her in force; they'd been nothing but watered wine to the full-bodied, fizzing champagne she enjoyed with Gryffyn.

Gryffyn. After her conversation with Lizzie, Keren had braced herself against his pull. She didn't want to love him—she didn't want to love anyone—but she feared that was where she was headed. She'd thought some distance was needed to clarify the boundaries of their acquaintance. And so, she'd met his greeting with cool detachment. Had managed it, in fact, for the length of . . . oh, an entire sentence.

But something had flashed across his face at her trite pleasantries—irritation, disappointment, she wasn't sure which—and her heart had twisted painfully. She'd been helpless against the spell that continually drew her to him, but how her heart had lightened when she'd loosened her hold on it. Like a spring foal, it gamboled, delighting in every look, every word shared between them. She was a sad case indeed, and although she worried that the end of their association would devastate her, she couldn't help her continual glances in his direction.

Their party had been an odd nine in number, an unfortunate circumstance that Keren had quickly rectified with an eleventh-hour entreaty to Miss Litton. Henry's governess had joined them to round out the females, and she sat next to Gryffyn at his other side. Keren lifted her wine glass and watched them now, brows lifting when his lips curved at something Miss Litton said. Keren straightened. When had Henry's governess become so amusing?

"Mr. Kimbrell," Keren said, and both Kimbrell gentlemen looked her way. "Won't you share the tale of your grand rescue at the cliffs? I'm certain our guests would enjoy hearing it." The elder Mr. Kimbrell looked toward his son, whose neck had reddened. Keren felt a twinge of remorse for causing Gryffyn's discomfort, but at least he was no longer smiling at Miss Litton. Lizzie cast an amused glance at Keren, her expression bordering on a smirk which Keren ignored.

"Yes, do tell us how you managed to extricate young Henry," Mrs. Richardson said. "You must be terribly brave." She punctuated the sentence with a delicate shiver. Keren was certain the reaction must have been forced, and she frowned. How did one shiver at will?

Gryffyn studied his wine longingly before replying. "'Twasn't nearly so grand as it sounds, Mrs. Richardson. To be sure, 'twas no more than anyone else would have done."

"You must have been terrified, Miss Litton, to know your charge had escaped your care," Mrs. Richardson said.

"I—it was my off day," Miss Litton said with a glance of apology toward Keren. "I didn't attend the picnic."

"Henry was in my charge—" Keren began, but Mrs. Kimbrell interrupted.

"We were all of us caring for Master Henry," she said. "Why, there must have been twenty ladies or more keeping a watch on him, but he was much too quick for any of us. He has quite the inquisitive mind, you know."

Keren smiled at Mrs. Kimbrell gratefully. While she accepted full responsibility for losing sight of Henry at Oak Hill, she had no wish to lay her faults along the dining table for Mrs. Richardson's inspection.

"He's nearly past the age of a governess," Mrs. Richardson said to her father. "I'm certain the structure and discipline of school will better serve him."

Miss Litton paled, and Keren felt the blood drain from her own face.

"Well," her father began with a frowning glance toward Keren's end of the table.

"I'm afraid you're mistaken, Mrs. Richardson," Keren said quickly, ignoring her father's frown. "School will *not* better serve him. He's not ready to leave Camborne."

"But you're not his mother," Mrs. Richardson said sweetly, nose twitching. "Certainly, that's a decision to be made by his parent. You must wish to marry, Miss Moon, and set up your own house. I'm sure it will be a relief to pass the burden of managing your brother to others."

Keren's eyes slid to Gryffyn at the mention of marriage, and she quickly pulled them back to Mrs. Richardson. "Henry's not a burden, and he's not ready for school," she repeated then motioned to Simons to send for the next course.

Keren lifted her wine once more as a delicate sole in lemon sauce was spooned onto the guests' plates. With one last frowning glance toward her end of the table, her father neatly turned the conversation back to the Truro exhibition.

"While I wish you great success in your endeavor, Davies, I have fixed my hopes on Mr. Kimbrell here. I'll have everyone know that Newford is as fine a town as Truro."

Gryffyn, whose blush had recovered from Mrs. Richardson's earlier attention, looked as if he longed to be elsewhere.

"Who will determine the winning entry?" Lizzie asked.

"Enys has enlisted a number of fine gentlemen from across the county to stand as judges," Davies said.

"His predecessor had quite the scandal on his hands at last year's festival," Langford said in frowning recollection. "Something about favoritism and bribes affecting the outcome of the contests, I believe. Let's hope Enys's judges are more impartial."

Moon nodded and said, "It's meant to be a blind

competition, and the judges won't know who the carvers are until after they've selected a winner. But regardless, the judges are well-respected and honorable gentlemen, so I can't imagine there will be any controversy. I believe Prinny's favorite for Truro's next member of Parliament will even participate. A gentleman by the name of Derrick Carne."

Silver clattered against porcelain, and Keren jumped. Mrs. Kimbrell retrieved her fork where it had fallen and murmured, "My apologies."

———

THOMAS KIMBRELL WATCHED HIS WIFE of nearly forty years sag onto the end of their bed. He lowered himself next to her and laid his hand atop her smaller, fragile one to quell her trembling. She'd let her hair down to fall across her shoulder in a soft, shining braid that even the years couldn't dim. The candle caught glints of burnished gold and threads of polished silver—riches well beyond the dreams of his youth—as she leaned her head against his shoulder.

"We have to tell him," she said.

"To what purpose?" he asked softly.

"He deserves to know the truth."

Thomas couldn't refute her statement, but to

unburden their truth would surely hurt her and Gryffyn both, and that was something he couldn't—wouldn't—allow. His wife continued, her voice faint in the room's stillness.

"Whether we choose to tell him or not, his own face will betray us. When he goes to Truro—" Her voice caught on a sob, and she gripped his hand tightly.

"I never should have agreed to this exhibition," Thomas said. "'Tis my fault we've reached this place, when I knew 'twould cause problems."

"You mustn't blame yourself, Thomas. You could hardly stop him, and he's long past the age of asking for your permission. He only wishes for your support."

"Aye, and if I'd not given it, would he have reconsidered?"

"I don't think so. 'Twould only have set him further from us. Our son is an ambitious carver, with large dreams and a talent to match, much like . . ." The unfinished sentence hung between them. *Much like you were.*

Thomas's ambition, long since tempered by other, more important considerations, had started them on this path. If only he'd listened to his wife all those years before. If only he'd not taken the job in Truro—He quickly struck that line of thinking before it could fully form, because if he'd not taken the job in Truro, they'd not have their youngest son.

He set his jaw and gave his wife's hand a reassuring squeeze. They rode a runaway carriage with the cliff's edge fast approaching. He couldn't change the past, but if there was a way to avoid the disaster that loomed ahead, he needed to find it.

CHAPTER SEVENTEEN

GRYFFYN SPENT THE NEXT DAY helping his father prepare stone facing for the new town hall. The work was something they'd planned to do after the Truro exhibition, but his father had expressed a sudden, inexplicable desire to see it completed post-haste.

His urgency had been as puzzling as it was pointless, for his father's movements had been unusually slow and plodding. The work had taken twice the time it should have, and when they finally finished for the day, his father had requested Gryffyn's help with repairs on their own home. It was but one more delay he couldn't afford if he meant to finish his piece for Truro.

The exhibition was fast approaching. He'd enlisted Jory and Alfie to help him carry Fortuna to Truro at week's end, and there was much to be done. Her torso still required more filing, and he hadn't even begun the detail work on her face. If he didn't find time for carving soon, there wouldn't be a statue worth submitting.

So, when a message arrived Wednesday from Miss Moon with a request to postpone Henry's lesson, he should have been pleased with the extra hour. Instead, he frowned in disappointment. Henry, she'd written, had developed a small cough, and they wouldn't be able to join Gryffyn at the cove. He shoved his disappointment aside and ignored the voice that suggested he call at Camborne to inquire after them.

Retrieving his leather apron instead, he went through the back door to where another lady awaited his attentions. Taking up his sanding file, he studied the drape of fabric about her hip. He set the steel file to the marble twice before he was satisfied with its placement, then he continued the painstaking work of spinning silk from stone.

——

KEREN LEFT MR. CLIFTON'S BAKERY with a paper-wrapped parcel of mince pies. She hoped the treat might cheer Henry, who'd been disappointed to miss his carving lesson. She'd indulged in a pastry for herself as well, to soothe her own regret. Despite her earlier, admittedly frail, intention to set some distance between herself and Gryffyn, she longed to tease more humor from him.

She glanced across the high street to his workshop. There was no movement beyond the window. Was he inside, or had he gone to assist his father elsewhere? How *was* his Truro project coming along?

Mr. Davies—who still remained at Camborne with his sister—had not achieved any success with his repeated inquiries the night of her father's supper. As little liking as she had for the man, Keren could well appreciate his curiosity about Gryffyn's submission.

An uncomfortable suspicion crowded her thoughts. What if his reluctance to share his progress was more than an artist's secretive temperament? Was it possible his work wasn't proceeding as he hoped? Or worse... He'd sketched her to assist with his carving. Had he found her uninspiring? Was *she* the cause of his reluctance?

She swallowed against an uncomfortable lump, then quick steps carried her across the cobbles before she could think better of the decision.

She paused at his door and glanced up and down the high street. The way was empty, and there were no faces at the windows opposite. No tell-tale neighbors to carry stories back to her father. She twisted the knob, and it turned easily in her hand.

She slid inside where the air was cool and dim, lit only by the light of the front window. "Mr. Kimbrell?" she called into the silence. She moved into the workshop slowly, allowing her eyes to adjust to the dimness. Henry's red-handled tools lay neatly lined upon a leather cloth awaiting his lesson, but there was no sign of Gryffyn.

Could she steal a peek at his marble? After a small hesitation, she moved past the worktable, past shelves of tools and small carvings to the rear door. She eased it open and entered the small stone yard to find it shrouded in canvas. Where it had once been open to the breeze, tarps now hung across ropes to cloak the sides and rear. Low enough to admit the golden morning sunlight but high enough to shield the space from curious eyes.

In the center sat the same ragged block of marble she'd seen when Gryffyn had first begun carving, and her heart made an uncomfortable turn. *This* was his Truro submission? Why, it was naught but a lump of unpolished stone, and the exhibition mere days away! Her brows drew together as sorrow pinched her insides.

She must have made a noise because shuffling sounded from the opposite side of the block, and Gryffyn's head came around the edge. His eyes widened on seeing her and he stood, a metal file hanging loosely from one hand. She saw then that chunks of stone littered the ground at his feet, and dust painted the toes of his boots white. Given that and the amount of dust covering his person, he must have been carving *something*.

"Miss Moon, is all well? How does Henry fare?" He wore a leather apron over shirt sleeves and buff trousers, and he wiped his hands on a linen as he approached.

She swallowed and forced a smile to her face. "Henry is resting," she said. "He's not the best patient, as I'm sure you can imagine."

"Has the fidgets, does he?"

How could he be so calm in the face of certain failure in Truro? Her eyes burned for him, and she blinked. After a brief hesitation, she nodded slowly. "Like a cat on hot bricks."

The dark shadow of Gryffyn's jaw was liberally sprinkled with stone dust. When his finely sculpted lips curved in a smile, she stopped breathing. Averting her gaze so she could think, she forced out the obvious question: "Is—is this your piece for Truro?"

"Aye." Surely, he would ask her to leave, and she would be relieved to avoid any awkwardness. But he merely watched her through thick, dark lashes. Then, swallowing once, he motioned to the far side of the stone and said, "Would you like to see her?"

Frowning, Keren jerked an uncertain nod.

He lifted a dusty hand to assist her through the debris then dropped it to his side, eyeing her white gloves. "My apologies for the dust," he said.

She gave a shaky smile at his understatement and set her parcel of mince pies on a low bench. "I've invaded your workshop," she said. "You can't think I don't expect to find a little dust." She followed him to step lightly through the stone shards, rounding his side of the marble with dread thumping at her temples. Her brain scurried to think of appropriate words of encouragement but what could she say?

She lifted her head and stopped. One hand flew to her mouth as she took in the piece before her. She stood silent and unmoving, unable to sort the superlatives crowding her mind. Exquisite. Brilliant. Magnificent. All competed for a place on her tongue, but she could only muster the sense to say, "Ohhh. Oh my."

"'Tis still a fair bit unfinished, o' course," he said into the silence. "I've yet to carve the details of her face, but..." His voice trailed off, and Keren's breath caught in her throat at his hesitation. That this man should harbor any uncertainty about his craft was humbling. And to think, she'd allowed him to see her poor fox—how he must have laughed! A giggle bubbled in her throat, and she swallowed.

Fortuna stood half-emerged from her marble, hair and skirts blowing in great waves to disappear into the uncarved stone at her back—the rough portion Keren had seen from behind. The statue balanced on one finely detailed foot while the other lay trapped, concealed in the marble behind her.

Translucent white "cloth" draped her figure, and she glowed, even in the filtered light of the canvas-draped linney. The impression of thin cloth was so realistic Keren couldn't help asking the ridiculous question: "Is—is this *stone*?"

"Aye."

Seized by the sheer beauty of the thing he'd created, her poor heart didn't know whether to flutter or pound or flop about. Finally, it settled into a shaky rhythm as she lifted a tentative hand to the cool marble. Belatedly, she recalled the impediment of her gloves and slowly tugged them from her hands.

She trailed a finger along a rippling fold. Despite his assurances that it was indeed stone, she was surprised to feel cold, unrelenting marble beneath her touch rather than silk. Like a mythical god, he'd captured the *wind*, for Heaven's sake. Halted its fury as it carved Fortuna's form from virgin rock. Her smile grew; she was giddy with relief.

"I can almost hear the winds rage as they sculpt her," she said softly.

"Aye, 'tis fitting, I should think." She looked a question at him and he continued. "'Taint a calm breeze that carves and shapes our lives, but turbulent winds. 'Tis left to us to decide if we'll emerge beautiful or broken."

There was much more to Gryffyn Kimbrell than Keren realized. Much more than *anyone* realized, she suspected. Without minimizing the trials of life, his words made them sound . . . surmountable.

She thought of her mother's death and her brother's, both of which had profoundly affected her. Carved her, even. How had she chosen to emerge from the rubble of those dark days? She shifted a little, uncomfortable with the answer that lurked at the edge of her mind.

While she wouldn't say she was *broken*, precisely, neither had she come out as strong and beautiful as she might have. That thought pulled her up short. *As she might have.* There was a wealth of potential in that phrase, and a sudden, unexpected flare of hope warmed her. Gryffyn Kimbrell had a rare power indeed, to spark such optimism.

As she studied his work, another illuminating thought struck her. "She emerges from the stone like the ship at the cove."

"Your observation of the cliffs was inspired, Miss

Moon. You've an artist's eye, and 'tis only fitting that you be the first to see her."

She was absurdly pleased—and highly skeptical —that the childish fancy she'd shared with him had precipitated something so magnificent. Then the rest of his words caught, and she said, "I'm the first?"

"Aye."

"Because I came to your workshop uninvited?"

"No, Miss Moon. I could have escorted you back inside, but I didn't. I allowed you to see her because I wished it."

"Fortune favors the bold, it would seem," she said airily.

He merely dipped his head in agreement.

She turned to study the figure from a different angle, then another. The stone "folds" draped Fortuna with gossamer-thin transparency, hinting at a pulsing, breathing form beneath. She felt as if she could peel back the silken fabric to find the supple flesh of a woman's leg.

Gryffyn lifted his file and rubbed lightly at a spot on the figure's torso. His long fingers smoothed away the dust from his efforts, and Keren flinched as if his fingers had caressed her own fevered skin. She reminded herself that while she may have been his model for the lady's skirts, the torso beneath the stone fabric was *not* hers. The admonishment was futile, though. Warmth bloomed in her cheeks and spread to her stomach. Her heart raced as his thumb made one final, slow sweep across Fortuna's rib, and she drew a shuddering breath.

Heavens. The man wasn't even *trying* to flirt with her, and still he'd stirred and boiled her into a quivering pudding.

He lifted the file again and held it up to Fortuna's arm. Then, glancing at Keren from the corner of his eye, he stopped.

"Would—would you like to try flirting?" he asked.

She stared at him. *Filing.* He'd asked if she'd like to try *filing*.

"You did provide the inspiration for her, after all," he continued.

Her eyes widened. "Oh, I'm sure I couldn't." Shouldn't.

He nodded. Was it her imagination or had his shoulders dropped slightly?

"What if I ruin her?" she whispered.

"Miss Moon," he said with a small smile. "'Tis a block of stone that's withstood the ages. To be sure, it can withstand your delicate attentions. And besides, I shall guide you in where to apply the file."

"*Delicate attentions*, Mr. Kimbrell? Do you believe my hands are incapable of carving then?" She herself doubted her abilities, but she couldn't resist teasing him.

"Delicate does not mean incapable, Miss Moon.

Indeed, I believe you would be capable of anything you set your heart to. Now, will you try it?"

She swallowed at the certainty in his gaze and the expectation that lightened his features. Surely, she should leave. It wasn't proper, just the two of them together behind his workshop, with no Miss Litton to maintain propriety.

She looked toward the door and opened her mouth to take her leave of him. But she found herself saying instead, "Yes, I should like to try it."

CHAPTER EIGHTEEN

GRYFFYN READ HESITATION ON MISS Moon's face, and he couldn't say he blamed her. With her pale blue muslin, fitty bonnet and lace gloves, of course she wouldn't wish to soil her finery with stone dust. He wasn't sure what he'd been thinking, to ask her if she'd like to *file*.

But then she surprised him. "I should like to try it," she said.

He waited for the quirk of her lips to indicate she was teasing him again, but her lips remained steady, her expression earnest.

He gave a short nod. "You'll wish to secure your gloves," he said.

She obligingly shoved her gloves into a pocket then loosened the ribbon beneath her chin and set her bonnet aside.

He removed his apron and held it out to her.

"This will help protect your dress."

She took the garment and looped it over her neck, tying the leather ties behind her. "Do I look a proper stone carver?" she asked, smiling.

He eyed her trim form, swallowed in one bite by his apron, dainty slippers peeking out from beneath her hem. "No," he scoffed. Then, softening his voice, he said, "To be sure, there's never been a stone carver quite so fetching."

Her smile widened and roses bloomed in her cheeks. He cleared his throat and used a linen rag to clean the worst of the dust from the file's wooden handle before passing it to her.

"I've been refining this section of her skirts," he said. "D'you see how the stone here is rougher than it should be?" He motioned to an unsanded fold in the marble.

She ran a slim finger along the length of the crease and nodded. "Yes, I can feel it."

"Now, imagine the direction of the wind that blows against her and align the file with it."

He waited while she studied the sculpture, gauging the flow of movement in the stone before adjusting the file. She looked up at him from beneath dark lashes, a question in her gaze.

"Aye, 'tis almost there," he said. He hesitated then reached a hand over hers and adjusted her grip slightly. There was a reason ladies wore gloves, he thought, as the smooth coolness of her bare alabaster skin distracted his better sense. Her fingers were long and tapered, the bones delicate to his larger, rougher hand. His pulse thumped loudly in his ears, and seconds passed while he tried to regain his focus.

He'd nearly succeeded, but then she turned her head. Mere inches separated them; he could see the nearly-black outline of her irises, feel the whisper of her breath on his cheek, smell her warm orange-blossom scent. She had a tiny, mesmerizing freckle at the corner of her upper lip. Her gaze was fixed on his mouth, and his lips burned beneath her steady regard.

The urge to close the distance between them was as strong as the winds he'd been carving, hammering at his mind's objections. She leaned closer, and he matched her movement, bringing their lips to within a hair's breadth.

But then his conscience stilled him. He was a gentleman, by deed if not by birth, and she a gently bred lady. She deserved a gentleman who would court her in earnest, who would offer more than a kiss stolen behind his workshop.

"Mr. Kimbrell," she whispered, and he felt the breath of her words on his lips. "Are you trifling with me?"

"Aye. That is, no." Her eyes darkened as he

closed the distance between them, and all thoughts fled his mind as he pressed his lips to hers. Her mouth was warm and impossibly soft beneath his. He tasted the alluring freckle at the corner of her upper lip and grew dizzy on her scent. His ears roared with his pulse.

Her hands rested against his chest, and he was certain she must feel his heart racing beneath the linen of his shirt. Something poked him. It was some moments before he realized through his kissing fog that they still held the file, his larger hand wrapped about hers, wrapped about the steel.

With effort, he lifted his head. Miss Moon's eyes fluttered open to reveal liquid pools, and her chest rose and fell rapidly, much like his own, he suspected. His free hand rested on her waist. She felt right—curved and warm and perfectly fitted to his palm. He slowly released her and stepped back. Cleared his throat and resisted the urge to loosen his collar.

He opened then closed his mouth, unsure how to proceed. What was the proper thing to say after such an encounter? He couldn't—wouldn't—apologize for something so sublime. Finally, he whispered, "Move the file along the rough spot."

She stared at him, confusion clouding her expression. She looked as if she'd kiss him again, and he waited breathlessly to see if she would.

Then she turned back to the stone, and he closed his eyes as relief and disappointment swamped him. He swallowed then continued.

"Apply enough pressure to smooth the stone but not so much to reduce it to dust."

After a brief hesitation, she did as he instructed. He crossed his arms and willed his heart back to its normal rhythm.

Some moments later, she lowered the file. Her color was high, pink staining her cheeks as she awaited his inspection. He used a rag to wipe dust from the place she'd been filing then, running a finger along the surface, he nodded.

"You've done a proper job of it. A little burnishing will see her rightly polished."

He was relieved to see the teasing light had returned to her eyes. "Well," she said, returning the file to him, "there's truly not much to it, is there? I think the skill required of a stone carver must be quite exaggerated." She watched him from the corner of her eye, her soft lips tipping up on one side as she untied his apron.

The air around them, which had grown heavy with want, lightened with the return of her teasing and he relaxed. "Aye," he agreed. "If a delicate miss such as yourself can accomplish the task, it must be a pure and simple thing indeed."

Her smile erupted in a laugh. She didn't rush to

cover the sound, and he was pleased for it.

His apron had protected much of her, but stone-white shavings still sprinkled her fingers and the tips of her half boots. She brushed at her hands in a futile attempt to rid them of dust before retying her bonnet beneath her chin.

"Thank you for allowing me to have a hand in carving Fortuna."

"'Twas my pleasure," he said. The polite words did an injustice to the depth of feeling coursing through him.

She seemed to realize it as well, for she watched him in silence for a beat longer before turning to take her leave. As he escorted her back through the workshop, she spied his sketchbook and paused.

"These are your drawings?" she asked. "The ones you did to prepare for Fortuna?"

"Aye."

"Shall we see how your carving measures up to the statue of your imagination?"

Unease filled him as she reached for the leather-bound book, and he hurried to take it up before she did. He was too many paces behind her though and, sensing his intent, she spun to face him, the sketchbook tucked behind her back.

"You've already seen my sketches at the cove," he said, holding his hand for the book. She eyed him, her familiar half-smile gracing her lips. Then, spinning once more, she turned from him and opened the book.

He pushed a hand through his hair and swallowed. The figure studies he'd captured during Henry's lessons were nothing of interest, to be sure—an anonymous bit of Miss Moon's skirt here, a windswept curl there.

But it was the *other* sketch that caused his stomach to twist nervously as she turned the pages . . .

—

KEREN SPUN AWAY FROM GRYFFYN, taking advantage of the moment to regain her equilibrium. Or to try, at least. Her brain felt like it had been swaddled in cotton, and she couldn't recall much of the past minutes, little beyond the all-too-brief meeting of their lips.

That kiss.

She'd enjoyed a few kisses from previous flirtations—not so many as others might assume, but enough to suspect that a kiss from Gryffyn Kimbrell would be wholly unique. She'd not been wrong. His kiss had been firm and tender, soft and hard, full of emotion and promise and heart. It had sent a bright, fizzing energy from her center to her toes and back.

As soon as he'd pulled away, she'd wanted

another. No, she *yearned* for another with an intensity that zipped and crackled along her veins. Even now, long moments later, her heart still had not found its normal rhythm.

But of the two of them, Gryffyn was the more sensible one. More's the pity . . . Her disappointment at his restraint still stung.

She set her pies aside and turned several pages of his sketchbook before she was able to marshal her thoughts away from his perfectly chiseled lips. His drawings were nicely done, although he was correct: they were little more than what she'd already glimpsed during Henry's lessons. She was hard-pressed to recognize her own skirts in them.

Then she reached one that was unlike the others, and her breath caught. Gryffyn stood at her back — she could feel his heat — and she edged away, lifting the book toward the window to study the page more closely.

He'd drawn *her*, not merely her skirts, as she'd stood at the water's edge with Henry. One calf was exposed as she lifted her hem to avoid the water, her head angled toward her brother.

She recalled the morning well. They'd reached the cove before Gryffyn, and she and Henry had passed the time exploring the edge of the surf while Miss Litton collected shells.

This drawing was not a hastily sketched figure

study like the rest of the pages. There was warmth and life and detail in this one and an intriguing blend of contrasts: the demure features of her face against the impropriety of her exposed calf. The modest lines of her dress against her bonnet-less head. And while she recognized the lady's profile as hers, she didn't recognize the spirit. With simple, bold strokes, he'd captured a person possessed of both strength and gentleness. Of *delicate capability.* He'd captured a lady Keren would like to know.

The silence around them stretched and lengthened, and she turned back to him.

"Is" — she swallowed — "is this how you see me?"

His eyes shifted to a point over her shoulder for a long second before coming back to hers. "Aye," he said softly. "'Tis a proper likeness."

She drew a shallow, stuttering breath. Longing — greater even than what she'd felt for their kiss — swirled and frothed within her at his blunt admission. She couldn't help the burning curiosity to know if he experienced the same depth of feeling. It prompted her to ask, quite boldly, "Do you harbor an affection for me, Mr. Kimbrell?"

The sudden dip of his brows sent her heart into a spin. Had she misread his sentiment? More importantly, what was she thinking, to ask him such a question? Regardless of his answer, there wasn't room in her life for more than idle flirtation. She couldn't—wouldn't—abandon Henry. And yet she waited, lungs frozen, for his reply.

He rubbed the back of his neck and looked at her through his lashes. Finally, he said, "My feelings are of no import, Miss Moon, as I don't intend to marry."

"Ever?" she asked in surprise. She'd never met another person her own age who didn't have matrimonial aims. *Everyone*, it seemed, was intent on pairing off, on making a match. As Lizzie had reminded her, to do otherwise was unnatural.

Gryffyn shook his head, and she exhaled a slow breath. His statement should have eased her, but an uncomfortable weight settled in her stomach instead. She pulled her lips into a smile and said, "We are kindred souls then, Mr. Kimbrell, as I, too, have no intention of marrying."

"Ever?" he whispered.

"I won't say never, for that's an awfully long time, but at least until Henry's of age. Although I suppose that amounts to the same thing, as I'll be much too old to attract any gentleman's notice by then."

"Miss Moon," he said. "I don't think the day will come when you fail to attract a gentleman's notice. Your spirit is much too large for that."

She straightened, and her smile came more easily

this time. "If I was of a mind to marry, Mr. Kimbrell, and if you were similarly disposed, I think we would suit quite well. May I ask—" She hesitated. The question was too forward, even for her.

"Aye?"

She pressed her lips, but the question wouldn't be stifled. "May I ask *why* you don't wish to marry?"

"I didn't say I don't wish to marry, only that I have no intention of doing so."

She frowned. "I admire you, Mr. Kimbrell, I do. But that's quite the silliest thing I've ever heard. If you wish to, and if you find a lady who holds you in affection, what's to stop you? Surely love can overcome any obstacle."

He watched her curiously, and she reconsidered her words. Oh!" she said as her stomach dipped.

"Miss Moon?" His brows flattened over his eyes.

"Have you fixed your affections on a lady who is already attached?"

His brows dipped in irritation. "No."

"A lady who is not a lady then? Perhaps someone unworthy of your affection?"

His brows reversed course and climbed toward his hairline. "No, Miss Moon." After a moment's hesitation, he added, "But have you considered that perhaps 'tis I who am unworthy?"

She snorted in disbelief. His face was an arresting one (handsome was too bland a word to describe him), and his name was well respected. He was clever and thoughtful and—yes!—amusing when one paid proper attention. There was no lady of intelligence who would not find him worthy.

"Mr. Kimbrell, I don't think the day will come when you're unworthy of a lady's affections." He smiled at her wordplay, and she continued. "You may be certain the right lady will accept your tarnish as well as your shiny bits."

"My shiny bits?" he asked.

"Yes, I'm sure you must possess a few." She'd meant to tease him, to steer them back to their harmless flirtation and away from the dangerous ground they skirted, but he remained unsmiling.

"Although," she tried again, "I suppose you'll become tremendously famous after Truro, and everyone will desire a Gryffyn Kimbrell carving. You'll leave Newford—why, you might even go so far as Paris and carve for the cathedrals there. A wife and children would only hinder your success, I imagine."

His lips finally curved up on one side in the barest hint of a smile. "To be sure."

His agreement reestablished a proper distance between them, but the weight in her stomach didn't ease.

He took the sketchbook from her. "You have my apology, Miss Moon. I should not have drawn you thus. 'Twas not our bargain, and I wouldn't wish to create trouble for you."

Their bargain. Trouble. There would be plenty of it if her father learned she'd been the object of a man's secret drawings. She sobered and eyed the sketchbook again. "If my father learns of this," she whispered, "he'll send me away, without Henry."

He nodded then slowly tore the sketch from the book. "I assure you, Miss Moon, I shall burn the page. You have my word."

He began to crumple the paper in his fist, and she placed a hand on his arm. "May I . . . may I have it?" she asked.

"Aye, o' course," he said after a small hesitation.

He handed her the sketch, and she tucked it in a pocket. She looked up at him with a small smile, prepared to take her leave, but stopped when she spied two figures approaching from the end of the high street.

"My father—he's walking with Mr. Davies," she said with a disbelieving gasp. He'd surely see her if she left now.

She retreated from the window. Her father was still some distance away. Perhaps they meant to stop at the bank or the post office, and she could slip away then. There was no reason to think they would come as far as the Kimbrell workshop, but then her father lifted a hand to indicate the stone carver's building. Davies nodded and the pair strode with purpose toward them.

"They're coming here," Keren hissed. She pressed a hand to her throat in alarm. If her father found her here, alone with Gryffyn and covered in stone dust . . . She glanced around frantically.

"Go through the back," Gryffyn said. "You can return to the high street through the alley by the Feather."

She nodded and hurried from him, shoving at the back door and ducking through a gap in the canvas. A narrow path ran behind the shops that lined the water, and she raced along the river's edge. With luck, Gryffyn would hold her father's attention long enough for her to escape down the alley and back to Camborne. As she reached the back of The Fin and Feather Inn, the door opened and Gryffyn's cousin Wynne emerged.

"Miss Moon," she said in surprise.

"Mrs. Teague." Keren greeted her with a short nod before glancing back to be sure her father hadn't stepped into Gryffyn's stone yard.

Wynne eyed her suspiciously before directing her own gaze down the river path. Keren supposed her actions must have appeared suspicious to the average observer, and Wynne was anything but average.

"Are you in need of assistance?" Wynne asked.

Keren forced a smile to her face. "No," she said. "I'm merely in a hurry. Henry has contracted a cough, and I thought to cheer him with some pies from Mr. Clifton's bakery." The pies! She'd left them in Gryffyn's workshop. She waited for Wynne to remind her that Mr. Clifton's bakery lay on the opposite side of the high street.

But after a slight pause, Wynne said only, "I was glad to hear your brother didn't suffer for his adventure at Oak Hill."

Keren checked her surprised at such an overture and said, "Thank you. We were grateful for your cousins' timely assistance."

Wynne nodded then narrowed her eyes at the fine stone dust on Keren's hands. Heavens! She'd forgotten to don her gloves.

"If you'll excuse me," she said with a nod. She stepped around Wynne and approached the alley that ran along the side of the inn.

"Miss Moon," Wynne called. Keren paused and glanced over her shoulder. "You've a bit of stone dust on your dress." She motioned to Keren's waist, and Keren twisted to see a large, very distinct handprint marking the blue muslin of her dress. Gasping, she brushed at it, but only succeeded in smearing the dust about. Face aflame, she spun and hurried away.

Her heart didn't slow until she reached

Camborne, where she brushed past Simons and hurried up the stairs. Once in her bedchamber, she closed the door firmly behind her then washed her hands and changed her dress. Only then did she remove Gryffyn's drawing with shaking fingers.

She held the page to her lips, breathing in the scents of paper and Gryffyn. The prudent thing would be to burn the page, cast it on the embers in her fireplace, but she couldn't bring herself to do it. Instead, she carefully refolded the page and tucked it in the back of her vanity.

He had no intention of marrying.

She had no intention of marrying.

Their shared lack of intention should have brought relief. Neither of them had any expectations for the other, so she needn't worry their flirtation would lead either of them to disappointment. So yes, relief should have poured through her, but her stupid heart raised a hand. It pointed out with smirking condescension that intentions were all well and good until love entered the fray.

CHAPTER NINETEEN

G RYFFYN HAD NO TIME TO sort his thoughts or review his conversation with Miss Moon, much as he longed to. The mayor and Davies were but moments from his workshop. He closed his sketchbook and tucked it out of sight, ignoring the ragged edge where he'd removed his drawing of Miss Moon. She'd surprised him by requesting the page, but of course, she'd wish to see to its destruction herself.

His thoughts on revealing his carving to Davies hadn't changed, so he hurriedly rewrapped Fortuna's tarp about her then returned inside to await the mayor's arrival.

"Mr. Kimbrell," Moon said jovially as they entered.

"Sir, 'tis a pleasure to see you. Mr. Davies." He nodded in greeting.

"I hope you don't mind the unexpected visit, but Davies and I thought to see if you've reconsidered giving us a peek at your work." Moon angled his head toward the back of the workshop, and Gryffyn nearly groaned to see he'd left the door ajar. His mind had clearly been on Miss Moon's hasty retreat rather than securing Fortuna.

"Is that it?" Davies asked, nodding to where the statue's tarp fluttered in the breeze.

"Aye, but I'm sorry to say 'tis still not ready for viewing," Gryffyn said. Then, with alarm, he spied one of Miss Moon's lace gloves on the floor. It must have fallen when she'd pocketed his drawing. He stepped to the side and covered it with his boot, nearly braining himself on one of the cabinets that ringed the shop as her father sauntered about to examine his carvings.

"Will you at least share the theme of your carving?" Davies asked. "'Twould be an embarrassment for certain if we were to submit the same thing."

Gryffyn crossed his arms, careful not to move his foot. If the men found anything odd in his fixed stance, they refrained from comment. "I don't think there's any danger of that occurring," he said to Davies. "The possibilities are endless, and the odds we'd choose to carve the same thing must be impossibly small. And even if, by some quirk of fortune, we did submit the same subject, 'twould surely come down to the carver's skill and execution."

"He has you there, Davies," Moon said. He lifted the fox in the window and held it to the light, turning it from side to side. After several more minutes of irritatingly persistent questions about Gryffyn's submission, Davies finally excused himself to post a letter.

The mayor turned to watch him go, and Gryffyn hurriedly pocketed Miss Moon's glove. As the door clicked shut, Moon's brows lowered. "I didn't think he'd ever leave."

"Sir?"

"Are those mince pies I smell?" Moon pointed at a parcel on a low stool. Miss Moon's pies. She'd forgotten them in her haste.

"I—yes, I believe so."

"My son William had a fondness for them," Moon said, his eyes unfocused in remembrance. He shook himself and added, "I imagine Henry does too, although Keren would know better."

Gryffyn frowned and waited for the mayor to state his purpose. Moon didn't keep him waiting long.

"I'm not blind, Mr. Kimbrell," he said with a long stroke of his side whiskers, and Gryffyn's stomach sank. Had the mayor seen his daughter's glove beneath Gryffyn's boot? Gryffyn recalled the oft-repeated stories of Moon's well-aimed right hook and wondered if he'd need to duck soon. He outweighed the mayor by two stone or more, but he'd not engage in fisticuffs with the older man.

But when Moon continued, his words were not what Gryffyn expected.

"I've had the burden—er, the pleasure, that is—of five daughters. I make no secret that they've been both my triumph and my trial, though not necessarily in that order. But Keren—well, I'll make no bones about it. I've seen the way she looks at you. You've confounded her, and I think it does her good to be uncertain."

Gryffyn maintained a carefully neutral expression, unsure of Moon's intention.

"And while a stone carver is not quite the match I would have chosen for any of my daughters, the Kimbrell name is a well-respected one. She could do worse, to be sure. You have my permission to court her, if you're of a mind to do so."

Gryffyn turned his gaze to his hands. He wasn't sure what he should be feeling—surprise, certainly. Affront on Miss Moon's behalf, probably. Irritation at the mayor's presumption, definitely.

But hope and longing were unexpected. They winged through him to set his veins to fizzing before the reality of his situation returned.

His name—the well-respected one of which Moon approved—wasn't his to give. And even if he ignored that impediment—and he was sorely tempted—Miss Moon had not more than ten minutes past expressed her own intentions. Intentions which did not include marrying anyone, much less himself. She seemed perfectly content to enjoy a flirtation with him, although he supposed flirtation was not the right word for what lay between them.

Your manner is as it should be.

Every time he recalled her softly spoken words, which he'd done often since Moon's interminable supper, his stomach dipped as if he'd fallen unexpectedly. The sensation was both alarming and thrilling at the same time. He'd graduated from full-on infatuation to love; he *loved* Miss Moon.

Laughter—the barmy sort reserved for the hopeless and ironic—bubbled in his chest. He inhaled deeply and pressed it down, forcing his thoughts to settle. Forcing reason to return. "I appreciate your approval, sir," he said slowly.

"But?"

"But 'taint necessary."

Moon frowned. "I know Keren's behavior can be—"

Gryffyn interrupted and hurried to add, "I assure you, my reticence is not on account of your daughter, sir, but myself. To be sure, she's a fine lady who deserves much better than a stone carver."

Moon's frown deepened, whether in disbelief or disagreement, Gryffyn couldn't be sure. The mayor scrubbed a hand over his face. "My apologies, Kimbrell, if I misread the matter."

Gryffyn opened then closed his mouth. He didn't know what to say, so he remained silent.

Finally, with a short nod of resignation, Moon took his leave. Gryffyn watched the mayor's back as he strolled down the high street, and he couldn't help feeling he'd let Miss Moon down.

He sat heavily on the low bench beneath the front window. Considered the conflicting questions and dilemmas knotted together in his mind. He closed his eyes and imagined sketching, his charcoal flying across the page. The activity usually helped untangle his thoughts, but when he recognized the lines emerging in his mind as those of Miss Moon's face, his eyes flew open in irritation. Clearly, sketching would not be sufficient to sort this particular tangle.

Tomorrow, he and his father were set to extend a hedge near Weirmouth. If his father's pace remained as slow as it had been, they'd pass some hours in one another's company. It had been years since Gryffyn had decided to keep what he knew about his origins to himself. But for the first time in a long while, he considered speaking with his father. Asking for the truth about where he'd come from.

He tested the thought, rolling it on his tongue like a dram of whisky. It burned, much like the whisky, but perhaps the time had come to put his questions to rest.

Then, and only then, could he decide what to do about Miss Moon.

———

THE NEXT MORNING, GRYFFYN DESCENDED to the kitchen well before the sun crossed the horizon. He'd gotten little sleep the night before, and his chest tightened at the thought of the conversation that lay ahead with his father. It was one thing to know in his heart that he was not a true Kimbrell, another altogether to acknowledge it aloud.

The glow from Mrs. Quick's fire danced on the stone landing, and he heard humming before he rounded the doorway. *Spanish Ladies*, if he wasn't mistaken, as Mrs. Quick had a liking for the sailors' songs.

He expected to find his father waiting for him, but their housekeeper was the only one present. She stopped humming as he entered the kitchen.

"You'll be lookin' for yer da," she said. "'E's already gone. Passed 'im on me way up."

Confused, Gryffyn thanked her. He thought they were to leave together for Weirmouth, but he must have misunderstood. He'd collect his tools from the workshop before making the trip to the neighboring village on his own.

He wrapped a piece of bread from last night's supper in a cloth, along with a wedge of cheese. Tucking his meager breakfast into his pocket, he let himself out the door.

Autumn was upon them, and a chill sharpened the early-morning air. Wind fluttered the crisp leaves of the trees as he walked. His breath fogged before him, and he dug his hands deeper into his pockets, taking comfort that the morning's frost would soon melt away. Newford rarely took the full brunt of the colder months like villages further inland.

A thin orange glow touched the horizon by the time he reached the workshop and let himself in. The interior was dark, so the faint light coming through the open back door immediately caught his attention, and he frowned. No sound came from the stone yard beyond, but he distinctly remembered securing the workshop the day before. He'd made a habit of double-checking the locks since his cousin had found Henry exploring. He'd no wish for the lad to fall on a chisel or tip a headstone onto himself.

Davies. Had the man come to steal a peek at

Fortuna? His frown deepened and he moved on silent feet to the back of the workshop, easily navigating the familiar space in the meager light. But when he reached the open door, he stopped, confused.

His father stood in profile, shadowed against the lightening sky as he gazed at Fortuna. Her tarp lay in an untidy heap to one side, and his father's arm hung limply, a mallet dangling from one hand.

"Father?" Thomas Kimbrell started and turned. His face was pale and Gryffyn was struck by how tired he appeared. How clearly the years were etched upon his features. "I thought we were to extend Trewyck's hedge today."

After a long second, his father lifted his hand. "I came to retrieve my old mallet. 'Tis a better fit for my hand than the one I acquired last month."

Gryffyn nodded. His father had often remarked on the new mallet's awkward handle, but he couldn't ignore the impression that his father was not being entirely truthful. But why would he lie? And if he wasn't there to retrieve his mallet, why had he come? He had to know Gryffyn would have readily shown him Fortuna if he'd asked.

"You've done a proper job with the proportions and the balance," his father said in a raspy voice. "'Tis masterfully executed—certainly better than I could have done. To be sure, she'll win in Truro."

The praise struck Gryffyn solidly in the chest. "Thank you, Father. But I will always disagree that my carving is better than yours. How could it be, when you taught me all I know?"

"'Tis as it should be. A father's greatest wish is to see his sons surpass him." His lips curved in a small, closed-mouth smile, and Gryffyn thought he detected the sheen of tears in his sea-blue eyes.

"Will you come?" Gryffyn asked. "To Truro?"

His father was silent for a long moment before saying, "There's much to be done here, but I'll look forward to hearing how she fares."

Gryffyn nodded. Given his father's opposition to the Truro competition, he'd not expected him to make the short journey, but he couldn't deny his disappointment. He swallowed against a heavy lump in his throat. His father's shoulders curved, and Gryffyn was unsettled again by the defeat in his posture.

"Is anything amiss, Father? You seem out of sorts this morning."

"No, son. 'Tis simply the weight of the years catching up with me." And with that, he straightened and propped the mallet on his shoulder. "Shall we make for Weirmouth so we can return in time for Mrs. Quick's lobster pie?"

"Aye." Gryffyn secured Fortuna's tarp then followed his father, glancing back once as he reached the workshop door. The statue stood still and silent, but he couldn't forget the image of his father standing beside her with hammer in hand.

The rest of the day passed slowly, as if they trudged through a staggy bog. After a brief showing from the sun, it hid behind the sky's grey skirts. The cold persisted, and a slow, mizzly rain began to fall. They worked steadily to extend Mr. Trewyck's hedge, the handles of their tools cold and slick in the damp.

His father grew even more taciturn than usual, although several times Gryffyn caught a speculative gaze on his face as if he intended to speak. He never did, though, and as the day wore on, it was as if the years multiplied on his father's face. His skin grew ashen, the lines about his eyes and mouth more pronounced. Gryffyn's chest tightened at the thought that he may not have many more years with his father, even as his questions burned his throat.

No, he thought. Now was not the proper time to broach the matter of his birth. Lead weighted his feet, and he moved through their task as slowly as his father.

CHAPTER TWENTY

T HE WEEK'S END CAME MUCH too soon for Gryffyn's liking. He and his father had completed Mr. Trewyck's hedge (which had, in fact, taken them well into the twilight hours), and he'd spent the last day and night in his workshop carving, filing and polishing Fortuna's features in the dim light of a ring of lanterns. Pausing every fifth stroke to savor the memory of Miss Moon, clad in his apron and covered in stone dust, hadn't sped things along, but he was nearly finished. He wiped his forehead with his sleeve, wincing to feel the grit that coated him.

He still had no answers to his questions. Whenever he looked on his father's wearied form, the words simply died on his tongue. He possessed enough self-discernment to recognize his inaction was as much a reluctance to overset his father as it was an avoidance of his own fears. There was something to be said for keeping unpleasantness safely locked away, and since the tightness in his chest eased whenever he abandoned his questions, he convinced himself silence was the proper course.

But that wasn't to say he'd managed to silence Miss Moon's words. They looped over and over in his mind, causing his hand to still and his gaze to grow distant at an annoying frequency.

Love can overcome any obstacle.

I think we would suit quite well.

And his current favorite: *The right lady will accept your tarnish as well as your shiny bits.*

Could she be persuaded with her own arguments? He didn't think she was indifferent to him.

And could *he* simply let go of his questions and accept the Kimbrell name as his own to give? Years of holding and nurturing his secret close to his heart had left him with shadowy corners, but Miss Moon brought light with her wit and warmth and gentle strength. Perhaps it would be enough to fill him. Perhaps he could convince her they were well matched.

Perhaps, perhaps. Even with his uncertainties, a burgeoning hope spread like warm honey into the deepest parts of him. He straightened and set aside his burnishing cloth.

Fortuna was finished.

Alfie and Jory would arrive soon with a cart to help him make the journey to Truro. There was little time to be mooning over Miss Moon. He smiled to himself at the turn of phrase, convinced he'd gone as barmy as Jory if he was finding amusement in his own jests.

With an empty cart, the trip to Truro was naught but an hour, two at most depending on the condition of the roads. But with Fortuna weighing them down, they'd allowed three. He checked his watch; he was already late, and he still needed to wash and shave. He secured Fortuna's tarp and hurried home.

When he descended the stairs, hair damp and his boots hastily shined, his parents waited for him. His mother approached with a tremulous smile, gripping her hands tightly. Her face was pale, the skin stretched over her fine bones, and she looked as if she'd passed a restless night. She reached up and straightened his neckcloth.

"Travel well, love," she whispered, then she wiped her cheek.

"What's this?" he asked. "Tears? 'Tis naught but a day's ride there and back." Indeed, his brothers had often traveled throughout the duchy with never a tear shed that he'd seen.

"Aye," she agreed. "But 'twill be a long day." She patted the front of his coat and turned toward his father with a sniff. His father stared at her for a long moment before giving her a tiny shake of his head.

Gryffyn watched them, wondering at their odd behavior. He would return later that day. Nothing would change, except he hoped to have a heavier purse and a lighter cart if Fortuna found a new home in Truro.

He flipped his watch open, and his anxiety increased. He was twenty minutes late. There was no more time to make sense of his parents' actions. Alfie and Jory would be waiting for him, and if he didn't leave now, they might not make it to Truro in time.

"Good-bye, Father," he said, pressing his cap on his head.

"Son," his father blurted. "There's something I need to tell you."

"Father," he said, moving toward the door. His tone was shorter than he intended. He softened it and added, "I'm late. I must go."

"But there's something you should —"

"Can we discuss it when I return? I don't want the judges to disqualify my submission."

His father hesitated, jaw tight, before nodding tightly. "Godspeed, son."

Gryffyn hurried down the hill toward the workshop but slowed when he saw Miss Moon. She was walking with Henry and Miss Litton, and when she spied him, she adjusted their path to intercept him.

"Miss Moon. Miss Litton," he greeted. He resisted the urge to look beyond them to see if Jory and Alfie had arrived, but only just. "And Henry, I trust you're recovered from your cough."

"I am," Henry said. "And Keri says we're to travel to Truro today for the exhibition. Father said if Newford's attendance doesn't outstrip Truro, at least we'll embarrass Falmouth. Did you finish it — your carving, that is? May we see it?"

"Aye, fully recovered, I see," Gryffyn said. Miss Moon smiled at him over Henry's head, and his stomach dove and swooped in a routine he'd grown all too familiar with. "I'm afraid you'll have to wait to see my statue in Truro, though. 'Tis already wrapped and ready for the journey."

"I'm certain you'll win," Henry said, and Gryffyn thanked him for his confidence, even if he himself wasn't so convinced.

His urgency must have shown, as Miss Moon said, "You must be in a hurry to leave, but I — we — wanted to wish you good *fortune*."

She smiled, then he recalled the lace glove in his pocket. He removed it and, ignoring Miss Litton's curious glance, he said softly, "You dropped this."

"Thank you, Mr. Kimbrell." Then leaning closer, she whispered, "You may keep it. For luck."

CHAPTER TWENTY-ONE

THE HIGH CROSS, TRURO

"I DON'T KNOW WHY YOU couldn't have carved a smaller piece," Alfie grumbled from behind Fortuna's left hip. "This 'bit of stone' as you've so poorly called it is heavier than one of Jory's bells."

"And twice as wide," Jory added with a grunt from Fortuna's other side.

"All the submissions were required to be this size," Gryffyn said.

"You'd think we'd at least have had the privilege of an advance peek at this monstrosity. We're family, after all." Alfie's complaints were muffled by Fortuna's tarp as the cousins bent in unison to settle the statue on her wheeled dais.

Gryffyn looked around the edge at his cousin.

"You'll see it soon enough. And besides, the competitors were instructed to keep the submissions concealed today so the judges aren't privy to who carved them."

"You know our cousin has always been a man of mystery," Jory said.

"Aye, I've had it from Wynne that he has secrets aplenty."

What was his cousin going on about? "You might find you have more strength, Alfie, if you save your wind."

With Fortuna finally arranged on her platform, they straightened and stepped back, faces red from their exertions. The air was crisp and lively with the sounds of Truro's harvest festival. Stalls ringed the High Cross to fill the square with the scents of savory pie and cider, and a man across the cobbles hawked apples.

"A bucket fer two coppers!"

The cousins stood before Truro's assembly rooms, where a row of carts had drawn up and the other contestants were busily unloading their submissions.

Gryffyn gazed up at the building's facade with a stone carver's appreciation, noting the smooth, finely dressed stones and tight joints as well as the rich ornamental plaques decorating the upper floor. His father had spent time in Truro as a young man, and Gryffyn wondered if he'd had a hand in the buildings around the High Cross.

"Let's hope this thing wins," Jory said. "I'm not certain you'll convince Alfie to load it back onto the cart."

Gryffyn snorted. As much as his cousins pained him, they could be counted on to help a man. Alfie wouldn't let him down.

"I'll help so long as we don't tarry in Truro. I mean to have a good night's sleep so I can make an early start in the morn."

"Tomorrow's Sunday," Jory said. "You wish to make an early start with Vicar's sermon? Are you feeling aright, cousin?" Jory and Gryffyn frowned at one another.

"Aye," Alfie replied with a grin. "I overheard Mrs. Pentreath say the vicar's niece will arrive soon *and* that she's unattached."

Jory closed his eyes on a sigh while Alfie surveyed the crowd. Gryffyn tightened the ropes securing Fortuna's tarp then looked up as three men crossed the cobbled square toward them. One carried a notebook in which he penciled Gryffyn's name.

"Ye'll be number five," he said. "All contestants must remain behind the cordon with the public." He tossed a thumb over his shoulder to indicate the rope circling the exhibition area in the center of the square. Rows of chairs were lined before the rope, and spectators had already begun to gather in anticipation of the judging.

Gryffyn watched uneasily as the other two men wheeled Fortuna away, her dais catching on the uneven cobbles. "Where are they taking it?" he asked as the man with the notebook began to move down the line of carts.

"They're wheeling it into place for the judging."

"They'll use caution?" he asked the man's retreating back.

"Aye." The man spoke over his shoulder as he hurried on, and Gryffyn forced his uneasiness down. He felt much as he imagined a parent might when a child became lost in a crowd. He drew a slow breath and released it.

"Why the numbers?" Jory asked.

Gryffyn turned back to his cousins, grateful for the distraction. "'Tis to be a blind competition with anonymous submissions. The carvers won't be revealed until the judging is complete and the winner is announced. 'Twould seem there was quite a scandal some years back, and the judges were accused of bias toward certain livestock."

"Aye," Alfie said. "'Twas quite the to-do. I recall reading about it in the papers."

As they began walking toward the exhibition area, another cart drew up, and two block-shaped men dressed in rough linen climbed down. George Davies met them and began directing the unloading of his own tarped statue.

"Easy, lads," he said as the men staggered beneath the statue's weight. "I'll not have your ham-handedness."

When it was clear Davies had no intention of lending any assistance other than the verbal sort, Gryffyn and Jory stepped forward and helped the men lower the statue to the cobbles.

"Ah-ah, Kimbrell," Davies said. "I suppose you think to steal a peek at my submission, but the time for comparing technique is passed."

Gryffyn responded with a grunt from behind the tarp as something poked him in the rib. A child's arm or foot, perhaps, although it could have easily been a parsnip or an eel. He adjusted his grip and lowered his end to the ground.

The man with the notebook hurried up to log Davies' submission. "All contestants must remain behind the cordon with the public," he recited. "Ye'll be number six."

Gryffyn and Jory straightened, and Davies nodded once at them in dismissal.

"Well, that's a fine thank-you," Alfie said as they continued on.

Carriages stopped and surrendered their passengers at the edge of the square before departing for the mews. The day's anticipation could be heard in the low buzzing of the crowd, could be felt in the fine hairs on the back of Gryffyn's neck. He kept a tight rein on his nerves as the time for the exhibition drew near.

"Pie," Alfie said, rubbing his hands. "We need pie." He moved toward a stall where a gap-toothed woman stood behind wooden boxes of handhelds.

"Whattayer fancy?" she asked. "Per'aps pork or eel? Us'll 'ave turnip pasties, too."

Jory quickly gave the woman a coin for a pork pie, but Alfie dithered over the array of choices, finally choosing one each of pork and turnip. He offered one to Gryffyn, who shook his head. He was too anxious to eat.

As Alfie bit into his treat, flaky pastry clinging to the corner of his lips, Gryffyn glanced toward the exhibition area behind the ropes. A group of well-dressed men in top hats had begun to gather—the judges, he presumed. They stood behind the row of canvas-covered lumps that awaited their unveiling. There were now eight submissions. Numbered placards had been placed before each, and Gryffyn quickly located his lump behind number five. His nerves eased the tiniest bit before thoughts of the judging to come scattered them again.

He'd done a proper job with Fortuna, but he didn't know if the judges would see her as he did.

The last few days and nights had been a rush of carving and sanding and polishing to put a face on Fortuna, and now thoughts of all the things he should have done erupted—lines and angles he should have carved differently, spots he should have polished more.

He drew another heavy breath, then he spied Miss Moon and her family stepping down from their carriage. Dressed in a pale green gown and a demure bonnet, she appeared much as the other young ladies in the crowd, but he knew better. Miss Moon was quite unique and unlike any of the other young ladies present.

She glanced up and, by some stroke of providence, found his eyes in the crowd immediately. As Mayor Moon began to lead her away, she glanced over her shoulder with a tiny half-smile, and Gryffyn's nerves settled. No matter what the judges thought, Miss Moon had seen Fortuna, and the wonder on her face was enough to satisfy him.

"We should find our seats," Alfie said, brushing crumbs from his coat.

———

KEREN MAINTAINED A SERENE SMILE as her father led them through the crowd to greet his political acquaintances. His youngest daughter having no remarkable accomplishments of which he could boast, he emphasized her singular skill in arranging herself at the end of his string of daughters.

"Ho, Blackmore, how does your mother fare? You recall my youngest girl . . ."

Or, "Well met, Mr. Squibbly. My daughter Mary sends her regards. You'll recall, she has a fine ear for the pianoforte. And permit me to introduce my youngest . . ."

They also greeted a number of familiar faces from Newford—Keren spied Mr. and Mrs. Pentreath near the soap maker's stall as well as two of Mrs. Pentreath's sisters. Her father would be pleased with his constituents' numbers. He was not one to suffer a second-place showing gracefully, whether the contest was one in truth or perception.

Henry and Miss Litton trailed them at a more leisurely pace, taking time to examine the wares in the stalls. A row of canvas-covered statues had been collected in the exhibition area, and she wondered which one was Fortuna. They all looked much the same.

Her eyes repeatedly found Gryffyn, which was not such a remarkable feat as he stood a head above most of the spectators. His cousin Alfie held a pie in each hand, and they moved across the square like a small shoal of Kimbrells swimming through the crowd. She smiled and tucked her head before her father could question the source of her amusement.

"We should find our seats," Miss Litton said before Keren's father could tow her through the crowd to meet Truro's mayor. She excused herself, disentangled her arm and happily followed Miss Litton and Henry to a row near the front.

As the time for the judging drew near, the crowd milled about looking for the best vantage point. Keren had to crane her neck around a group of ladies to locate Gryffyn, seated only a short distance away with his cousins. As she watched, he tapped his coat pocket where he'd tucked her glove, and she hid a smile. He turned then and caught her gaze, his lips curving before Alfie drew his attention once more. She fanned herself slowly; despite the chill in the air, she'd grown quite warm.

Henry chattered eagerly to Miss Litton, expounding on everything from the size of the crowd to the delicious scents emanating from the stalls to the precise number of chairs arranged before the cordon.

"How do you think they came to find such a good number of chairs, and all of them matched?"

Keren didn't hear Miss Litton's response as a voice interrupted from her other side. "I'm pleased to see the exhibition has drawn such an impressive crowd."

She turned to find Mr. Davies had taken the seat next to her. "My father will be sitting there," she said, irritation overriding etiquette.

"Of course. I'll just hold the seat for him, shall I?"

She sighed and turned her attention back to the front, where Truro's mayor had stepped up to a podium. He tapped the wood twice with his knuckles, and once the crowd quieted, he began to speak. He introduced the judges in an overlong speech full of *ahems* and *therefores*, and the crowd grew restless again.

Finally, the judges moved to the first in the row of concealed statues. Keren held her breath as two men untied the ropes and removed the statue's tarp. A shout of appreciation went up as St. Piran was revealed, and Keren drew in a breath. The statue was impressive in its own right, but it had the added admiration of the tinners, who, judging by the volume at the back of the crowd, had shown up in force. She placed a calming hand on Henry's shoulder as he bounced on his seat.

"St. Piran will be hard to surpass," he said. "But Mr. Kimbrell is clever. His statue will deliver a crushing defeat."

"Do you think so?" Keren asked, amused by his certainty although it matched her own. She, however, held the advantage of having actually seen Gryffyn's work. And if anyone had carved a stone half as clever as his silk-clad goddess, she'd eat her bonnet strings.

The judges scratched in their notebooks and conferred with one another over St. Piran. One pointed at a detail near the base of the statue, and the crowd leaned forward in a collective effort to hear their words.

Despite her confidence, Keren's hands grew damp in her gloves as each piece was unveiled to the judges' slow evaluation. The crowd's excitement could be heard in the rising and falling of voices as each submission was revealed. Keren pressed back a knowing smile, waiting for Fortuna's turn. She knew Gryffyn must be anxious, although he appeared calm, arms crossed and coat straining across his shoulders as he sat with his cousins. But then the judges unveiled the fifth statue, and he tensed, scrubbing a hand over his face. Something was wrong.

"'Tis quite a piece Mr. Kimbrell has carved," Miss Litton whispered from the other side of Henry.

Henry's brows dipped behind his spectacles and Keren said, "I beg your pardon?"

Miss Litton nodded toward the statue at the center of the crowd of judges. "I overheard someone say Mr. Kimbrell's statue is number five."

Keren shook her head slowly. Miss Litton was wrong. Number five was most definitely *not* Fortuna.

CHAPTER TWENTY-TWO

A LFIE SHIFTED IN HIS SEAT as Truro's mayor drumbled on with his lengthy introduction. Gryffyn could sympathize as his cousin turned first one way, then the other in a bid to find some comfort. The chairs were spindly bits and had clearly not been fashioned for men of their proportions.

"Alfie," Jory said shortly as he took an elbow to the ribs. "Cease your twisting about. Look, they're about to begin the judging."

The crowd's attention turned as the judges shuffled toward the first in the line of statues. Gryffyn glanced toward Miss Moon once again and frowned to see Davies had joined her. The carver sat quite close, his sleeve brushing her arm. Where was her father—shouldn't Moon be seated with her? He studied the crowd and located Moon standing near the cordon, arms crossed as he watched the proceedings from the side.

Jory nudged him, and Gryffyn turned as the first statue was unveiled. It was a well-executed carving, finely done with excellent proportions. The stone itself was sublime, a clean, pure white marble without the darker veining from magnesium or iron or other impurities. Gryffyn rubbed his hands on his trousers and pulled in a slow breath. Fortuna would have some proper competition.

"'Tis Guinevere?" Alfie asked.

Jory pulled his head back. "St. Piran. How d'you confuse a bearded bishop with Arthur's queen? 'Tis no wonder you've not found a lady willing to keep company with you for more than a fortnight."

His cousins' familiar, whispered banter eased Gryffyn's tension until the judges reached number five. He leaned forward and balanced his elbows on his knees, breath lodged in his throat. Jory quieted Alfie with an elbow nudge, and they turned their attention to the front as well.

Two men untied Fortuna's ropes and removed her tarp. As the canvas fell away, Gryffyn's heart stopped. Confusion knitted his brow as astonished gasps went up across the crowd. His cousins stilled, and he felt their bewilderment keenly.

Number five was finely carved, but it wasn't Fortuna. A god-like figure with distorted features dangled a plump child before his open mouth. Cronus, Gryffyn thought, trying to recall his classics. Greek god of time and, having devoured his own children, perhaps the worst father in all of Creation.

Alfie was the first to recover from their collective shock. "You've certainly secured the crowd's interest, Gryff."

"Aye, the proportions are . . . well done," Jory added slowly. Loyally.

Gryffyn shook his head, too stunned to speak. The child's flailing arm was about the right size and position to match the protrusion he'd felt on Davies' statue. And Cronus was just the sort of lurid, shock-inducing subject Davies would carve.

He glanced up to see the other carver wearing a pleased expression. Despite the numbered placards, the man clearly didn't realize his statue was in the wrong place. What had happened? Where was Fortuna, if not in the fifth position?

Gryffyn dropped his head and rubbed his temples as he considered how to address the mistake. He couldn't correct the matter now; revealing himself as Fortuna's carver risked disqualifying her. After the judging was complete, he and Davies would simply have to explain the confusion to Enys.

The judges murmured among themselves and spent excruciatingly long minutes in front of

Cronus, but whether their study was due to admiration or alarm, Gryffyn couldn't say. The crowd began to grow restless; there were still three more submissions to be unveiled.

Finally, the judges moved to number six and repeated the process. Ropes were untied, and the canvas fell away. Gryffyn held his breath as Fortuna was revealed. The crowd stilled in hushed silence until Alfie spoke.

"Why, 'tis Miss Moon," he said in whispered surprise.

Confused, Gryffyn glanced toward Miss Moon. She stared at number six—at Fortuna—but instead of the flattering awe she'd displayed in his workshop just days before, her mouth formed a perfect O of what appeared to be . . . shock? Gryffyn frowned until Alfie's next words drew his attention once more.

"Some fool has carved Miss Moon."

"Aye," Jory said with a snort. "'Taint an obvious likeness, but 'tis clear enough."

Gryffyn followed Jory's gaze to where Fortuna battled her winds. She stood proudly among the other carvings, and his own pride filled his chest.

Then his cousins' words settled on his brain, and he tried to sort them. Finally, realization sent shocked awareness zipping through him. It flashed from his stomach to the tips of his fingers as he finally saw what Alfie and Jory were going on about. In his haste to finish his submission, to put a face on Fortuna, he'd not noticed her resemblance to Miss Moon.

Oh, it wasn't a precise match, as Jory had said, but there was enough of Miss Moon in the angle of the chin and the curve of the cheek for an observant person to connect the two. To be sure, an observant *father* couldn't miss the likeness—a fact which was only confirmed by Alfie's next words, spoken in a low voice.

"Judging by Moon's expression, we're not the only ones to recognize his daughter in the piece."

With dread, Gryffyn looked toward the mayor, who was aiming a fiery glare at his daughter. Miss Moon studied her gloved hands, face averted from her father's displeasure, as Henry bounced on his chair with delight.

Miss Moon would not appreciate what he'd done, nor would she believe the act had been unintentional. He could hardly believe it himself. He recalled her distress at seeing his drawing of her and could only imagine how she must feel to know he'd *carved* her likeness for all to see. Did she believe he'd betrayed her for the sake of the competition?

His jaw tightened until his teeth hurt.

He willed her to look up, to see the apology on

his face, but her gaze remained fixed on her hands. His stomach grew hot and queasy until he thought he'd be ill. He glanced around for a path through the chairs, just in case. He'd have to navigate his cousins' knees and feet . . .

Truro's mayor stepped up then to address the crowd, and he realized that while he'd sat in a pool of his own misery, the remaining statues had been unveiled.

"Friends and fellow citizens," Enys began, "the judges have determined a winner, and 'tis with great pleasure and delight that I announce the piece that will grace Truro's High Cross."

He left the words to hang, and a murmur rumbled and rolled through the crowd as the spectators guessed at the contest's outcome. It was clear they were thoroughly enjoying the event, but Gryffyn only wished for an end to the day he'd eagerly anticipated for weeks. The mayor consulted a paper then rapped on the podium with his knuckles. Gryffyn closed his eyes as the man finally continued.

"The winning submission is . . . number six, carved by Mr. George Davies of Falmouth. Mr. Davies, please approach and collect your purse."

Gryffyn snorted an ironic laugh and rubbed a hand over his face. Number six. Fortuna.

The crowd applauded and the noise swelled

around them as Gryffyn's emotions were pitched about like a cutter on stormy seas. Added to his misery for the distress he'd caused Miss Moon were the twin feelings of elation and dismay.

Elation that Fortuna had won.

Dismay at the ridiculous muddle that named Davies the carver.

"I thought you said Davies completed his piece some weeks past," Alfie said.

"He said as much." Gryffyn's voice was hard as he stared at Fortuna. He stood. He needed to speak with the judges. Alfie and Jory rose and followed him as he began to move toward the cordon.

"I suppose 'tis only coincidence then that his piece bears a resemblance to Miss Moon," Jory said.

Davies, who had also begun moving toward the judges, was hampered by the milling crowd. Gryffyn looked beyond him to Mayor Moon. Confusion rather than anger furrowed the man's brow as he stared at his daughter. He'd clearly reached the same conclusion as Jory. Having only met her at Moon's supper, Davies could not have carved her likeness on a piece he'd completed weeks before. She couldn't have possibly served as his inspiration, much less posed for the man.

"Don't worry overmuch, cousin," Alfie said, clapping a hand on Gryffyn's shoulder. "Although it didn't win, your Cronus is bound to be the talk of

Truro for some time to come."

"'Taint mine," Gryffyn said through clenched teeth, stopping and turning to his cousins. He forced his jaw to relax as he removed his cap and ran a hand through his hair.

After a moment of confused silence, Jory said, "What d'you mean?"

"They confused the order of the submissions."

"You didn't carve the . . . the ghastly piece then?"

Gryffyn's brows dove into a steep V. "No."

Jory puffed his cheeks in relief. "Aye, well, that's all right then," he said. His cousins' sagging relief would have been humorous if Gryffyn hadn't been so conflicted over what to do next.

"Then which one—?" Alfie stopped speaking as his gaze landed on Fortuna. "Ah. Miss Moon. Wynne thought there might be a breeze blowing there."

Jory followed Alfie's line of sight and his reasoning. "You won?" he whispered. "Gryff, you won! Hurry, you must tell the judges there's been a mistake."

Jory moved to approach the judges himself, and Gryffyn pulled him back. He scrubbed a hand over his face and wondered how his eager anticipation of the day had devolved to this. By some ridiculous quirk of fate, Moon now believed his daughter's likeness on Fortuna's face was naught but coincidence. If he knew the carver to be Gryffyn rather than Davies, her secret would be out. Her father—nay, everyone—would know she'd been his model. It wouldn't matter that she'd only permitted him to draw her hair and skirts. She'd be ruined, and her father's displeasure fully justified.

He scowled. He could almost believe Fortuna mocked him from her stone base, having lent her mischievous hand to his current circumstances.

He didn't know what to do.

Miss Moon watched him, confusion of her own playing across her face. She glanced toward Enys and the judges and opened her mouth as if to speak. Gryffyn's breath caught. Would she alert them to the mistake?

No, he urged her with a slow shake of his head. And there it was: his answer.

He couldn't reveal himself to be Fortuna's carver. He couldn't be the cause of Miss Moon's ruination, no matter the hours, days and weeks he'd spent carving Fortuna. He closed his eyes and inhaled deeply.

"What?" Alfie said, tugging on Gryffyn's arm. "Will you not speak with the judges, tell them—"

Gryffyn ignored him. Davies, having navigated the crowd, neared where Gryffyn stood with his cousins. He'd alert the judges to the mistake soon enough, unless . . .

"Mr. Davies," Gryffyn said.

The carver paused and Gryffyn held out a hand. "Congratulations on your success."

Davies frowned at Gryffyn's outstretched hand as the crowd began to close about them.

"Gryff—" Jory spoke from his elbow, but Gryffyn hurried to continue.

"'Tis a fine piece you've carved," he said.

Confusion warred with suspicion on the other carver's face, suspicion emerging the victor. Davies leaned in and whispered, close enough not to be overheard, "What game are you playing, Kimbrell? I gather number six belongs to you?"

"Not today." Gryffyn lifted his brows and waited for Davies to accept his hand.

As Davies finally, slowly, raised his hand to shake Gryffyn's, a voice called out.

"Mayor Enys."

Miss Moon had risen, and her clear voice lifted above the milling crowd. Henry sat at her side, wide-eyed behind his spectacles while Miss Litton tried to disappear into her seat. Gryffyn shook his head, but Miss Moon ignored him and continued.

"Mayor Enys, there's been a mistake."

———

THE CROWD STILLED AND ENYS looked up. Keren waited while he scanned the spectators until his eyes landed on her. Frowning, he said, "I assure you, miss, the judging was fair and unbiased."

The silence of the crowd was loud in her ears, a rushing not unlike Fortuna's winds. It thrummed beneath the echo of Gryffyn's words: *'Tis left to us to decide if we'll emerge beautiful or broken.*

Decide.

She could decide to remain silent, to choose the easier path, but it wouldn't be the right one. She glanced at Gryffyn, and he shook his head at her once more.

She thought of Shropshire, and a life away from Henry. She could avoid it if she demurred and took her seat again, but to remain silent would surely leave her a bit more broken on the inside.

She'd known the risks when she'd agreed to Gryffyn's mad bargain. It was true that he'd exceeded the terms of their arrangement by carving her likeness in Fortuna's features, but she couldn't find it in her to be angry. Awed, yes. Perhaps even a bit prideful. But angry? No.

"The mistake to which I refer is not in the judging, but in the identification of the carver." A murmur swelled across the crowd. "I see Mr. Davies is approaching." She motioned to where Davies stood with Gryffyn, and heads turned toward them in unison.

"I'm certain he intends to inform you he did not

carve this piece. It was carved by Mr. Gryffyn Kimbrell of Newford."

Mayor Enys gazed at her skeptically then finally asked, "And how do you know this to be a fact, Miss . . . ?"

"Miss Moon," she said, gripping her hands more tightly to still their trembling. "And I know this to be true because I assisted Mr. Kimbrell as his . . . That is, I served as the model for Mr. Kimbrell's carving."

A collective gasp went up, and she chanced a peek at her father. An alarming shade of crimson painted his face. She jerked her gaze back to Enys before she could lose her courage.

"You're Moon's daughter?" Enys asked.

"Yes."

"Which one?"

She hesitated. She knew what he was asking: was she the painterly daughter, or the one with musical talents? Perhaps Moon's charitable daughter?

"I'm Miss Keren Moon," she said. Then, steeling her spine, she added, "The large-spirited, well-intentioned, too-forward-for-prudence, delicate-but-capable, Shropshire-bound one."

Surprised laughter from the crowd behind her warmed her cheeks. Henry stood up next to her, and she placed a reassuring hand on his shoulder.

"My sister is correct," Henry said. "Fortuna was carved by Gryffyn Kimbrell. I've seen his sketches and know it to be true."

Keren tilted her head at him in surprise. He'd seen Gryffyn's drawings? He knew she'd been his model, and yet he'd said nothing of the matter to their father. While she wouldn't wish him to be deceitful, his restraint indicated a heretofore unseen discernment in his thoughts and manner, and she smiled.

Enys turned from her to Fortuna and back again before nodding. "And where is Gryffyn Kimbrell?" he asked the spectators.

The crowd shifted expectantly, and Gryffyn raised a hand. "Here, sir."

With a heavy sigh, Enys said, "Approach the judges. You too, Mr. Davies."

———

GRYFFYN STOOD BEFORE ENYS, WHO was flanked by a sea of top-hatted judges. His dismay and elation had only grown with Miss Moon's revelation. How were two such incompatible emotions possible in the same person at the same time?

No one had been able to determine how the statues had been incorrectly placed. Davies and Gryffyn both denied any knowledge of the error, and while Gryffyn didn't particularly like the man, he couldn't believe him so lost to ambition to think a deliberate manipulation of the exhibition's outcome would go unchallenged.

Enys had spoken terse words to the individuals who'd organized the event. They in turn suggested it was the mayor's insistence on a blind competition that had resulted in the confusion. In the end, the matter of their statues had finally been sorted, and Gryffyn had been confirmed as Fortuna's sculptor.

The competition's purse was heavy in his pocket—and the thrill of success heady in his mind—but at what cost to Miss Moon? Large-spirited, well-intentioned, too-forward-for-prudence, delicate-but-capable Miss Moon? And never forget: Shropshire-bound. Would her father truly send her away?

The obvious solution to the dilemma he'd created for them was marriage. While he thought she might prefer it over exile to Shropshire, he'd rather not be cast in the role of the lesser evil. He'd rather not force her to make a choice at all, but it was too late for *rather nots*.

Worse than these thoughts was the singular fear that looped in his mind: Did she believe he'd betrayed her trust for the sake of his statue?

Guilt soured his stomach even as the judges approached to congratulate him one by one.

The last judge, a man by the name of Carne, removed his top hat and stepped nearer. He was tall—taller even than Gryffyn's own notable height. Despite his years, Carne's dark hair held only a trace of silver. A lock fell across the man's smooth forehead, and Gryffyn's gaze met rich brown eyes shadowed by dark lashes. He felt as if he looked into the shaving mirror above his own washstand.

"Kimbrell," the man said, frowning. "Of the Newford Kimbrells?"

Gryffyn continued to stare. Then, recovering his manners, he cleared his throat and said, "Aye. 'Tis a pleasure to make your acquaintance."

Carne ignored his attempt at the pleasantries. His expression remained hard as he asked, "Who are your parents?" Carne's words had the short, refined clip of the upper class, distinctly at odds with Gryffyn's own rolling timber.

He paused before replying, "Thomas and Mary Kimbrell." He didn't know why, but he immediately regretted providing their names. He felt as if he'd betrayed them in doing so, but he could hardly decline to answer such a simple question.

Carne sucked his teeth, and Gryffyn's unease grew. Who was this man? Anyone could see they shared a kinship of sorts. Was he an uncle? A cousin? Despite Gryffyn's own questions about his birth, he refused to believe Carne could be his father. He was much too ... everything. Too cultured. Too intense. Too tall. Too cold.

"Thomas Kimbrell ..." Carne's jaw tightened as he spoke the words. "I knew an accomplished sculptor by that name years ago. I've several statues of his in my garden."

Gryffyn nodded and relaxed enough to say, "Aye, that sounds like my father."

Carne continued as if Gryffyn hadn't spoken. He lowered his voice to say, "Kimbrell carved his statues, and then he took my wife."

Gryffyn straightened and frowned, certain he'd misheard. His father was not in the business of wife-stealing.

Carne's brow lowered as he studied Gryffyn, his face hardened in anger. "And I see he took much more than that besides."

Before Gryffyn could respond to that cryptic statement, Moon's bellow sounded behind him.

"Kimbrell!"

Gryffyn turned and received the mayor's well-aimed fist on his jaw. He stumbled back and met the cobbles with a heavy thump, taking down two of the judges with him. He looked up, flexing his jaw.

Eyes flashing, face florid, Moon spat, "You'll make this right."

Gryffyn gave the man a terse nod—were fists necessary when the path forward was so obvious it required neither persuasion nor coercion? Then he spied his cousins. Alfie, Jory and Gavin. He frowned. Why was Gavin here?

Gavin pushed through the crowd and reached a hand down to help Gryffyn up.

"Why are you here?" Gryffyn asked.

"'Tis your mother, Gryff. I'm sorry to say she's taken ill."

CHAPTER TWENTY-THREE

S CENERY PASSED LIKE SMUDGED PAINT as Gryffyn raced along the road to Newford on Gavin's horse. He forced a breath in then out, his jaw stiff beneath what must, by now, be a magnificent bruise. The day had been too much.

The buzzing anticipation of the exhibition.

The debacle of Fortuna's misplacement, followed by Miss Moon's bold admission.

His own foolishness at carving the lady's likeness.

Then there had been Carne and his accusations.

Moon's fist.

The bone-deep fear that Miss Moon, who had no wish to marry, might never forgive him for placing her in such an undesirable position.

And now, his mother's illness.

Some part of him was sure to crack beneath the weight of so many thoughts.

Then he recalled his mother's teary eyes when he'd left that morning. His father's attempts to speak with him, if only he'd stopped to listen. They'd known. They'd known he'd encounter Carne, and they'd let him walk, unwittingly, into the man's ire. He knew he should be angry with them, but none of that mattered now. He still had his questions, of course, but they paled against his concerns for his mother's welfare.

Gavin said she'd suffered an attack of some sort. Dr. Rowe thought it must be her heart. Gryffyn reached the lane leading to their home and urged the horse faster.

The yard was empty, the house quiet when he entered, his boots loud on the wood floor. He took the stairs three at a time until he reached his parents' bedchamber. His father met him at the door. His face was pale and grey, like the ashes in the firebox, and his eyes were rimmed in red.

"How is she?" Gryffyn asked.

"Sleeping."

Gryffyn nodded, and relief that he wasn't too late caused his shoulders to sag. "What does Rowe say? Will she recover?"

"He doesn't know. Per'aps. 'Tis in God's hands."

His father had withered even further in his absence. Mere weeks past, he'd been the hale man who'd raised Gryffyn and his brothers with quiet strength. But now, he was naught but a husk of a man who could barely stand without reaching for support. No matter the secrets he'd kept, Gryffyn couldn't bear to see him reduced to such an empty shell.

"How d'you fare, Father?" he asked. The term *Father* felt both familiar and odd on his tongue.

Thomas rubbed a shaking hand along his neck and his eyes filled with tears, but he said only, "Right enough. Your grandfather has been here, and your uncles. I imagine your brothers will arrive soon enough. Will you come and sit?"

Gryffyn entered their bedchamber to the ever-present scent of his mother's rose water. It wrapped him in a warm, soothing embrace as he crossed the room. She lay still, paler and more ashen than his father, and he pulled a chair close to the bed. He tried to be quiet, but her eyes opened slowly as he sat, and she reached a hand for him. He took it and pressed her thin fingers in his as his father took a seat at her other side.

"Did you win the competition, love?"

He smiled. As ill as she was, she thought of him first. His eyes burned, and he blinked. "Aye," he whispered.

She squeezed his fingers. "I knew you would. And your Miss Moon? I'm sure she must be quite overdone with your success."

"Aye. She's overdone."

His mother closed her eyes once more. She was quiet, and he thought she slept again, but then she whispered so softly he had to lean closer to hear.

"And did you meet a man with the name Derrick Carne?"

"Mary," his father began.

She opened her eyes. "I want to know if he met Carne," she said, her voice firmer than it had been.

Gryffyn said softly, "I met him."

"And d'you wish answers to your questions, love?"

Did he wish answers? Aye. No. He didn't know, but he couldn't continue on as he had been. He needed answers, whether he wished them or not.

"Aye," he whispered.

"Mary, are you sure this is what—"

"He should know the truth," his mother said. "And I wish to be here when he learns it. Tell him, Thomas. Please."

His father sighed and relented with a short nod. Elbows on his knees, he stared at his hands before saying, "Carne is your father. I imagine you've worked that out for yourself by now."

Gryffyn remained silent. He dropped his mother's hand and leaned back, crossing his arms.

"I met him nearly thirty years agone when I accepted a commission at his estate near Truro."

"Statues for his garden," Gryffyn said.

His father looked up. "Aye. The commission was a lucrative one, and lengthy. Some eight months and more. Your mother and I took a cottage in Truro, where we lived for the duration. It was small, but it suited our needs. Your brothers didn't take up as much space then as they do now. But your mother was in the family way again, and we didn't wish to be separated, you see."

His mother reached for him again, and Gryffyn uncrossed his arms. Her thumb moved slowly over the back of his hand, soothing his hurt as only a mother could do. His father pulled in a large breath and continued.

"Over the months, your mother became acquainted with Carne's wife. She was a kind and gentle lady—not bigger than a minnow. She was in the family way as well, so they grew close as ladies do. But her husband—"

"Carne is not a kind man," his mother said, and her hand tightened on Gryffyn's.

His father rubbed a hand over his face. "We occasionally saw bruises on Sarah and"—he swallowed—"burns. I suspect there were many more injuries we couldn't see," he continued.

"Sarah Carne—she was my mother?" Gryffyn's voice caught on the words.

His mother closed her eyes briefly. When she

opened them, they were softened by tears. "Yes." She swallowed before continuing his father's tale. "She was distraught when your father's —when Thomas's—commission with Carne ended. We'd grown quite close, as your father said, and she didn't have other friends or family nearby. Certainly, no one to distract her from her troubles."

She paused and inhaled slowly. Her hand was weak in his, and Gryffyn worried over the strain the story was placing on her. "Mother, there's no need—" he began, but she silenced him with a shake of her head.

"Your father had begun to make quite a name for himself by then," she continued. "He'd secured another commission, and we were to travel to Bath for the winter. Sarah was despondent at the thought of being left alone with only her husband for companionship, and she was terrified about bringing another soul to live under his cruelty. We invited her to come with us, as our guest, but Carne refused."

His father picked up the thread of the story, and his mother relaxed against her pillow. "We'd been in Bath for a month or more when Sarah arrived. She'd defied her husband and came to us, bruised and broken. She feared for her babe, and rightly so. She stayed with us and began to heal, but then ..." He swallowed and studied his hands again before continuing. "But then we lost our babe—a girl." Gryffyn's heart twisted to hear such raw grief on his father's tongue. "And within a day, Sarah birthed her own child. You." He smiled at Gryffyn, and the pain in Gryffyn's heart eased some to see the love there.

"The birth was hard on Sarah," his mother said. "She was a frail thing, and already heart-sore from her treatment at Carne's hands. She died within hours, but she begged us with all the love she had for you to keep you safe. And so, we did. You were the blessing we didn't know we needed, love."

Gryffyn frowned, taking in their words. He still couldn't believe the cold, harsh man he'd encountered in Truro was his father. "But what of Carne?" he asked. "He must have learned where his wife had gone."

His father covered his face with one hand, and Gryffyn braced himself for the rest of the story. "Aye," his father said. "Carne found us in Bath the night of Sarah's death. I—" He stopped, eyes closed.

"Your father did what had to be done," his mother said. "He placed our daughter in Sarah's arms. Carne buried them together."

The chair scraped the floor as Gryffyn tried to stand, but his mother's grip tightened on his hand.

"You gave up your child," he whispered. "You gave up the right to bury her, to mourn her properly. Why?" His ears felt like they had cotton wadding in them. His pulse pounded thickly, and he forced a breath in, then out. He rubbed his free hand against his chest.

His mother smiled. "I can't believe you have to ask that. Don't mistake me, love. I mourned our daughter, as is a mother's right. I still do. But you became ours that night as well, and I couldn't let you go to that man to be treated so cruelly as he'd treated Sarah, no matter that you were rightfully his. And your father, bless him, he didn't hesitate to do what I asked of him."

Gryffyn stared at her, trying to find his mother in the image she'd painted for him. She'd always been a strong lady, stalwart and brave, but he'd never imagined she'd go to such lengths. He'd never imagined she'd *steal* a child.

"I know your flaws, love, and now you know mine," she whispered.

"*Our* flaws," his father said, straightening. "It may have been your mother's bravery that prompted our actions, but I'd do it again if need be."

"But you risked transportation or *worse.*" His parents watched him in silent acknowledgment, and Gryffyn directed his next words to his father. "You stopped taking the fancier commissions. You carve nothing but headstones and hedges."

His father nodded. "Not long after we returned

to Newford, I carved a statue for Moon's entry. I gained a number of other commissions from that job—promising work for wealthy gentlemen—but I found I'd lost my appetite for working with the upper class. And with your hair and eyes, you were becoming the very daps of Carne. I couldn't risk encountering anyone who knew Carne, who might have suspected what we'd done."

"Your objection to the Truro competition," Gryffyn said as pieces began to tumble into place. "The hours we spent on the town hall and Trewyck's hedge . . . They were all because you didn't want me to encounter Carne."

His father pressed his lips but remained silent.

"And the other day, when I found you behind the workshop with Fortuna . . ." Gryffyn's breath caught in his throat, and he couldn't continue with such an ugly suspicion.

"I—it occurred to me that if your submission were damaged, you'd have to withdraw from the competition," his father said softly. "But I couldn't do it. I couldn't destroy such a thing of beauty, much less rob you of your achievement."

Gryffyn looked across the bed into his father's eyes, at the pain and regret and love shining there. He sank back against the chair, weary and spent. Finally, he pulled his hand from his mother's, and she let him go. "I knew I wasn't yours," he said slowly, "but I didn't know how. I'm so different from you both, from my brothers. I heard you arguing one afternoon about returning me."

His mother choked on a sob and his father nodded, eyes closed. "I'm sorry son. We should have given you the truth long before now. But the argument you heard wasn't about returning you. Never think that. Carne's new wife had just borne a son. We worried that in taking you, we'd denied you your proper birthright. But we never once thought to return you. You were ours in every way that mattered."

Gryffyn leaned forward and dropped his head, stabbing his hands through his hair as his heart turned in his chest.

They'd never thought to return him. Had never meant to give him up.

That simple truth eased a silent ache that had pulsed in him for nearly two decades.

CHAPTER TWENTY-FOUR

A HOT, THICK TENSION THAT even Henry couldn't miss filled the Moon carriage. The silence was oppressive as Keren and Miss Litton faced her father and Henry for the drive back to Newford. Henry opened his mouth once then closed it again. He shifted on the seat, only to still when her father barked a gruff order. Then, pulling a small sketchbook from beneath the seat, he turned to a clean page and began drawing. It was a new habit he'd taken up after his incident at the Kimbrell picnic, and she was glad to see the action ease the furrow on his brow.

Keren watched him as the carriage rocked and tried to memorize his features. How much would he grow before she saw him next? Her breath shuddered in her chest on the thought, and the enormity of her situation crashed about her: she was but moments away from being buried in Shropshire, away from Henry, away from Gryffyn. A sob climbed her throat, and she pushed it down.

Despite her earlier courage (stupidity?) in Truro, she longed to wind the clock back and return to her bed. How she wished she'd never agreed to Gryffyn's ridiculous bargain. But no, she couldn't regret that because, without his bargain, she'd not have known these past weeks with him.

She'd not have known *him*.

But there was no getting around her father's displeasure. It was best to settle matters quickly and firmly, lest the tension in the carriage suffocate them all.

"I shall have Molly begin packing for the journey to Shropshire," she said into the silence.

That snagged Henry's attention, and he looked up from his sketchbook, brows dipping behind his spectacles. "Are we taking a holiday?" he asked.

The ache in her throat threatened to erupt in a sob, and she forced a smile. Tears wouldn't move her father and would only give her a headache. Pushing out a slow breath, she said to Henry, "I'm to visit our great-aunt Agnes for a bit."

"I think I remember her," he said, nose wrinkled in thought. "She's the one that wears trousers, isn't she? And she smells funny. How long will we be gone?"

Keren inhaled once before saying, "I'm to go to Shropshire, Henry, but you'll remain here with Miss Litton and continue your lessons."

She wondered if she could persuade Gryffyn to continue Henry's carving instruction, then she realized the folly of that notion. Her father wouldn't allow the arrangement to continue, not after the day's revelations. She turned to him with a pleading look.

"Father, if Mr. Kimbrell is amenable, you must allow Henry to continue his carving lessons."

Her father's face fell in a great, thunderous frown that set his side whiskers to quivering. He clenched his fist on the seat next to him. His knuckles were raw, and she winced at the memory of Gryffyn's stunned expression as he'd landed on the cobbles in Truro. For all her father's concern about propriety, he couldn't seem to keep his own manners about him when it came to his daughters.

At his continued silence, Keren whispered, "Please don't punish Henry for my mistake."

"You're not going to Shropshire," her father said, the timber of his voice low and gravelly in the small confines of the carriage. "This disaster is too large to ship off."

"I'm not?" Keren said. "It is?" She frowned, wondering what punishment her father had in store for her if not exile to Aunt Agnes.

"There's nothing that will fix this short of marriage, no matter that Kimbrell is against the notion."

Hope gave her heart wings even as she recalled Gryffyn's intentions regarding marriage. Then the import of her father's statement penetrated her thoughts. "What do you mean, no matter that he's against it? What do you know of Mr. Kimbrell's intentions?"

Her father shifted on the seat and wouldn't meet her eyes.

"Father?"

"I gave him permission to court you."

"He asked to court me?" Her stupid, foolish heart leapt in her chest.

"No," her father admitted. "I went to his workshop. I told him he had my permission if he wanted it."

Keren turned her head away. She already knew the rest of the story.

"He declined," her father finished.

"Of course he declined," she said, turning back to him. "He has no intention of marrying. And he's not like Langford; hitting him won't change his mind."

"A man doesn't carve," her father's voice rose to bounce off the carriage ceiling and he lowered it, though she could see the effort pained him. "A man doesn't carve a lady's likeness for all to see without consequences. He'll make this right."

Keren smiled sadly as she realized the full measure of the day's disaster. Gryffyn's mind wouldn't be swayed by her father's fist, but he'd offer to marry her just the same. He'd accept responsibility for carving her likeness and set aside his own intentions in order to salvage her reputation.

In truth, marrying him would be the best of all possible outcomes. She would remain in Newford, close to Henry. Tongues would wag for a bit, but they'd settle once the initial flurry of gossip passed. Her father would be appeased, and she'd have Gryffyn's gentle teasing to look forward to for the rest of their days.

The thought should have warmed her, but an icy chill frosted through her instead. She was Mayor Moon's greedy daughter, it would seem, unsatisfied with crumbs. She didn't want Gryffyn like this. Not when he had no choice but to marry her.

They'd reached Newford and the carriage traveled the length of the high street. She turned from her father's frown to gaze out the window. How different their return felt from when they'd left that morning. Gone was the anticipation of the exhibition. Henry's ever-present energy that was usually enough to fill ten carriages was subdued.

She spied Mrs. Pentreath, newly returned from

Truro and walking with another matron near the post office. They leaned their heads together and whispered to one another as they watched the mayor's carriage pass. Word of her disgrace had already reached Newford, and her father scowled his displeasure. He wouldn't be moved from his position, but neither would she.

"You won't force Mr. Kimbrell's hand on this, Father, or mine." Her voice grew stronger even as a heavy weight settled more firmly in her chest. "I'll go to Shropshire before I marry him."

—

GRYFFYN LIFTED HIS SANDING BLOCK from the headstone he prepared, dismayed to see naught but a ploofy cloud where there was meant to be a rose. He'd rubbed the edges clean off the flower he'd just carved. Sighing, he took up his chisel to begin again. Perhaps with the proper angle, he could transform the vague petals into those of a camellia instead.

After his parents' revelations, he'd left his mother resting in her bed and his father hovering about her. Unable to bear pacing the parlor, waiting for her condition to change for good or ill, he'd come to the workshop to finish his father's commissions for the day. And, if there was any good fortune to be had, to banish his thoughts. But judging from the condition of the poor headstone, he'd seen little success with either endeavor.

He finally tossed the chisel aside and sank onto the low bench beneath the front window. Elbows on his knees and confusion weighting his stomach, he hung his head.

He had no notion what to do about Carne. The man had long believed Gryffyn's parents had stolen his wife and now, rightfully so, his son. Carne had legal right on his side. Whether he intended to press that fact remained to be seen. To do so would require he claim Gryffyn as his son, and that, Gryffyn thought, meant he'd lose his parents twice—once to any legal punishment and again in name. Was it any wonder his parents had been reluctant for him to travel to Truro?

He also had no idea how to proceed with Miss Moon. He'd sent a note round earlier that he would call at Camborne, but he hadn't been able to move his feet in that direction yet.

Admittedly, it was hard to consider such things with his mother lying in her bed, but he was fully aware of the ill turn he'd done Miss Moon. He owed her a marriage proposal, but he'd consider himself fortunate if she'd accept his apology. He couldn't forget her open-mouthed shock when she'd seen Fortuna's face for the first time.

Regardless of the lady's willingness to forgive,

her father must be waiting for him.

Before he could persuade his feet to move, though, the door to the workshop opened and a shadow stretched across the floor before him. He lifted his head then lifted it some more, surprised to see Derrick Carne standing before him. With a deep inhale, he stood.

"Kimbrell," Carne said. With his top hat, his height brushed the workshop's low rafters.

Gryffyn nodded reluctantly. "Carne."

Carne looked about the workshop. His disdain for Gryffyn's working-class surroundings was apparent in the curl of his lip. With naught but a cursory glance toward the carved figures in the window, his gaze returned to Gryffyn and his dust-covered person.

This man was his father. Gryffyn still couldn't quite wrap his mind around the fact. No, he thought, not his father. His *sire*. There was a distinct difference.

"I've come for but one purpose," Carne said, and Gryffyn's brows edged up in inquiry. "My son and heir comes of age soon. If you think to lay a claim to your birthright, know that I will deny it. And if you press the matter," Carne continued in his gentry-class tone, "I shall see to it that the magistrate is made fully aware of your parents' crimes. That's the agreement—the *only* agreement—I'm prepared to make. My silence for yours."

Relief relaxed Gryffyn's shoulders.

Carne didn't intend to acknowledge their relationship. That he assumed Gryffyn would risk his parents' good name—and their freedom—for material gain told him all he needed to know about the man.

"'Tis sorry I am you've traveled such a fair distance," he said, giving his rolling Rs extra license. "But I've no notion to what you refer. As I told you in Truro, my parents are Thomas and Mary Kimbrell."

Carne studied him for a long beat, eyes narrowed, before he nodded. "We understand one another then." And without another word, he left the workshop.

Gryffyn returned home and shared the news of Carne's visit with his father while his mother slept. Thomas closed his eyes and nodded.

"I'm sorry, son," he whispered again. "We've deprived you of your rightful place—"

"Stop," Gryffyn said, careful to keep his voice low. "You gave me much more, and I'd not have you think otherwise."

His father's blue eyes shone and the truth of Gryffyn's words caused his own eyes to burn. Regardless of the fact that he wasn't their son, Mary

Kimbrell was his mother and Thomas Kimbrell was his father. He'd been christened a Kimbrell, and a Kimbrell he would remain. His father gripped him in a firm hug, and some of the weight in Gryffyn's chest lifted.

If only he could settle the matter of Miss Moon so easily.

—

KEREN WATCHED FROM THE DRAWING room window as Gryffyn approached Camborne on foot. Her heart twisted at his beloved form, his shoulders rounded beneath the weight of the day's events. She'd been surprised to receive his note not an hour past, given his mother's poor condition. She supposed it spoke of his determination to do the proper thing, that he would come calling while his mother lay ill.

As it was, she'd had a devil of a time convincing her father not to storm the Kimbrell residence. In the end, she'd persuaded him of the poor image he'd present to his constituents, were he to descend in a fury upon the Kimbrell household at such a time.

As Gryffyn neared, she studied his features in the shadow of his cap. He wore his serious face. Admittedly, it wasn't much different from his teasing face, but she'd come to know him over the past weeks. His current expression was one he wore when he was trying to solve a particularly difficult problem with his stone. The difference now was that *she* had become his difficult problem.

Her stomach sank further to see the firm set of his jaw and the tightness of his perfectly chiseled lips. This wasn't merely his serious face. This was his I've-come-to-propose-although-I've-no-intention-to-wed face. No matter how she might wish to, she didn't delude herself that he'd suddenly developed a desire to marry her. Nothing had changed between them but the day's unfortunate revelation that she'd been his model. Well, she wasn't having any of it.

With a disgraceful lack of decorum, she ignored the bell pull and opened the drawing room doors. "Simons," she called.

He started from his post near the entry then, spying her framed in the doorway, approached with a short bow. "Yes, Miss Moon?"

"Mr. Kimbrell is approaching. I'm certain my father does not wish to be disturbed."

As the servants had all witnessed her father's dark mood on returning from Truro, Simons nodded in ready agreement.

"Please inform Mr. Kimbrell that neither I nor my father are at home."

"Yes, Miss Moon."

When had she become such a timid mouse? She

wasn't as bold as she believed herself to be if she couldn't withstand a perfunctory proposal from Gryffyn Kimbrell. She ignored that thought and softened her voice to ask, "Has a basket been delivered to the Kimbrell home?"

"Yes, Miss Moon."

"And is there any news of Mrs. Kimbrell?"

"Mrs. Quick says Dr. Rowe believes it to be her heart. They're hopeful of a recovery, but it's not certain."

Keren nodded, her own heart twisting for Gryffyn and his parents as Simons left to answer the knock at the door.

CHAPTER TWENTY-FIVE

GRYFFYN FROWNED TO HEAR THAT neither Miss Moon nor her father were at home to visitors, although he'd seen a curtain move at one of the windows. Simons stood motionless at the door, neither a twitch nor a flash of his eye to betray the truth.

Gryffyn nodded and turned away as the door closed behind him. Had it only been hours since he'd thought to persuade Miss Moon with her own arguments?

Now it seemed she had no wish to see him, although he couldn't blame her after he'd betrayed her trust in such a manner. His courtship had died a splendid death before it had even begun.

He rubbed a hand over his face, wincing at the throbbing ache in his jaw. He'd thought the mayor, at least, would have been anxious to settle matters between them. Truth be told, he was surprised Moon hadn't stormed his home already, although he was grateful for the man's unexpected restraint.

His feet were heavy as he walked back the way he'd come. He returned to find his home overflowing with relations. His brothers—all four of them—had arrived with their families, and several of his cousins had joined them. They'd packed into the small parlor where they kept his father entertained with hushed voices while his mother continued to sleep upstairs.

Gryffyn paused in the doorway, certain that nothing highlighted the urgency of a situation more than a mustering of the troops. Still, gratitude swept him as Alfie leaned close to his father and said something that caused him to smile.

"Gryff," Jory said from his side. "How d'you fare?"

"Better now," he said, relieved to find comfort with his family. *His family.* They may not have been his by blood, but they were his in all the ways that mattered. How could he have ever doubted that?

"Gryffyn," His eldest brother Tom greeted him. Fair and blue-eyed like their parents, he was shorter than Gryffyn, but broader in the shoulder, and his hug was of the not-so-gentle variety. "Congratulations on your success in Truro," he said. "We knew it would be a sure thing."

"Aye," said Daniel, who at three and thirty was next in line. His agreement came with a punch to Gryffyn's shoulder that he felt to his soles. "Jory and Alfie told us Truro was quite the muck-up. Moon must be over himself to see Truro show to such poor advantage."

"Aye," Gryffyn said. "Moon's over himself."

"Gryffyn." The deceptively sweet voice of his cousin Wynne broke into his brothers' greetings. "I've brought raspberry tarts, but you may have them only if you tell us what you plan to do about Miss Moon. The matrons are abuzz."

It was just like his cousin to use food to extort information from him. His neck grew warm at the sudden silence in the room.

"What's this about Miss Moon?" his father asked, a crease lining his forehead.

And so, Gryffyn explained how Fortuna had come to wear Miss Moon's features. He left out a few details, such as Miss Moon's flirting and the kiss they'd shared as she'd filed Fortuna's skirts, but he didn't doubt his relations would fill in the tale's missing pieces.

"Aye," Wynne said when he'd finished, "but what d'you mean to *do* about her?"

"Well, o' course he'll marry her," Alfie said. "He's good and compromised her for all intents, even if he hasn't had the pleasure of—" He stopped. "You haven't had the pleasure of the good bits yet, have you cousin?"

Gryffyn's ears heated, but he shook his head. "O' course not. But it makes no odds as the lady has no wish to marry."

"She doesn't wish to marry *you*, precisely, or she doesn't wish to marry *anyone*?" Wynne asked with a frown.

"Well, anyone, I suppose." But especially me, he added silently.

"Gryff," she said in exasperation. "You're not *anyone*. Have you not seen the way she looks at you?"

"Aye?" he said, unwilling to admit he had no idea what she was talking about. He didn't miss, though, that his cousins leaned closer to hear her words. At least he wasn't alone in his ignorance.

"She looks at you as if you carry the sun and the moon in your pocket. And you—you're no better."

His brows lifted at that.

"You watch her as if she's the last cup of water spilling across the desert sand."

"Sorry, cousin," Gavin said with a wince. "She's right about that last bit."

Gryffyn frowned. Was his love so obvious? Then he considered the rest of his cousin's words. *Did* Miss Moon gaze at him in such a barmy fashion? Certainly, she enjoyed flirting with him, but was it possible her affection ran as deep as his? If so, perhaps she *could* be brought round with a bit of persuasion. He rubbed a hand over his sore jaw.

"She'll not be pleased I've brought such unpleasantness to her door."

"Well o' course not," Wynne said, and his brothers' wives murmured their agreement. "Twas a daft thing you did. But your waters were all flowing to the same sea; your actions didn't do anything but hasten things along."

"It sounds like you have your orders, son," his father said.

"Didn't I tell you there was more to Miss Moon's pleasant manner?" The room stilled as his mother's voice, soft and thready, sounded from the doorway.

"Mary!" His father rushed to her side. His mother was pale, wrapped in a quilted dressing gown and balancing one hand on the door post. Her gold-and-silver hair had been brushed and braided, no doubt by Mrs. Quick's hand. "You should be abed," his father admonished.

"Oh, stuff! And miss the party? If these are to be my last moments, I don't intend to miss a single one."

The room stilled, silence hanging in the air, before everyone jumped. They cleared a path through the parlor, and Gryffyn's father led his mother to her favorite chair by the window. Daniel found a blanket and tucked it about her feet while Tom asked Mrs.

Quick to please bring a fresh pot of tea.

When the fuss died down and Gryffyn had poured his mother's tea, she said, "Now, how do you intend to secure Miss Moon's hand? Neither your father nor I have forever to wait around for more grandchildren."

"Well," he said, rubbing the back of his neck. "I suppose I must begin by apologizing . . ."

The men nodded sagely even as Wynne and his brothers' wives *tsked* their disapproval.

"Never say you mean to begin a proposal with an apology," Wynne said amid feminine murmurs of assent. "You'll have plenty of opportunities to beg her pardon once you're wed, but a proposal on the heels of an apology sounds a bit forced. You must tell her how you *feel*."

He wasn't entirely convinced of the truth of his cousin's words. Her own path to love had been strewn with its share of rocks and muck, after all, so it was possible she didn't know as much as she thought she did.

Gryffyn looked to his mother for her opinion. She smiled and cocked her head to one side. "I can't fault her logic, love."

And thus began a lively debate on the best strategy for gaining the lady's hand.

"You must have something to offer. A home and land. Ladies prefer gentlemen with prospects. Didn't you say the competition in Truro came with a purse?"

"Children. Ladies all want them. Tell her how you long to give them to her."

"Compliment her eyes."

"Nay, her smile."

"There's no need for words. Kiss her proper." That, of course, was Alfie's contribution.

Gryffyn's mother squeezed his fingers, and he leaned closer to hear her whisper. "Say what's in your heart, love, and you can't go wrong. And a kiss won't hurt your cause, if Miss Moon is agreeable."

———

GRYFFYN LEFT HIS COUSINS TO their debate and returned to Camborne. The day was getting on, so it wasn't, strictly speaking, proper calling hours, but he had no wish to leave the matter for another day. Simons answered the door and registered only mild surprise at seeing him again so soon after his last visit.

"I don't suppose Miss Moon is at home to visitors yet?" Gryffyn said.

"No, sir." The butler's gaze was impassive, but Gryffyn thought he detected regret in his tone.

"And Mayor Moon?"

"The mayor has gone out for the evening."

Simons' expression eased on that statement, so Gryffyn assumed it must be true.

He pressed his lips and nodded, prepared to take his leave yet again. Simons began to close the door, then Gryffyn stopped him. "What about Master Henry?"

Simons pulled the door wider again. A small smile threatened his countenance before he regained control. "One moment. I shall see if Master Henry is receiving."

Gryffyn paced the portico as he waited for Simons to return. Glancing up, his eye stopped on his father's stone statue gracing the top of Moon's curved gravel drive. It was exquisitely detailed and quite original—Moon could certainly boast having the only one of its kind in all of Cornwall.

He pressed fingers to his temples and closed his eyes on all his father had sacrificed over the years. His carvings could have gained repute as far as London or Paris, but he'd chosen his family over such acclaim.

Gryffyn wondered if, given the same choice, would he have made the right one? If Miss Moon could be persuaded to marry him, if they were blessed with children . . . would he be worthy of them? His chest warmed at the thought of building a family with her. As hard as he'd worked the past weeks, as much as he'd longed for a win in Truro, he'd been prepared to walk away from Fortuna. Of course, he would choose his family over fortune.

He and his father were not so different, after all.

The door opened again, and Simons said, "Master Henry will receive you now."

Gryffyn turned from his pacing circuit and followed Simons. As they walked to the drawing room, he peered down Camborne's wide hall.

Where was Miss Moon? Did she hide in the morning room where he'd found her painting her poor fox? Perhaps she'd seen him coming and had escaped to the back gardens. He didn't doubt she was avoiding him, although he'd not have thought her capable of such timidity. Miss Moon—Keren— was bold and forward. Imprudently so. If she avoided him because she avoided his proposal, would she not come out with it directly?

"Mr. Kimbrell!" Henry said when Gryffyn entered the drawing room. He bounced at his place on the couch as Miss Litton looked on from an adjacent chair. His lessons had clearly not yet covered the polite, restrained receiving of guests, but Gryffyn couldn't help the smile that came to his lips at Henry's enthusiasm.

"Henry," he greeted with a polite bow. "And Miss Litton. 'Tis a pleasure to see you, although I regret the hour."

Henry—every inch the gentleman of the manor—

sent Simons for tea, and Gryffyn spent some minutes receiving a pure and thorough accounting of the day's events. Henry regaled him with the entire tale, from the departure of the Moon carriage from Camborne that morning until Henry had seen Gryffyn laid out on the cobbles. That part, Gryffyn knew well.

"I'm sorry for that," Henry said, cocking his head to the side. "It looks a proper bruise, but did I not warn you about my father?" He shook his head to himself. "No matter how fine your sketches, I knew he wouldn't like them."

"Aye," Gryffyn agreed, rubbing his jaw. "You did warn me. And what"—he cleared his throat—"what of your sister? Did Miss Moon have anything to say of the day's events?"

"Oh, yes. She and my father had a fantastic row—"

"Henry," Miss Litton protested.

"Or rather, my father yelled while Keri—"

"Henry."

"—told him she won't marry. She said she'd rather go to Shropshire than marry, which doesn't make any sense. There's nothing in Shropshire but our aunt, and I know Keri would rather marry you. You don't smell half as bad as Aunt Agnes."

"Henry!"

The boy finally attended his governess, adding

defensively, "Well, it's the truth."

Gryffyn wasn't sure which part of the story Henry defended—Keren's preference for Gryffyn over Shropshire, or Gryffyn's superior scent. He chose to focus his attentions on the former, although he appreciated Henry's sentiment on the latter.

"She would? Prefer to marry me, rather?"

"Well, why else would she moon over that drawing you did of her? Ha! Moon!" Henry grinned at his joke.

Gryffyn's heart skipped. "She still has the drawing?"

"Oh, yes. She keeps it in her vanity." Henry stood as if to leave. "Do you want to see it?"

"No," Gryffyn said, holding a hand to stay Henry. "'Taint necessary, but I'm thinking you probably shouldn't be rifling your sister's things."

Henry nodded sagely as if the notion were a new one to consider and regained his seat.

"Henry," Gryffyn said. "Is that where your sister is? Has she gone to Shropshire?"

"Oh, no," Henry said. "Father took away her pin money and denied her the use of the carriage. She's at the cove."

Gryffyn stilled. "She's at the cove? You're certain?"

"Yes, didn't I say that already?"

"No, Henry, you didn't. But the sun will set

soon. Has she gone alone?"

Henry nodded. "It's where she goes to ponder—"

"Aye, ponderous thoughts," Gryffyn finished. The cove. If he hurried, perhaps he'd find her there before she had a chance to escape him once more. "Thank you, Henry. You've been most helpful." He stood to leave.

"But you haven't finished your tea."

Gryffyn paused then drained his cup. "Excellent tea. Thank you, Henry. Good day, Miss Litton."

CHAPTER TWENTY-SIX

KEREN ALLOWED THE GENTLE SHUSHING of the waves to soothe her as she stood at the water's edge. The westering sun was a great, red ball drawing near the horizon. Soon it would paint the sky purple and orange as it fell into the sea.

It was her favorite time of day, but her thoughts were less on the sun's upcoming display and more on the day's revelations, for they'd continued long after Truro.

She'd passed Gryffyn's workshop on her way to the cove. Her footsteps had hesitated, of course, which was why she'd been there in the street when one of the judges from Truro emerged and climbed aboard an unmarked carriage. He was the judge who so closely resembled Gryffyn. Carne, she thought his name was. It didn't take a tremendous effort of reasoning to conclude they shared a kinship. Their coloring was the same, as was their form, although Carne was a trifle taller.

He'd tipped his hat to her, and Keren was startled by the similarity in their features. He had Gryffyn's brown eyes, although Carne's were less ... Gryffyn. She didn't feel as if she were drowning in Carne's eyes, as if she wanted to spend her days teasing sparks of gold and amber from them.

All of this had pointed her to the obvious—if unexpected—conclusion: Gryffyn was base-born. She didn't know how or why he'd come to make his life with the Kimbrells, but it certainly explained why he was so much like them and yet so different.

Was *that* why he didn't intend to marry? Even as she pondered it, she knew it must be true.

Perhaps 'tis I who am unworthy.

She'd scoffed at his words days before, disbelieving that any lady of sense would find him unworthy. But his was an honorable soul. Of course, he would believe himself unfit for a genteel lady, no matter how little she cared for such things.

That he should believe such a ridiculous bit of nonsense caused her heart to pinch uncomfortably, and she pressed a hand to her chest as if that alone could ease the thing. She must set him straight on the matter.

The hairs on the back of her neck rose and she turned. He was there, atop the cliffs, silhouetted against the riotous colors of the sky. Her heart ricocheted against her ribs, a heavy thumping she was certain he must hear above the sea's murmur.

He set one booted foot on the first step, then the next, and she watched as he slowly descended the cliff.

When he finally reached her on the sand, he tucked his hands behind him and said, "Thank you for the basket." He winced as if surprised by the words, and she blinked.

"You're welcome. I hope your mother is improving."

"She doesn't grow worse, which is a blessing."

Keren nodded. "It seemed the proper thing, to send . . . foodstuffs."

His lips quirked. "Aye. And you've always done the proper thing."

She gave him a pitying glance. "Perhaps you haven't heard," she said. "I'm Mayor Moon's bold daughter—the one who poses for sculptors and . . . and meets them alone at sunset." She tossed her head to look about them at the sun's display, but his gaze remained fixed on her. A flush warmed her cheeks, and she swallowed.

"Sculptors?" he said. "As in more than one?"

"No," she whispered, turning back to him. "Only the one."

He stepped closer, and her breath caught at the amber fire in his eyes. It warmed her as if she stood before one of the cove's bonfires.

"I've been advised not to begin with an apology," he said, and her brows climbed. "But I can't speak what's in my heart without telling you how sorry I am for the trouble I've caused. 'Twas never my intention—"

"I know," she said. He rubbed his jaw and she added before he could continue, "I also know the circumstances of your birth are such that"—she stopped on seeing the confusion that clouded his eyes. "I saw Carne leaving your workshop," she finished.

He stepped away from her and turned, running a hand through his hair. The breeze from the sea cooled her skin where his warmth had been and set her curls to flutter about her cheek.

"You must not think me so shallow to be moved by such things," she continued to his back. "They matter not. A man's origins say nothing of his character. They say nothing of the fine man you are inside."

Her heart leapt at the declaration, victorious at having gained the upper hand over her brain. What would he make of a statement like that?

He returned to face her, staring intently into her eyes. His tone was low and earnest as he said, "No, I can see you've no concern for such things. Of course, you wouldn't. But as much as I adore you for looking past my tarnish,"—her brows climbed on that—"I'm afraid you have it wrong."

She frowned.

"*I* had it wrong," he continued, and his smile grew. "As it turns out, my origins—though not entirely blemish-free—are not as I had assumed. Aye, Carne is my father. I can't claim him, nor will he claim me, but my parents were well and wedded to one another when I was born. I shall explain it to you, but for all intents, the Kimbrells are my family."

While she tried to make sense of this revelation, his gaze angled down. She followed it to the stone beside them, where he and Henry had practiced their letters. "GK" and "KM" were carved boldly across the stone's surface.

"'Tis fitting," he said, "our letters carved side by side."

She smiled. "Someone who didn't know better might presume to make something of it."

He slowly took her hands in his and kissed her knuckles. She delighted in the soft feel of his lips across her skin, grateful she'd removed her gloves.

"Miss Moon—Keren."

A shiver skipped across her shoulders at the sound of her given name on his lips.

"You must know the depth of my affection. I love you. You once said that love can overcome any obstacle. I'm not one for fitty speeches, but if I was of a mind to marry, and if you were similarly disposed, I think we would suit quite well."

She smiled to hear her own words returned to her in his rich timber. Despite her mind's clambering, urging her to caution lest she race headlong off a cliff, she asked, "And are you? Of a mind to marry, that is?"

"Aye." He paused then asked the obvious—the only—question. "Are you?"

And that was the crux of it, wasn't it? The ponderous thought she'd come to ponder. Not Gryffyn's feelings for her, or hers for him, for nothing could be more certain. But rather, her willingness to let go.

She closed her eyes and tested his question, laid it alongside her sister's words: *Are you certain it's not you that needs Henry?*

She'd lost first Will and then her mother. She'd been alone in her grief. Unseen, unneeded, until the moment when she realized infant Henry was equally alone. He'd needed her then, and she'd held onto him for so long she hadn't realized how much she'd come to depend on him rather than the other way round.

Henry had her father and Miss Litton. And without the threat of Shropshire, Keren would never be far. Henry would be all right. She smiled and watched the sun set fire to the gold and amber sparks in Gryffyn's eyes as it dipped into the sea.

He waited for her answer, his fingers warm about her own. Was she of a mind to marry?

"Yes."

The breath whooshed out of her on the word and she tried to draw another, but he sealed her lips with his own. She melted—there was no other way to describe the swiftness with which her bones dissolved as he slanted his firm lips over hers, hands cradling her head as she gripped his coat.

Her eyes closed, no matter that she wished to see him. The swell of emotion that crested over her was simply too much. The pads of his thumbs stroked her cheeks, and she was surprised to feel cooling moisture there. He nibbled the corners of her lips, drawing a giddy smile from her before pulling away to kiss her eyelids. His arms were tight about her waist, and she leaned into their support as her legs didn't seem capable of holding her any longer.

When he finally released her some long moments later, she whispered again, "Yes."

EPILOGUE

SIX YEARS LATER

THE RAYS OF A LATE summer sun slanted across Newford's slate rooftops, casting the high street in deep shadow as Gryffyn walked toward his workshop. He'd passed a long day finishing a fountain at a nearby estate, but he wasn't surprised to see lantern light spilling from the workshop's front window. He suspected he'd find his father within, and he wasn't disappointed.

Thomas Kimbrell bent over a creamy white headstone, the flames of two lanterns dancing and lengthening about him. Henry stood at his elbow and quietly passed him a filing rasp.

Gryffyn and his father had created quite a reputation for themselves in recent years, with commissions scheduled for the next fourteen months.

Most recently, Mayor Moon had engaged them to carve a statue for the top of the high street, but Gryffyn's father still made time for headstones and hedges.

This, however, was no ordinary headstone.

His mother's heart had endured another six, beautiful years. Long enough to see two more grandchildren come into the world—Gryffyn's four-year-old Thomas and two-year-old William. Not long enough, though, to greet the one that was yet to come.

Gryffyn closed the door softly. "Father," he said. "I wish you would let me do the carving."

"You know I can't leave this to another," Thomas said without lifting his head. "Even one as skilled as yourself."

Gryffyn couldn't fault his resolve, though it had pained him to watch his father stare at the blank stone this month past. But perhaps now, in finally taking his chisel to it, he could begin to heal.

Gryffyn pulled a stool next to the worktable and settled atop it. "Have you given any more thought to the matter we discussed?" he asked his father.

Thomas glanced up once before returning his attention to the stone. "Aye."

"And?"

His father finally straightened and laid aside the file. Lifting a rag, he wiped his hands as Henry began gathering their tools. "And I accept your proposal."

Gryffyn's brows lifted. He'd come prepared with a number of persuasive arguments. "You do?"

"Aye, 'twill be an imposition, to be sure, but what is family if not a hindrance to one's peace? Although I can't fathom how you convinced your lovely wife to come live with an old man." His father's lips turned up at one corner as he spoke, and Gryffyn smiled.

He and Keren had let a small cottage these past years, but their family was growing. Their number would soon outstrip the available beds, and thoughts of his father, alone with only his memories for company, had pinched at Gryffyn's heart. So, when Keren had suggested they give up their cottage to live with Thomas, he'd kissed her thoroughly.

Henry turned to Gryffyn with a broad smile. "We're to live with Granfer?" he asked. "Truly?"

Henry's official place of residence, of course, was Camborne, with his father and stepmother. But anyone, on being asked his direction, would reply, "Why, Henry Moon resides with his sister and her husband. For all intents, he's one of the Newford Kimbrells, you know."

"Aye," Gryffyn replied with a smile. "'Twould seem so, although you'll be spending less time there soon." Henry would leave in a fortnight to begin the

Michelmas term in Exeter. His eagerness to go both relieved and distressed his sister, who would have been pleased to keep him with her always. Of necessity, Miss Litton's role had been transformed from that of governess to nursemaid to the younger children. It was a position for which her years of shepherding Henry had well prepared her.

The door opened, and Keren and Miss Litton entered the workshop, ushering the children before them. Little William fisted his mother's skirts, but Thomas quickly broke away to join Henry at the worktable. Their oldest son adored Henry, and Gryffyn was hard pressed to say who would miss his brother-in-law more when he was gone: Keren or young Thomas.

"Granfer," Thomas said, "Mrs. Quick is making a lobster pie for supper. She let me stir the sauce and sprinkle the salt, but not too much she said, or we'll pickle our insides."

He reached for a chisel as he spoke and tapped it ineffectually on a bit of stone Gryffyn kept about for his use. Henry reached over and gently removed the chisel from his grasp and handed him a smaller, green-handled tool. Gryffyn caught his gaze, and Henry looked toward the ceiling with a long-suffering roll of his eyes.

Gryffyn moved to the low bench beneath the window and scooped Will onto his lap, but Will was having none of it. He wriggled and stood on the bench to survey the carvings in the sill. Stretching his short arm, he retrieved a dolphin—his favorite. It was small enough for little hands but not so small to pose a problem when it found its way into little mouths.

"A lobster pie, you say?" Gryffyn's father asked. "Well, then. We'd best wash and dress for supper. We don't wish to appear at table in our boots and carving dust."

He held a hand for his grandson to take and, after some playful resistance, allowed Thomas to heave him from his seat and lead him away. Henry collected Will and his dolphin and followed with Miss Litton.

When the workshop was quiet once again, Keren fluttered a hand through Gryffyn's hair. She tugged his head toward her slightly curved belly.

He resisted but without conviction. "I'm stone-dusted," he said.

"I happen to like your dusty bits."

"I thought 'twas my tarnish you preferred."

"I'm partial to all your bits. But regardless of stone dust or tarnish, I'm prepared. I carry extra handkerchiefs, you know."

He tugged on her hand, and she settled on his lap. She was soft and delightfully rounded. He tucked his nose into the curve of her neck and inhaled her soft, orange-blossom scent.

"She knew," he said, voice muffled. He lifted his head and Keren laid a palm along one whiskered cheek. "She knew from the first that you were the match for me."

"She was a smart lady, your mother."

"Aye."

"And perhaps a tiny bit touched in the head."

He chuckled then sobered. "Did you ever think to find yourself attached to a stone carver?"

"Never in my wildest imaginings did I dream such a wondrous thing," she said. "But fortune favors the bold."

He smiled at that and helped her to stand. He crossed to the worktable to extinguish the lanterns then paused at his father's carving. Taking up a cloth, he brushed dust from the embellishment near the top of the headstone. His father had carved a simple rose, his mother's favorite flower. He could almost smell her familiar rose-water scent.

The tips of the petals were more defined on one side than the other. Frowning, he set the cloth aside and took up a chisel to even the points. But before he could lay metal to stone, something caught his eye, and he squinted. Moved his head from one side to the other. And smiled as what appeared to be a rose from one angle transformed to his mother's profile from another.

He looked up and spied a dampness in Keren's eyes to match his own. She'd seen it, too.

"They were fortunate to have found a match in one another," she said. "As were we."

He nodded, unable to speak.

"It grows late. We should return," she whispered.

"Aye, before Henry eats all of Mrs. Quick's lobster pie."

THE END

Thank you for reading!
If you enjoyed Gryffyn and Keren's tale,
be sure to claim your copy of the Hearts of Cornwall
prequel novella at klynsmithauthor.com.
Discovering Wynne is free to newsletter subscribers!

AUTHOR'S NOTE

I create a mood board of the visual references I use when writing. If you would like to see my inspiration for Gryffyn, Keren, Fortuna and their environs, please check out my Pinterest board at www.pinterest.com/klynsmithauthor/_saved/.

Matching Miss Moon is a book of fiction based on historical events and attitudes of the time. Below are a few themes that influenced this story.

WARNING: Spoilers ahead.

ADHD. Henry Moon—with his excessive questions, forgetfulness and difficulty concentrating—might be diagnosed today with Attention Deficit Hyperactivity Disorder (ADHD). Gryffyn Kimbrell also exhibited milder signs in his childhood; whether that was ADHD or a result of his troubling concerns over his place in the Kimbrell family, I'll leave for the reader to decide.

The first clinical description of ADHD may be attributed to George F. Still in 1902, at which time the condition was termed an "abnormal defect of moral control." However, there are accounts of individuals with similar symptoms dating back to the Bible. Reports have suggested that later figures such as Cromwell, Mozart, or Lord Byron could have had ADHD. Other early terms for the condition included "mental instability", "unstable nervous system" and "disease of attention."

As with any diagnosis, ADHD presents in varying degrees, and no two people experience the same signs, symptoms or response to treatment. Readers familiar with the challenges of ADHD may feel it was oversimplified in this story; it was not my intention to minimize the condition, but rather to highlight some of the challenges Henry might have faced, as well as strategies that have proved successful in some cases, such as art therapy (Gryffyn and Henry's sketching) and the use of visual cues (the colored handles on their carving tools, for example, and Miss Litton's statement that they're "forever leaving notes about Camborne to remind [Henry] to clean his teeth or complete his French lesson"). You can read more about the early history of ADHD at www.wjgnet.com/2220-3206/full/v5/i4/379.htm.

Stone Carving. Of all the visual arts, stone carving is, for obvious reasons, one of the most enduring. Two sculptures in particular were the inspiration for Gryffyn's *Fortuna.*

Veiled Christ by Giuseppe Sanmartino features a shroud so realistically transparent that people thought the sculptor had managed to turn a real veil to stone. No words can describe it; you really should see it for yourself. You can find some incredible images and read more of this magnificent piece's story at https://www.amusingplanet.com/2019/12/the-unbelievably-delicate-marble.html.

The West Wind by Thomas Ridgeway Gould was the inspiration for how Gryffyn addressed the issue of balancing *Fortuna's* weight on such a delicate ankle. Gould faced similar challenges that he solved beautifully by distributing the weight of *The West Wind* between the figure's ankles and the flowing drapery behind her. You can learn more at https://mag.rochester.edu/seeingAmerica/pdfs/21.pdf.

Artists' Models. Models of the Regency era had a lower social standing than today's muses. They were generally affiliated with the working class, and to pose for an artist for any purpose beyond the acceptable family portrait was considered fast, if not condemnable. Given this attitude, it's easy to understand Gryffyn's dilemma and Keren's fears. I'm so happy Jory was wrong when he said, "I doubt you'll find [a lady] willing to risk her reputation, no matter how respectable the artist."

BOOKS BY K. LYN SMITH

Something Wonderful
The Astronomer's Obsession
The Footman's Tale (Short Story)*
The Artist's Redemption
The Physician's Dilemma

Hearts of Cornwall
Discovering Wynne (Prequel Novella)*
Jilting Jory
Matching Miss Moon
Driving Miss Darling
Kissing Kate

Love's Journey
Star of Wonder
Light of a Nile Moon
Stars of Twilight Fair

* Subscribe at klynsmithauthor.com
for these free bonuses!

ABOUT THE AUTHOR

K. Lyn Smith lives in Birmingham, Alabama with her real-life swoony hero. Her debut novel, The Astronomer's Obsession, was a finalist for the National Excellence in Romantic Fiction Award, and many of her other titles have been shortlisted for awards such as the American Writing Award, the Carolyn Reader's Choice Award, the HOLT Medallion and the Maggie Award.

When she's not reading or writing, you can find her with family, traveling and watching period dramas. And space documentaries. Weird, right?

Visit www.klynsmithauthor.com, where you can subscribe for new release updates and access to exclusive bonus content.

Made in the USA
Columbia, SC
27 November 2024

47775526R00200